An Excerpt fron

"Aunt Carlotta
inquiry to a gray-haire
and soft as a downy pill

The woman's fixed stare changed to joy. "Mosey! Come in here, girl. I haven't seen you in, good grief—"

"I know, I know. I always say I'm going to drop by, but you know how it is."

"Uh-huh, uh-huh, I know *just* how it is." The woman her grandfather had hired as his first paralegal came from behind the desk to give Mosey a hug and an affectionate pat on the hand. "Carlotta's not here just now. She'll be back after lunch." She pushed back the sleeve of her dark gray suit coat to check her watch. "Twenty minutes, maybe thirty? She'd love to see you. I know she would. Can't you wait?"

"It's nothing important. I was just wondering about some family stuff."

"Everything's okay, I hope." Dot knitted her brow and stared at Mosey over silver-rimmed, cat-eye readers.

"I was just thinking about something Daddy used to say and thought Carlotta—"

"I doubt she'd know anything about that," she said with a wink, "but you can ask." Tugging at Mosey's coat sleeve, she led her to the large leather couch where, from the time Mosey was big enough to wiggle free of her mother's grip, she jumped and tumbled without the slightest reproof from Dot Cowsley. Mosey sat, and Dot looked pleased. "Now, then. What was it you wanted to know?" She tapped her foot impatiently against the bare wooden floor.

Murder in High Cotton

by

Kay Pritchett

Murder in High Cotton: A Mosey Frye Anthology

Contact Information: info@thewildrosepress.com

Cover Art by *Kristian Norris*

The Wild Rose Press, Inc.
PO Box 708
Adams Basin, NY 14410-0708
Visit us at www.thewildrosepress.com

Publishing History
First Edition, 2022
Trade Paperback ISBN 978-1-5092-3945-0
Digital ISBN 978-1-5092-3946-7

Published in the United States of America

Dedication

For my Delta family, whose stories have long amused
and inspired me.

Acknowledgments

My thanks to Teresa Nicholas for calling to my attention the profound attachment Deltans have to their houses. With your permission, I have used your fitting words as an epigraph to *Murder at Waite House*.

And to Frans de Waal, for permission to reference your book *Our Inner Ape*, which fell into my protagonist's hands just when her first stigmatized property set her sleuthing on the trail of Delaney Crump's killer.

Murder at Waite House

A Mosey Frye Mystery, Book 1

So often the history of Southerners isn't just the history of our forebears, but also their houses.

~ Teresa Nicholas, *Delta Magazine*

Prologue

In getting to know the people of a town, late-comers may place little importance on the houses of their acquaintances. To them, it's the person that truly matters, not the house. But when children grow up in a town, their knowledge of the neighborhood ripens in a particular way. As infants and toddlers, they breeze along the sidewalk in their strollers. A few years later, they go out on their own to pump their bicycles up and down the street. In the course of play, they gather impressions of their neighborhood—maybe the houses even more than the people who live in them. If the child is a curious youngster, as was the protagonist of this story, she might wander down the alley behind her house, gaze at a shadowy back stoop or a row of lawn chairs lined up for a scrubbing or fresh coat of paint. It's in early adulthood that she finally breaches the thresholds of various dwellings and chats with the residents, getting to know them a little better. Be that as it may, the foundation of her regard—albeit fabricated from naïve observations—remains rock solid and is apt to alter little despite correction or contradiction. In the mind of the girl who has beheld it all her life, a house stands for something, and that is unlikely to change.

Chapter One

December 29, 2008
Waite House, Hembree, Arkansas
Stay away from Waite House, Daddy had said.

Mosey Frye sat fidgeting in the cab of her old truck. With a shiver, she turned up the collar of her pink flannel shirt, a Christmas gift from her husband Robert. Amazing taste her Robert had—knew her better than she knew herself. Nice flannel, nice shade of pink, Bobby. Pretty pearl buttons. She looked in the rearview mirror, plucked at her honey-colored bangs, pushed them to the left, then the right. Wide-set blue eyes—the color of lapis lazuli—stared back absently. She drew a tube of lip gloss from a satin pouch and painted her lips a radiant pink, then blotted them on the back of her hand.

She'd come to take a look at Waite House, though she was still undecided about whether to list it or not. "Is there even a choice here, Mosey?" That's what John Earle Shepherd, owner of Shepherd Realty, had said. And she'd had to agree. It made little sense—no sense at all—to turn down the opportunity of a lifetime. Any realtor would have jumped at the chance—except Mosey. She'd been a little frightened of the place since childhood.

Stay away from Waite House, Daddy had said.

She was waiting for her best friend Nadia Abboud.

Mosey had asked Nadia if she'd like to see Waite House, inside and out, and Nadia had responded, "Of course, but why?" To which Mosey had said, "I'm clueless about staging—you know that." To which Nadia had said, "Who do you think you're fooling?" To which Mosey had said, "I'll buy you lunch." So, even though she'd never said a word about it, there it was: Nadia *knew*.

Mosey frowned at her watch. Eight forty-five and no Nadia. "C'mon, girlfriend. You're late."

A brightly jacketed book lay on the floorboard, the libretto of Mozart's *Lucio Silla*—a Christmas gift from Nadia, the one who really knew her better than she knew herself. She flipped past the introduction and came to the opening lines: *Ah ciel, l'amico Cinna, Qui attendo invan. L'impazienza mia.* She tapped out the music on the steering wheel. "Ah ciel...ah ciel," she droned. Not right. She tapped again. Still not right. She tossed the book on the dashboard and slid across the seat to the passenger window. Her operatic aspirations had died at the altar, which is why her wedding pictures caused her to wince a little. She wiped away a circle of fog and squinted at the façade of the big Victorian. "Ah ciel...ah ciel...ah ciel."

She scrambled in her satchel for a pad and pencil and wrote as she mouthed the words: "Faded colors, uh-huh, disrupted by the branches of oaks and dogwoods..." She put her pencil down and laughed. "Not bad, girl, for a piece of cheeky prose." She slipped her pad and pencil into her jacket pocket, climbed down from the cab, and slammed the door. She wasn't in the mood to *describe* a house, *list* a house, *stage* a house— though Nadia had generously offered to lend her

3

whatever she needed for the staging. Mosey's career in real estate had hardly begun, but already she was bored stiff. It was a job, though, and she needed the extra cash. John Earle had been kind to take her on despite her utter lack of experience as a realtor.

She perched on the bumper of her truck, then the curb, then leaned against the passenger door and stretched out her long legs. "Nice boots, Bobby, nice boots." She checked her watch again and glanced up and down McAllister, expecting any minute to see a crop of dark hair fluttering in the wind. Where in heaven's name was Nadia?

With no one in sight, she turned again to scrutinize the house—which was a tad overstated. The ground floor loomed tall. "Waste of good lumber, if you ask me." Had *she* said that, or was it her daddy? When he was alive, he'd plied her with opinions by the bushel, as if anticipating an early death. His impetuous offspring had hardly noted most of them, but others, with which she roundly agreed or disagreed, periodically came to mind.

She surveyed the façade, taking notes for her description. *White trim accentuates the height of mullioned windows traced boldly against olive drab clapboard siding.* She punctuated her sentence with a squiggle and shifted her eyes, first to the brick drive that led onto McAllister and then to the grounds on either side. The landscaping was severe, her preference being for gardens with an aura of simple pleasantness. *Clipped yews, tall and wide, line the circular brick drive, adding a stroke of fresh green to a landscape...* She paused to think. *A dreary landscape of pale grayish-yellow grass?* She laughed at her own silly mockery. "Nope, better not put that."

From the sidewalk, Mosey checked both directions before turning to admire the stone steps that led to the spacious veranda. There was a time, back when she and Nadia were children, that Waite House was *the great big house with the long flight of steps*, just as the Church of the Open Door was *where Aunt Lil married Bunt Whittington for the second time*. On Halloween night, she and Nadia would scramble up those steps and scoop a handful of candy from a basket set out by Eason Waite's spinster aunt. *Girls, take one, just one.*

Back then, wicker settees and comfortable, cushioned chairs stood all along the north side of the veranda, waiting composedly for a friend or relative to drop by, take a seat, and sit a spell. But the latter-day Waites—the few who'd remained after Eason passed the house to a close cousin and moved his family and good furniture to Bayou De View—seemed ill fitted to the customs of their forebears. She supposed, to them, the pretty wicker furnishings had been *de rigueur* solely in a decorative sense. Like many of Hembree's artifacts, things that owed their intransience to indolence more than interest, they'd remained in place until one day…they'd simply vanished.

As a matter of fact, the current inhospitality of the entrance—no place to sit, no hanging baskets of ferns to diffuse the rays of the afternoon sun—portrayed quite truthfully the manner of Waite House's most recent custodian, the now deceased Delaney Crump. He'd been of a bilious temperament, so Mosey had heard. Not at all the type to sit on the porch in the evening, sip a cool drink, and wave at his neighbors. He would just enter the house through the add-on garage where his speedy, two-seat convertible sat alongside his sleek, custom-built crossover. Nobody ever saw him except when he was picking up the paper or checking the mail.

Mosey had always regarded the house, despite the formality of the exterior, as a place where something ghastly could occur and, as a matter of fact, now *had* occurred. Six months earlier, the police had found Crump on the floor of the study with a .38-calibre bullet in his chest. Though a half-year had passed, the house still bore an aura of wickedness—no, too strong a word. Malice, unseemliness, maybe. She imagined Delaney lying dead only a short distance from where she now stood. Her throat went dry.

Delaney Crump, who was he to you, silly?

She swallowed and sputtered out, "Nobody, Daddy, nobody at all."

She walked to the back of her truck and dropped the tailgate, then shoved a tire toward the front of the truck bed. She rummaged through a stack of mud-spattered signs and found one that read Open House. She hesitated, then left it in place. Prone to backing away from snags of an emotional nature, she was still dithering between "yes, I'll list it" and "no, I won't." She closed the tailgate and strode along the drive toward the steps.

"Hey, Mosey," came a voice from a half-block away. Tall, brunette, with flirty eyes and full lips, Nadia approached at a steady gait. The clip of her high heels on the pavement gathered speed. "Sorry I'm late."

"You're *always* late."

"*You're* always late."

"Who says?" Mosey turned away and moved toward the house. It wasn't unusual for her to snap at

Nadia and Nadia to snap back, like a couple of nervous border collies. This morning was no different, though with the temperature close to freezing, it was too chilly to dawdle.

"I've been freezing to death out here," Mosey yapped.

"Hush, girl, it's not that cold."

"You're crazy." Mosey hastened toward the house. "*In queste mura Sai, che non è sicura la tua vita.*"

"What?"

"Your life is not safe—"

"What?" she said again, running to catch up.

"It's from Mozart, silly. A person could *die* here—or something like that."

"Oh, I see. You've been reading that book I gave you."

Mosey smiled broadly. "Um-hm."

Flanked by her friend, she trudged up the steps of the empty Victorian and, near the entrance, drew a key from her jeans pocket. The mahogany French doors gave in to her tactful push, allowing the slender twosome to enter side by side.

Mosey stopped still in the middle of the spacious foyer and took a look around. "Within these walls, your life is not safe."

"Stop that, would you?" Nadia scolded, her words echoing within the cold hollowness of the house.

"You ever been inside a stigmatized property?" Mosey strode to the staircase at the right side of the foyer and, keeping an eye on her friend, took two steps up, two down.

"Plenty of times," Nadia said.

Mosey returned to the middle of the foyer. "Oh,

well, I suppose in *your* business—"

"What's that supposed to mean?"

"Nothing, silly." Mosey chuckled.

"Well, I *have* been to a lot of estate sales, if that's what you're getting at."

"Chill, Nadia. I said I was just kidding."

They glanced circumspectly toward the room closest to the entrance, each searching for traces of the grisly event. "I don't see any yellow tape or sign of an investigation." Mosey stretched her shoulders and slipped her hands into her back pockets.

"Course not," Nadia said, letting her leopard-skin tote drop to the bare wooden floor. "They would have gotten rid of all that before the estate sale."

"Well, they *still* haven't solved the crime."

From the foyer, Mosey surveyed the downstairs: study on the left, parlor on the right, and a wide corridor that ran from the entrance through the dining room to the kitchen. A mustard-colored rug covered the heart of pine flooring in the parlor, but, in the study, the carpeting had been taken up. "The body circled in blood…" the newspaper article had read. Recalling the disturbing phrase, Mosey abruptly looked away.

From across the foyer came the sound of Nadia pacing off the measurements of the largest room. "Big rooms," Mosey observed as she walked toward the parlor.

"Twenty by twenty," Nadia said.

"High ceilings."

Nadia looked up at the light-blue plaster above her head. "Fourteen, fifteen feet?"

Mosey took out a metal tape measure and slid it up the wall. Loose particles sprinkled down. "I hope that's just dust and not mold," she said, pulling a tissue from her pocket.

Nadia sniffed. "Doesn't smell like mold."

Mosey snapped her tape measure shut and dropped it in her tote. "Fourteen feet, nine inches."

"That light fixture is obviously antique...stained glass shade...Art Nouveau." As Nadia backed toward the wall, her eyes came to rest on the blue paisley wallpaper that ran from the chair rail to the crown molding. "Terrible pattern," she said. "Unfortunate shade of blue. What would you put with that?"

"You're the expert," Mosey said.

"My clients have better taste."

Mosey rolled her eyes. "It's a little bold but typically Victorian. The trim's pretty, don't you think?" She knelt on one knee and slid her hand along the wide molding. "It's in good condition for an old house."

Nadia, still focused on the walls, pulled a lime green scarf from around her neck, draped it over a light sconce, and backed away. "This color might work."

"Hmm" was Mosey's wavering reply.

"I've got a lime green settee at the store...just the thing to brighten up these walls. By the way, I don't guess you know *where* it happened?" She flipped the light switch.

"The study...in front of the windows. Somebody from a house across the street saw something."

They entered the study, where bare windows welcomed in the bright rays of the morning sun.

"That's ironic." Nadia passed her hand over the washed-out walls.

"What's ironic?"

"This color. Blue is supposed to be the color of

tranquility."

"Yeah? Well, it fell short here."

Nadia shaded her eyes and stared through the bay window at the sprawling Queen Anne across the way. "That's the Raines house. See, Mosey, that's how a house ought to be set, not like they set them these days. Have you seen the apartments they're building by the park? Terrible taste, terrible." She shook her head in displeasure.

Mosey, deaf to her friend's commentary, picked up a wheat-colored damask cushion from the window seat and turned it over.

"I met the owner a couple of weeks ago." Nadia gazed at the Queen Anne. "He came in the shop, he and that young wife of his."

"How young *is* she?"

"Mid-thirties. Our age more or less. He's gotta be sixty, but youngish and attractive."

"Old rich guy, young woman. Hmm." Mosey put the cushion down and sat. "Is she pretty?"

"If you like the type."

"What type's that?"

"Blonde."

"Hey!" Mosey glared at her friend.

"Not like *you* blonde, silly. Platinum out of a bottle."

"They been married long?"

Nadia ignored the question and posed one of her own. "Could you hear a gun shot from over there?" She knelt on the cushion next to Mosey.

"Course you could." She twisted in her seat. "You could hear a shot from my granddaddy's rifle." She paused. But that was a rifle. A pistol? She wasn't sure.

While Mosey remained at the window, calculating the distance between Waite House and the Queen Anne, Nadia crossed the foyer in the direction of the winding staircase. "What's up there?"

Mosey reached into her pocket and pulled out a crumpled sheet of paper. "Upstairs…six bedrooms, three baths, a nursery, and a laundry room."

Nadia, hands on hips, shook her head. "You'd think they would have brought somebody in to wax these floors." She picked up her tote and hung it over her shoulder.

"John Earle told me he sent his people over."

"If you ask me, John Earle's people did a lousy job." Holding on to the railing, Nadia hunched over and tilted her head to look up the stairs. "Where was the baby when it happened?"

Mosey thought back to the piece she'd read in the *Gazette*'s online archives. A man from across the street, Matthew Raines, hearing two shots, had called the police. When the officers arrived, they'd entered through the back and, searching the premises, had found Delaney Crump's body face up on the study floor. "According to the paper, the baby was upstairs in the nursery."

"And nobody down here but the dead father?"

"That's what it said."

"Where was Jane?"

"Jane? She divorced Delaney long before the murder."

"But if the baby was here…?" Nadia questioned.

"He was here all right, but Jane…? I have no idea."

"Know anything else?"

"Nope." Mosey shook her head, then, looking at

Nadia, added, "I'm here to have a look around, suggest a price—that's all." She folded the crumpled sheet and put it in her pocket.

"And I suppose nobody knows *why* he was killed? He didn't seem to me the type to get himself shot."

"Well, he was rich, wasn't he?" Mosey said. "That'd be motive enough. But, come to think of it, they ruled out robbery pretty quick. He was still wearing his *luxury* wristwatch." She waggled her head. "Nothing was missing except his keys."

"His keys?"

"That's what the *Gazette* said."

"Well, it's a tragedy," Nadia said. "A handsome, well-to-do cotton broker—"

"—divorced and with a new baby," Mosey added.

Nadia twirled on one heel, as if to capture a prospective buyer's impression upon entering the house. "A grand place, I'd say. An easy sell."

"Maybe."

"*Maybe* she says."

"Let's check up there." Mosey climbed the staircase with Nadia behind. They peeked into room after room until they had located the nursery, distinguishable by its fairytale wall covering.

"Poor child," Nadia said.

"Yeah, he won't remember his father."

They surveyed the rest of the second-floor rooms, then went downstairs for another look. The dining room and master bedroom, papered likewise in the original Victorian patterns, were similar in style to the parlor. The paisley print of the front room stopped at the corridor, yielding to a faux marble in the dining room and a floral in the master bedroom. In the remodeled kitchen, a fresh coat of off-white semi-gloss showed off new appliances, countertops, and cabinetry.

"Oh, my, cherry cabinets," Nadia said with a frown.

"Don't match the house."

"Not a bit. I'd have thought Delaney Crump—"

"—would've known better?"

Mosey approached the window above the apron sink and gazed out on a courtyard with an Italianate fountain. The water was still, and dead leaves covered the surrounding tiles. An unopened newspaper peeked out from under the leaves. She ought to take a look at the backyard. Nope, too dang cold. She'd check it out later.

In spite of the gloominess, which was common to vacant properties in winter, the spacious layout of the house and its well-crafted trim convinced Mosey she was likely to find a buyer in Hembree, or, if not, in a nearby town. Conakry, Gideon, Mound City—none of them had any nice old homes to speak of. Hembree, on the other hand, with broad lawns and stately houses, a town square and the quaint Tavernette, was known state-wide for its charm. And Waite House, generously proportioned and in suitable condition, would sell quickly. Of course, it would—why not? She checked her pocket to make sure she had the key, then gave the kitchen another once over. "You ready, Nadia?"

"I guess so." She opened an empty cherry cupboard and closed it. "I'd better get to the store. You think you'll list it?"

"Not sure."

"We could fix it up a little, bring in some furniture, maybe that lime green settee and some sort of rug for the study…something bright to contrast with the walls."

"That'd be nice. You got time for that?"

"Returns, that's all I've got at the store. Just let me know as soon as you decide. You *will* list it, right?"

"Probably."

As Nadia headed down McAllister toward the antique shop, Mosey hung back, gazing not at the property but at the sky, where swelling storm clouds were edging out a narrow patch of blue.

Stay away from Waite House.

"I hear you, Daddy."

Chapter Two

Morning, New Year's Eve, 2008
Mosey's House

Mosey set her cup on the jumbled counter and paged through *The Hembree Shopper* looking for her ad. "Holy moly!" she cried. She folded the page and dropped it into her tote. The open house, scheduled for twelve—or so she thought—was at eleven. She tossed the rest of the paper aside and shuffled through a stack of unopened mail for her to-do list. *Change sheets, clean bathroom, straighten up, thaw meat.* She had all that left to do plus *stop by the liquor store, buy flowers, and cook dinner.*

The phone rang.

"Hey, it's me," came Nadia's voice. "Did you see the morning paper?"

"Not much of it. I'm in a hurry—why?"

"Second page, national news. Got to run, bye."

"Confound it," she muttered, grabbing the *Gazette*. Why was Nadia always doing that...telling her to look at this, look at that with no explanation? She turned to the article: "Beaumont Real Estate Agent Found Strangled in Vacant Building." She gasped. "Another one. Good lord." She'd read about a similar case a few weeks before. A Texas woman, broker at a large firm, had been strangled in a parking garage in a high-end section of Dallas. Getting to the final paragraph, she read aloud: "Nothing has come to light linking the two victims or their assailants." Hmm, two victims…or their assailants.

She sipped her coffee and, taking a last bite of Danish, picked up Robert's dirty plate, stacked it on hers, and headed to the sink. She twisted the radio dial. "Good jook song," she whooped. She shuffled away from the sink toward the coat rack and, grasping a wire hanger, tapped out the backbeat on the sideboard—da-da-dah, da-da-dah—till the lyrics came again. *Uncle John, Uncle John…* As the chorus was ending, she dried the last cup, slipped an arm into the sleeve of her corduroy jacket, and opened the door. "The pork!" Turning back, she retrieved the partially thawed roast from the refrigerator, tossed it in the sink, and headed out the door.

Five minutes later, she'd arrived at Waite House. She staked the open-house sign in the lawn, then strode along the drive and up the steps. She took a big breath of cool air before inserting the key. If only the azaleas were in bloom, she pined, as she glanced across the front of the house. A gardenia, a honeysuckle, anything fragrant. But in the dead of winter, Mosey found nothing to excite the senses save the faint woodsy scent of the yews. She tapped with the key on the peeling doorframe. "I should've had John Earle touch that up." She pushed back the French doors and, with some reluctance, stepped inside the house.

Six months had gone by since Delaney Crump's murder, but his "ghost" lingered—at least in Mosey's mind.

Delaney Crump, who's he to you, girl?

"Why, nothing. I've never laid eyes on the man

more than once or twice in my life—as if it's any of your business. But, Daddy, this house is in desperate need of purgation, *hell,* sanctification." She said it loud enough for any ghosts to hear. "But at least it's starting to look a little better, lived in, even." She caught sight of a rolled up rug propped against the doorframe on the study side of the foyer. They'd gotten the blood stains up, but every time she entered the room, her eyes fell on the bare floor. She flopped the rug over and unfurled it. "That's better."

On the parlor side of the foyer stood the fiddle-leaf fig she'd brought from her own living room, thinking maybe something green and alive might help to dispel the grim atmosphere.

Her thoughts wandered from Crump to his ex-wife Jane Middleton. Mosey hadn't seen her in ages, but, yes, she could still *see* her: long chestnut hair, the stature of a beauty queen... She couldn't imagine how a modern woman like Jane, progressive, talented, could have tolerated the stuffiness of Waite House. Jane and the house, not a good match. Jane and Delaney, not much of a match, either. She and Nadia had regarded the marriage as risky, not that they knew Jane or Delaney all that well.

Both Jane and her daughter had vanished soon after the murder. The local and state police hadn't been able to find a trace of them in the Hembree area or the numerous quadrangles they'd mapped out across the state. They'd done all they could, then called in the FBI to extend the search. So here it was six months later, and Jane and Candice were still missing.

With no one to take care of the baby, Crump's mother had come in a prop plane from Mound City and taken temporary custody. Delaney's sister had shown up a short time later, cleared out the house, and hired an attorney—Pelezo by name—to take charge of the sale. The whole business was gradually drawing to a close, or so it seemed…but without closure.

Mosey, don't you go gettin' any bright ideas, ya' hear?

"I'm not, Daddy. Just putting two and two together."

Once she'd decided to list the property, she and Nadia had set about staging the front rooms. An ornately framed print of Van Gogh's *The Red Vineyard* gave the foyer the focal point it needed. As Nadia had predicted, the lime-green settee perked up the blue paisley walls of the parlor. Across from the settee, they'd angled two cane-back dining chairs covered in a coarse-woven fabric—nice touch of texture—and, for the corner nearest the chairs, they'd brought in a solid elm table—a pricey little item—above which Nadia had tacked up a faux antelope skull with long, curvy antlers. The room, Nadia had insisted, needed a touch of whimsy, and Mosey acquiesced, though she didn't take to antelope skulls any more than to the head of a ten-point buck. Mosey's fiddle-leaf fig—*au courant*, according to Nadia, in magazines of the trade—had brought the entire grouping to life. Admiring the glossy, dark green leaves of the fig, Mosey remembered the other spot of greenery she'd intended not for the parlor but the study. She headed to the kitchen and gave a shake to the macho fern she'd left soaking in the sink overnight. Out of the corner of her eye, she saw that the back door was slightly ajar. Huh, that's strange. She took a closer look. Not only was the door open, somebody had wiped his muddy feet on the mat.

Go home, Mosey, you silly girl.

"Hush, Daddy, would you just hush, please sir? These constant admonitions are not helping."

She pressed hard against the door. "Everything's fine, just fine." She twisted the lock and, grasping the knob, pulled back. It latched. The footprints, on closer examination, looked like a man's shoe, surely did. She took the broom from the utility closet and briskly whisked the mat, then picked up the fern and headed to the study.

North window, good spot for a fern, she decided. She set the plant on the library table. "Books," she mumbled. "It'd look homier with books settled around it, yeah." She gathered up a few handfuls of colorful paperbacks from the bookshelf, as many as she could balance on her outstretched arm, and stacked them around the fern. On her way out of the study, she grabbed her phone from her tote and tapped "Nadia" on her contact list.

"Hey, it's me. Let me ask you something. When we closed up yesterday, could we have forgotten to lock the back door?"

"At Waite House you mean? I'm sure I locked it, even checked it—why?"

"I'm here for the open house, and it wasn't locked. Somebody was here. There were muddy prints on the doormat." She stared down the corridor at the back door.

"Maybe the lawyer stopped by."

"Pelezo? Yeah, could be."

"Any customers yet?"

"Not so far," Mosey said. "I just got here."

"Before you leave, make sure you lock up. I don't want my stuff sitting over there in an unlocked house."

"I *didn't* leave it open, I'm telling you. Somebody's been here."

"Whatever. Call me later, okay?"

"If I can. Dahlia and Tommy are coming in. I've got a ton of stuff to do."

She slipped the phone in her pocket and rechecked the door. Then wiped up the water from the fern and walked back to the study.

From the window seat, she gazed out at the front lawn, in hopes that, any minute, a car would pull up at the curb. She checked the time on her phone. It was still early.

A watched pot never boils.

"You're making me nervous, dang it. Could you cool it, just till I get out of this place?"

I warned you—

"Daddy, hush now. Please hush."

She knelt on the rug in front of the window seat and began pulling items from her tote. "Flyers describing the house," she mumbled, as she separated the stacks. Historic Society pamphlets...business cards...maps of Hembree in case an out-of-towner showed up. She'd also brought the document the seller's attorney had provided, giving a detailed account of the crime that had taken place at Waite House on May 23, 2008. According to John Earle, she'd need to disclose all that should anyone express serious interest in the house. She gathered up the stacks and arranged them on the table in front of the books.

John Earle had given her a pep talk on the phone the night before. "Now listen, Mosey, there's no choice here, you understand?" "I know," she'd answered. But even if *he'd* thought so, it was minutes away from the open house and she was still of two minds. "If I sell it, I'll make a bundle, but…"

She sat on the window seat and focused on the Queen Anne across the street. Crump and the Raines—what was the connection there? So what if Raines had called the police. Didn't sound like anything out of the ordinary to her. If she were to hear shots in her neighborhood, she'd dial 911—wouldn't anybody? She couldn't imagine why not. But all that aside, Crump and the owners of the Queen Anne were neighbors…and rich. Moved in the same circles, most likely. Delaney and Raines's wife must have been about the same age. *A thirty-eight-year-old cotton broker, longtime Hembree resident and graduate of Blanchard College…* That's how the *Gazette* had described the victim. *Recently divorced from Jane Middleton Crump…* Hmm. Which pointed to another angle of the unsolved mystery. Where in the name of heaven were Jane and Candice?

She turned away from the window and looked up at the high ceiling—in pretty good shape, though a coat of paint wouldn't have hurt. And then there was that other business, totally unrelated, she muttered to herself. Those Texas real estate agents—both women. What lunatic was going around strangling women realtors?

She got up and stretched, then picked up a book from the library table. *Our Inner Ape*, it was called. She'd filched it from her anthropologist husband's nightstand. He'd said he'd bought it for her, but she hadn't read it. She'd found the title a bit off-putting. But that December morning, the last day of 2008, with nothing better to do than stand there and gape, she brushed the cover off with the sleeve of her jacket and began flipping through the chapters. She came to the heading "Violence," stopped, and silently read about an act of aggression that had taken place at Gombe National Park. Frodo, a chimpanzee, had decided to do unto humans as chimpanzees sometimes do unto members of their own species. He'd snatched a human baby off a girl's back and, before anyone could stop him, skedaddled into the rainforest to enjoy his meal.

"Well, that's pleasant." She laid the book on the table but reached for it again. On the back flap, there was a picture of the author Frans de Waal. Where was he going with this? Would he argue human violence mimicked the behavior of *our closest living relatives*? Huh. She thought about that: our closest living relatives. So, she was a primate? She'd have to ask Robert. She didn't think of herself as a primate.

A knock at the door pulled her back into the present. "Coming," she yelled. She straightened her dark-wash denim pencil skirt and buttoned the second button of her jacket. As she entered the foyer, she could see a tall, heavy-set man peeping through the etched pane. She opened the door, and he immediately stated his name.

"I'm Professor Hopkins," he said, then added, "*Evan* Hopkins."

Before she could utter a word of welcome, he placed a calling card in her hand, wiped his brown oxfords on the mat, and stepped—proud as you please—into the foyer. "I've come about the house," he said, closing the doors behind him.

"Of course," Mosey stammered.

"Any offers yet?"

She squared her shoulders. "None so far."

"I *might* be interested."

He moved toward the corridor, sneaking a peek at the rooms on either side. "What are they asking?"

"Wouldn't you care to see the rest of the house first?"

"I know it well enough," he said, turning toward the parlor, then the study. "They haven't made any changes, have they?"

"The kitchen's been updated." She wondered how he would react to the cherry cabinets. He seemed stylish, soberly dressed but stylish. But did his taste extend to décor? "Would you like to see?"

He looked down the hall toward the remodeled kitchen and replied curtly, "Fine, I'll take a look."

"Let me hang up your coat," she offered, though, so far, her efforts at slowing down the pace of the encounter were getting poor results.

"Well, all right." He removed his overcoat, exposing a handsome, two-button wool blazer.

She hung the coat in the hall closet and hurried to catch up with her hasty guest, who had entered the kitchen ten steps ahead of her. She caught up with him at the stovetop, where he stood looking up at the copper hanging rack—from which nothing hung—then down at the speckled granite island.

"Do you like to cook, Professor Hopkins?"

"I—"

"My father liked to cook," she added. "I thought maybe—"

"I've cooked all my life," he cut in, his voice firm. "I've never thought if I *liked* it or not."

23

She shouldn't have said that. Too personal, she expected.

Girl, you ask too many questions.

"Daddy."

"Did you say something?" Hopkins looked at her out of the corner of his eye.

"No," Mosey said, "just thinking out loud."

He continued with his cursory inspection of the rooms, as Mosey ticked off the exceptional features of the house. "Seven bedrooms, four baths. All the space a family could need. Would you want it for you and your wife?"

"I'm single."

It hadn't occurred to her a bachelor would be in the market for such a property. Still, she could imagine him there in his pajamas and robe, making a pot of coffee, scrambling an egg, reading the paper. "Elegant staircase, isn't it? The laundry room is upstairs—and the nursery." Surely he wouldn't care about that, unless— Well, no. She doubted he had grandkids. "The garden's lovely—will be in spring. Beautiful neighborhood. Nothing else like it in Hembree."

The taciturn gentleman responded with drones.

On the way out, he peeked into the parlor again. "That's a nice settee," he said. "Looks good in the room."

"It's on loan from Abboud Antiques. Do you know the shop?"

"I know where it is."

"Nadia kindly helped me with the staging."

He nodded and stepped back into the foyer.

A quarter of an hour later, after he'd retrieved his coat and left, she approached the closet. Earlier, when she'd opened it, she'd caught a glimpse of something on the floor. Sure enough, a pair of lavender crocheted mittens lay on a piece of carpeting between the broom and dustpan. She bent to pick them up but stopped herself, thinking she'd better leave them where they were. Not that there was anything unusual about finding a child's mittens—Candice had lived there after all. But now she was missing, as was her mother. Mosey closed the closet door and tripped quickly to the study window before Hopkins could get away. He'd made it across the lawn and down the sidewalk to his gray four-door sedan, which was parked not in front of Waite House but at another lot across and down the street. "I've seen that man before—I know I have." He opened the car door and, starting to get in, paused just long enough to cast an indignant frown in her direction.

Chapter Three

New Year's Eve, 2008, 3:00
Mosey and Robert's House

The pork—not Hopkins or the lavender mittens—was on Mosey's mind as she drove up the driveway and stopped just short of the garage. Her guests had arrived ahead of her—ahead of Robert, too, by all appearances. His hatchback wasn't in the garage or at the front of the lot.

Dahlia opened the kitchen door and pointed in the direction of the counter crowded with fresh greens and serving dishes. "I'm making dinner." She laughed and high-fived Mosey, who, in turn, handed her a loaf of crusty bread and a bottle of Malbec.

"I am *so* sorry I wasn't here when you arrived." Mosey gave her friend a hug. "Where's Robert? He's usually home by now."

Tommy looked up from fishing for capers at the bottom of a jar. "He ran out for a bottle of vodka. Dahlia's making martinis…pumpkin martinis."

"Yu-u-um." Mosey rubbed her palms under a stream of water and gave them a quick shake.

"The pork roast is in the oven," Dahlia said.

The aroma of garlic, rosemary, and lemon tempted Mosey to open the oven door a crack.

"You'll let out the heat!" Dahlia scolded. "Come over here and tell me what you've been up to. I haven't had an e-mail in weeks."

"Not much." Mosey chose a ripe tomato from a basket of vegetables. "Trying to sell houses." She seeded it, cut it into sections, and reached for a cucumber.

"Robert said you've listed Waite House."

"Yes, that's where the open house was." She scooped up the pieces and dropped them into the salad bowl.

"Do they know any more about the murder, or Jane and little—what was her name?"

"Candice. But you know Jane had another baby. With Delaney," she clarified. "A little boy."

Before Mosey could finish bringing Dahlia up to date, Robert pushed through the door. "You're here." He handed her a bouquet of mixed flowers. "You want me to put them in water?"

Mosey gave him a peck on the cheek. "Yes, please."

"And for you, ma'am," he said, turning to Dahlia, "the best the liquor store had to offer."

"That's a great brand," Dahlia said. "Excellent."

"It's New Year's Eve. Might as well celebrate in style." Then, turning to Mosey, "How'd it go?" he said. "Any luck?"

"Not exactly. I'll tell you later."

Dahlia poured half the vodka into the blender, spooned in pumpkin puree and spices, and dropped in a couple of ice cubes. She closed the lid and pulsed the button. "Where's the cheesecloth?"

"Lower drawer on the far right."

Dahlia snipped a piece of cloth and placed it over the mouth of the pitcher, then slowly strained in the cold mixture. She filled four glasses and garnished them with cinnamon sticks.

After multiple clinks and "cheers," the men sat down at the dining room table to finish their drinks, while the women, setting their drinks on the table, popped in and out of the kitchen. The chatter revolved around Mosey—most particularly her recent venture into real estate.

"Waite House," Tommy said, "that's a valuable listing."

Mosey nodded.

He leaned forward in his chair. "Mosey, you aren't spending all your time at the office, are you?"

"Not at all," Robert intervened. "Besides, she stays out of trouble that way."

"I wouldn't bet on it," Dahlia said, coming in with bowls and a ladle for the soup. "Sounds to me like she's dropped down in the middle of a murder case."

"You're kidding," Tommy said.

"Yes, she's kidding," Mosey said, handing cocktail napkins around. "Why does everyone think I'm getting mixed up in the Crump case just because I've listed the house?"

"Mixed up, no," Dahlia corrected, "but you could end up in the wrong place at the wrong time. Tell them about that strange client of yours."

"I didn't say he was a client."

"But he's interested."

"Maybe."

"I didn't know you had a potential buyer," Robert inserted. "Who?"

"Evan Hopkins—you know him?"

"Brady Hopkins's father? He used to teach at the

College. Sociology, history…" Robert said, snapping his fingers.

Mosey reached for her tote and dug for the calling card she'd received from her only visitor.

"Evan Hopkins," she read, "Professor Emeritus of Geography, Blanchard College."

"Geography, of course," Robert confirmed. "That's Brady's father." He moved from the table to the fireplace and, placing his glass on the mantel, lifted a log onto the irons.

"This whole business," Tommy said, joining Robert by the fireplace, "is becoming entirely too familiar. We all knew Jane a little, and now you know this guy Hopkins."

"I didn't say I *knew* him." Robert lit the logs with a piece of kindling and tossed it into the flames. "I just used to see him around the social sciences building. I did know his son somewhat. Brady married a distant cousin of mine, but they split up, and I've never heard anything more about him—or her, either." He reached into his pocket for a handkerchief and wiped his hands.

"Roast's ready," Dahlia called from the kitchen. "Shall I carve it in here or bring it to the table?"

"Let's start with the soup," Robert answered, "and then I'll carve the roast."

After dinner, Mosey, Robert, and their guests carried snifters of brandy into the living room and, sitting by the fire, traded news of old acquaintances. Hopkins was forgotten along with Brady and the now missing Jane Middleton, until Dahlia, spotting a Blanchard annual in a stack of books beside the coffee table, pulled it out and paged to her and Mosey's senior pictures. "Hey, look at that. You're right next to

Jane…Fulton, then."

"Let me see," Mosey said. "Jane Ellen Fulton, BA in French and Art. Huh, a lot of good it did her." She handed the book back to Dahlia.

"What's that supposed to mean?"

"Nothing. I just don't think a BA in the humanities is worth much, not around here."

Dahlia read aloud: "Anne Moseby Frye, BA in Psychology and Music. You think you might actually *do* something with your psychology degree?"

"I already am." She laughed, holding out a candy dish filled with divinity and bourbon balls. "You meet all kinds of screwballs selling houses."

Dahlia picked a bourbon ball. "Seriously, though," she responded.

"I *am* serious."

"So you're content with this…arrangement?"

"Content?" Mosey said, breaking a piece of divinity in two. "Well, I don't know if I'm content. Distracted. I guess you could say I'm distracted—for now."

"You make these bourbon balls?"

"What do you think?" Mosey laughed. "Gift from John Earle," she said, holding up a decorative tin.

****

The following day, Dahlia and Tommy continued their road trip to Nashville, and Mosey and Robert, despite the chilly weather, decided to hike up Shingwauk Mound. They parked the car in the visitors lot and followed the trail to the top. There was nothing up there, no viewfinders or benches, just an amazing view.

"I don't know why we don't do this more often,"

Mosey said. A puff of wind whipped through, blowing her hood off her head. "B-r-r-r, it's cold."

"You want to head back?"

"Not yet." She hooked her arm through Robert's.

Except for Shingwauk and a smaller mound nearby, there were no elevations on the landscape, nothing to look at really but the flat alluvial plain and the meandering river. An icy haze lifted off the water and floated over the trees, swaddling the barren limbs in pale gray mist. The fields that stretched along the river were empty. It was New Year's Day, and nobody was working. Everything had stopped.

"I like it up here in winter," Robert said, scanning the view.

"You do?" She tucked her head into his shoulder.

"You cold?"

"Yeah." She pulled her hood up and tightened the cord.

"Let's go," he said, giving her a pat on her gloved hand.

"I never did finish telling you about the open house."

"Was there anything to tell?"

She followed him toward the dirt path. "Well, yeah, I mean—"

"What?" He glanced back.

"That guy Hopkins."

"What about him?"

"I didn't let on to Dahlia, but he did disturb me just a little," she confessed.

"Huh."

"Not so much while he was there but after he left."

"How long did he stay?"

"Not long. Maybe it wasn't Hopkins…maybe it was one thing and then the other: weird Hopkins, then the mittens."

"Mittens?" Robert stared back at his wife.

"I found a pair of child's mittens in the hall closet after Hopkins had gone. Probably belonged to Jane's little girl."

"All a tad creepy if you ask me." He stopped to catch his breath. "But you know," he continued, "if you think about it, there isn't anything alarming about Hopkins *or* the mittens." He opened his canteen and passed it to Mosey.

She took a drink and handed it back.

"It isn't so strange," Robert said, pausing for a drink, "that something belonging to Crump's stepchild should be left in the house—if, in fact, they *were* her mittens. And Hopkins, well Hopkins always was—how would you describe him?" He turned and continued down the path.

"Shoot," Mosey exclaimed. "I forgot to ask Dahlia and Tommy about the Texas murders."

"What Texas murders?"

"You didn't see it in the paper? Two real estate agents were killed, one in Dallas a few months ago and now another one in Beaumont."

"Give them a call. Better yet, check it out online."

She wondered if he'd have been so indifferent—at least, apparently so—had she told him about the open kitchen door and the footprints. He could wax scientific, do that professorial thing, whenever the occasion called for it, but she knew deep down he was a worrier. She decided to keep it to herself for a while longer, save him a few gray hairs.

Chapter Four

January 5, 2009, 3:30 p.m.
Waite House

At Mosey's insistence, John Earle sent his people back to Waite House to touch up the floors in the foyer and hall. Once they'd left, she curled up on the window seat in the study to read *Our Inner Ape*. She perused the first chapter and, comprehending de Waal's intention, set the book aside. In his view, human behavior, both good and bad, were traceable to the conduct of chimpanzees (*Pan troglodytes*) and bonobos (*Pan paniscus*). It was an interesting hypothesis, she had to admit. She wondered if Robert would agree.

"Bonobos, bonobos," she repeated aloud. Why was she just now learning about bonobos? They were the good apes, amicable, sexy, superior to their chimpanzee relatives. Hopkins, she mused, wasn't a bit amicable. Must be a chimp.

She began to rethink the murders—Crump's and the Texas realtors'—in light of the primatologist's findings. Could murder be a natural act stemming from some sort of residual aggression? A consequence of biological heritage? Seemed reasonable. She thought back to what de Waal had said about the motives of human aggression. Jealousy, fear, lust, material gain.

The dose of scientific rationality had left her more curious than concerned. She retrieved her cell phone from her tote and keyed in "realtors murdered in Texas." But seeing a text from Nadia, she opened it and read:

—Hey, sorry to bother you but I need that settee. I've got a buyer. I can lend you another one every bit as nice, okay?—

—Fine— Mosey texted back. *—I'll meet you at the store in half an hour.—*

She pulled up in front of the plate-glass window at Abboud's Antiques but, seeing that Nadia was occupied, went inside. She walked past Nadia and her client—a woman inquiring about a set of miniature soldiers—and made her way toward the back, dodging china, crystal, and other fragile items crammed together on tabletops and shelves. As she went, she kept an eye out for a settee suitable for the Waite House parlor. Finding nothing up front, she entered the back room where Nadia kept the bulk of her sofas, settees, and chairs, arranged in long rows with narrow spaces in between. A man was bending over an over-stuffed chair, running his fingers along what appeared to be a worn spot on the arm.

"Professor Hopkins."

He stood erect and nodded in her direction. "Ms. Frye, I believe. Anything to report about the house?"

"No, but I hope you're still interested," she said.

"Oh, well, I just might be. I need to talk to my accountant."

She smiled surreptitiously. He was interested for sure though not entirely ready to admit it. "Buying furniture?" She squeezed into the second row and sat on a plum, camel-back love seat.

"I'm not here to buy, not necessarily," he said.

"One does look, though. It's a hobby."

"I'm returning the settee you admired," she said. "Nadia, the store owner, let me borrow it for the open house, but now it seems she's got a buyer."

Instead of responding to her remark, he somewhat abruptly took his leave, sliding sideways along the aisle.

Well, that was rude. She followed him with her eyes to the front and out the door. As far as she could tell, he hadn't even glanced in Nadia's direction. But, judging from her friend's expression, she'd anticipated a final word. Nadia turned back to her customer, who was holding a miniature of an Egyptian camel rider in one hand, a dispatch motorcycle rider in the other.

"Which do you think?" the client said. "You know my husband's collection better than I."

"He tends to like exotic figures, doesn't he? Take the camel rider, and if he wants to exchange it, he may."

"That settles it then, and I'm sure he'll like it."

Nadia wrapped the miniature soldier in tissue and dropped it in a gift bag.

"But, if he doesn't," the client said, "we'll be back."

Once the woman had left, Nadia turned to Mosey. "That's odd."

"What?"

"That man who ran out of here a minute ago—he was the one asking about the settee. Did you see him? He left without a word."

"That's Evan Hopkins," Mosey said in a whisper, as if he were still around, "the man who showed up at the open house."

"Really," Nadia whispered back.

Mosey said nothing more, though she continued to wonder about the inscrutable professor. So far, he hadn't done anything she might regard as sinister. But as much as she relished the thought of unloading Waite House, she was a little wary of future encounters. Something John Earle had told her about safety for real estate agents suddenly came to mind: "If anything raises the hair on the back of your neck, girl, you get out of there soon as you can. You might feel like a dummy, but never you mind that. Just leave." Sounded like good advice. She was pretty sure she'd know right off if a client posed a threat. Hopkins was brash, yes, but so far, he hadn't raised the hair on the back of her neck.

Even though the sale of the settee had been left up in the air, Nadia and Mosey proceeded with the exchange. They agreed on the plum camel-back and loaded it onto Mosey's truck.

"Okay, let's go," Nadia said. "Back to the chamber of horrors."

Under different circumstances, Mosey might have laughed. But the tedium of dealing with a stigmatized property and an off-the-wall client was starting to wear on her nerves. The chance meeting with Hopkins hadn't helped. Was he buying the settee but not the house? Or maybe the settee *for* the house? She cranked the engine and pulled away from the curb. "So, what do you think of Hopkins?"

"A little abrupt," Nadia replied.

"Weird as heck, if you ask me. Turns out he's a retired geography professor, somebody Robert used to bump into around the college. Hopkins's son Brady was married to Robert's distant cousin—briefly, he said."

They reached their destination and carted the new settee around to the back, so as to enter the house at ground level. They made the exchange. Then, back at the shop, found a spot up front for the lime-green settee.

"Let me know," Mosey said, heading for the door, "if you hear from Hopkins."

"You running off?" Nadia picked up a cloth and set to polishing the rungs of a satinwood dining chair.

"I have to pick up a contract at the office and check my messages."

"Anyone interested in the house besides Hopkins?"

"Not yet."

"Sorry," Nadia said, "I thought by now, but I guess in this market…"

Mosey thanked Nadia for her help and headed to Shepherd Realty.

****

Activity in the Hembree housing market had dropped off considerably in the past year, and Mosey had begun to mull over the idea of canvassing, though it did seem like a terrible bore. She sat at her desk drumming her fingers. A plus, however, was that it would give her a perfect excuse to visit Delaney Crump's neighbors, Matthew Raines in particular. She might be able to get a look at that big Queen Anne of his, maybe even learn something more about Crump's murder.

What's he to you, silly?

"Delaney? Nothing, Daddy, nothing. How many times do I have to say it?"

Mosey looked at the black-and-white photograph that hung on the wall across from her desk, a picture of her father and grandfather at a fishing camp on Lake Chico. A big fish dangled between them. *I'm gonna catch me*... She'd heard them both say that many times. But today *she* was the one saying it, though not about a fish. She reached for her tote. The brochures from the open house were still there, enough of them to get her foot in the door of a good half-dozen houses. She could be at the Raines house in five minutes. She continued drumming her fingers, thinking through her plan. She'd wait till six or six-thirty when she'd be more likely to catch him at home. In the meantime, she'd drop in on some of the other McAllister residents. They, too, might have information relevant to the murder. They might even know something and not know they knew it.

On her way out, she stopped at the desk of Saffron Smiley, John Earle's personal assistant. "Saffron, you think I can go out canvassing dressed like this?" She glanced down at her deconstructed skinny jeans and boots.

Peeping over her newspaper, the attractively dressed African American lady—about Mosey's age—looked her up and down. "They've seen worse." She went back to her paper.

"Thanks," Mosey said emptily.

"You asked, sista. You want me to lie?" With a waggle of her head, she took a second glance at Mosey's bottom half and uttered a knowing "uh-huh."

Mosey walked away humming the jook song she'd had stuck in her head since the day of the open house. *Uncle John, Uncle John*...

"A *woman*...singing a song like that, uhn-uhn. Your momma's turning in her grave."

"Momma liked jook songs just fine. Ask John

Earle if you don't believe me."

"Uh-huh."

"And if anybody calls—"

"I know."

"Right."

****

Nobody was home at the house on the east side of Waite House, so Mosey crossed the street and followed the sidewalk to the house next to the Raines property. It was a less grand Victorian of the shingled style with rocking chairs scattered across the porch. She knocked.

A stunning woman answered the door. She wore a long, striped tunic and a brightly patterned scarf that pressed down a mass of tightly plaited braids. "Can I help you?" she said.

"I'm Mosey Frye, and I'm the real estate agent for the Crump property. I was hoping to see if you knew of other houses in the area that might go up for sale. If you have a minute—"

"Sure, I could spare a minute or two," she said, in a British accent. She led Mosey into the front room. "I'm Mae Baker. Won't you have a seat?" She gestured toward a mission-style sofa. Between the sofa and the leather chair, where her hostess had perched sidesaddle, was a table set for tea. A ceramic pot and cups sat atop a teak tray.

"Sorry, you must be expecting company."

"Well, yes," Ms. Baker said, "I have a friend coming a little later."

"If this is a bad time…"

"You're fine. Please, have a seat."

"Are you a newcomer to Hembree?"

Ms. Baker answered with a shake of her head.

"I've lived here off and on for years. I moved here with my parents when my father took a job at Blanchard. He was Associate Dean till he retired. My parents are back in England now."

"Of course, I remember him," Mosey said brightly. "Dean Baker. I went to Blanchard. So, I'm guessing," she continued, feigning disappointment, "you're not interested in selling?"

"Well, actually it's a possibility."

Mosey smiled and handed Ms. Baker her card. "I'm with Shepherd Realty. You must know John Earle Shepherd—he lives around the corner. If I could ever be of service…"

"Perhaps you could." She glanced at the card and tucked it inside the book she'd placed on the seat of the chair. "I'm wondering what prices they're asking for houses in the Historic District these days. Like the Crump house, how much?"

"It's listed for a million ninety-five."

Ms. Baker uttered a little gasp of delight. "That much? Would you say this house is comparable?"

Mosey dug in her tote for a brochure and handed it to her host. "Well, the styles are different. The square footage must be less. Do you know the square footage of your house?"

"No idea. I guess I ought to, but it's not really *my* house."

"I'd be happy to give you a guesstimate, if I could take a quick look around."

Ms. Baker said she was happy to oblige and showed Mosey through the rooms of the nicely furnished dwelling, spacious but with the feel of a rustic cottage. The foyer, living room, and dining room were partially paneled in hickory with chair railings in warm sorrel. The bedrooms were painted in neutral shades with wainscoting on the lower two-thirds of the walls.

"Your rugs are beautiful," Mosey said, admiring the wool floor coverings that stretched throughout the downstairs. "Would they stay with the house?"

She smiled. "I haven't thought that far ahead, but I suppose they might as well. My next place will be smaller, probably a condo. My parents wouldn't want the rugs—too expensive to ship them back to England."

Mosey pulled a calculator out of her tote. "The house is about three thousand square feet," she said dropping down on the sofa, "and at two hundred and sixty dollars a square foot—that's just an estimate, you understand—you might expect to list for…about seven hundred eighty thousand. Sound about right?"

"I'd have to think about it and talk to Mom and Dad. But I'll be honest—that's a good bit more than I'd imagined. Houses around here have become quite dear, haven't they? I wouldn't want to be *buying* one."

"Yes, especially in the Historic District. The rest of Hembree, well—"

"I know. I hear the bottom has fallen out."

"It's improving, but not what we'd hoped for."

Ms. Baker offered to make tea, but Mosey said, "Oh, I don't want to put you to any trouble."

"Or maybe you'd prefer a glass of sherry?"

"That would be lovely."

Ms. Baker crossed to the sideboard on the opposite wall and poured two glasses of Bristol Cream from a crystal canister.

Mosey took the glass and sipped. "Delicious."

"We bring it from London. It's about time for

another run."

"Are you planning a trip?"

"Well, I'm always planning."

"I know what you mean. Robert and I have been talking about taking a trip to England for years. We never go. There's always something."

"I won't be going right away. My mother's out of the country...visiting her sisters in Haiti."

"Your mom's Haitian. I think I knew that, actually. But you were born in England, right?" Mosey babbled on, at a loss as to how to segue into a conversation about Delaney Crump. But determined to broach the subject, even if clumsily, she said, "You know I've listed Waite House. The open house was just the other day."

"Oh?"

"I suppose you've seen the house."

"I've been there fairly often over the years, back when Evan Hopkins lived there, and then a few times after Delaney purchased the house."

"I didn't know the professor had ever *owned* Waite House. You know him, then, Professor Hopkins?"

"Yes, I know him. He and my father were close friends. I'm younger, but Evan and I still call on each other from time to time."

"So, he owned the house?"

"Evan is related to the Waites, and when Eason moved away...God, that's been a long time ago...he let him have the house. They were close, grew up together."

"Didn't know that." Mosey sipped her sherry. "Was he related to Delaney Crump, then?"

"No, Delaney was more or less Evan's protégé. He

gave him a good deal on the house. Otherwise…"

Ms. Baker stopped, leaving Mosey to wonder what was to follow. Otherwise…he couldn't have afforded it. Otherwise…he wouldn't have wanted it. "Otherwise he wouldn't have been interested?" she ventured.

"No, Delaney was quite fond of the place. But, well, he'd just gotten started in the cotton business and—"

"Quite a successful start, I'd imagine," Mosey cut in.

"But after he and Jane Fulton—Jane Middleton, rather…" She stopped mid-sentence. Something outside the window had apparently caught her attention. She set her glass down. "I'm sorry," she said, getting up. "I was expecting someone later, but I see she's here already." She waved through the window at a woman who had gotten out of a car. "But you must come again."

"Oh, goodness," Mosey said, "I didn't mean to stay so long. Thank you, Ms. Baker, for your time, and the delicious sherry."

"Call me Mae."

"Then you must call me Mosey."

On her way out, she crossed paths with the visitor, a woman a good bit younger than Mae. She was wrapped snugly in a tam and scarf, and only a narrow strip of face was exposed. Mosey looked into her pretty gray eyes, a tad cheerless, but pretty. The woman nodded, and Mosey nodded back, then crossed the street toward Waite House.

"One more stop, and I'm heading home," she muttered. The open house sign was still staked in the yard, Mosey having inadvertently left it behind. She toted it to the back of her truck and lifted it in.

The lights were on at the Queen Anne, and three cars were parked in the drive. Before heading over, she glanced back at Mae Baker's place. "That's funny," she mumbled. The plantation shutters, open when she was there, were now closed.

Chapter Five

January 5, 2009, 6:00 p.m.
Raines Residence

The imposing Queen Anne was gray with light cream trim. It sat at a fair distance from the street, and the land around it was thickly planted with live oaks and magnolias. A tall wrought-iron fence surrounded the property, and a richly designed gate discouraged the intrusion of strangers. Mosey hesitantly pushed back the gate and, with the last rays of the setting sun to light her way, walked the winding slate path to the veranda.

Near the front of the house she encountered the gardener, who, pulling his wheelbarrow off the path, allowed her to pass. He tipped his hat.

"Good evening," Mosey said.

"All right," responded the man with a slow nod of his head. She smiled at the greeting, heard commonly in her youth but rarely nowadays.

Gathering her courage, she rang the doorbell.

A young woman with dark hair and eyes opened the door part way and stared out irreverently. "Are the Raineses expecting you?" she softly drawled.

"I don't have an appointment, if that's what you mean, but if I could possibly see Mr. Raines, it'd only take a minute."

The woman stepped back, allowing Mosey to enter the foyer. "Wait here." She pointed toward a mauve, spoon-back two-seater, then faded into the darkness of the corridor.

Once the butleress was out of sight, Mosey looked through the parlor door to discern the arrangement of the room, which, according to the *Gazette*, was where Raines was sitting when he heard shots ring out from across the street. Near the middle of the elegantly decorated space stood a high-backed sofa and two upholstered chairs with a coffee table in between. Several rosewood chairs were scattered about the room, the focal point of which was an ivory-colored grand piano. Raines would have had to be sitting either at the piano or in one of the upholstered chairs to see Waite House. Over there, she said to herself, focusing on the chair nearer the windows. Unless, of course, he was playing the piano. But at eleven o'clock at night? Not impossible, she supposed. The windows along the south and west sides of the room were tall and shuttered. Wouldn't the shutters have been closed? Hmm.

The young woman's return brought Mosey's scrutiny to a halt. "Mr. Raines says he can see you now."

Mosey followed her along the corridor, glimpsing at tapestries of hunting scenes on the left and richly framed portraits on the right. At the first open door, she stopped and waited to be invited in.

"Come in, come in," came a voice from within the room.

The study, dark-paneled and stuffy, might have been a dignified space in the past but now had acquired the look of a ghoulish game room. Mahogany shelves, jam-packed with dusty gadgets, lined the walls. And, nestled among the gadgets, pheasants, ravens, and owls gawked warily from glass eyes. Raines pushed back from his workstation, housed in an Edwardian armoire, and got to his feet. "Matt Raines." He smiled, waving a hand toward a chair near his desk.

"Mosey Frye." She sat and dropped her handbag onto the carpet, a luxurious silk Persian—oh my. No expense spared here. "Sorry to bother you, Mr. Raines, but I'm the agent handling the sale of Waite House. I was thinking that you might just, uh, be aware of other properties in the neighborhood—if anyone's thinking of selling, I mean." She handed him her card. "I'm with Shepherd Realty."

"Well," he said, "have you spoken to Mae Baker? She's thinking of moving back to England." Raines, trim, lanky, and rather handsome for his age, sat back down in his swivel chair and propped his elbows on the arms. He made a steeple of his long fingers and stared over it guardedly at Mosey.

"Yes, I talked to her today."

"That's the only house I can think of, other than the Crump house."

"Come to think of it," she said, "if two houses went up for sale on the same block, well—"

"I see what you mean." He leaned back and smoothed his longish, silver hair.

"But then, these houses are such gems, and yours is quite beautiful." Not this room, she thought, looking around, but surely there must be one or two beautiful rooms in this huge house of his. "I would love a tour," she chanced, emboldened by her eagerness for information. She wasn't hoping for much, but any little clue would do. "Sorry," she added. "I didn't mean to be forward."

"Well, I suppose I could give you a short tour." A wry smile revealed a set of perfect teeth. He turned off the monitor and headed toward the door with Mosey at his coattails. As they went, he tossed out a few remarks about the furnishings, many of which dated from the initial occupancy of the house in 1880. "You won't see a lot of these old library tables." He tapped one as they passed. "If my wife weren't so taken with them, I might have sold that one to the young lady at Abboud Antiques."

"Then you know Nadia?"

"I met her recently. We ran by her store, just to look around—Charlotte and I."

She paused to admire an arrangement of antique wall mirrors. "I can't imagine parting with any of these beautiful pieces. They must be heirlooms. But Nadia would make you a good offer, should you want to sell."

"Much of it came down from my great-grandparents. But I must confess, I'm a collector."

While Mosey looked from mirror to mirror, Matthew paused at a bookcase and pulled a large volume from a set of books pressed between scrimshaw bookends. "So that's where you've been." He brushed a cobweb off the cover. "I've been looking all over for this." He handed it to Mosey. "*Sketches from the Dream Island of Birds.* It's a first edition. Are you familiar with Charles Van Sandwyk?"

"No, can't say I am." She flipped through, stopping at a picture of a bird in flight. " 'Follow your dreams,' it says. Are you a bird watcher?"

"Not really. However, I see them in my sleep, as did Van Sandwyk. But I've never painted them."

This man isn't a chimp, he's a bonobo. "Maybe

you should try your hand at it."

"Do you like to read?"

"Love to read." She handed him the book.

"What sort of books?"

"Whatever I pick up…opera, anthropology."

He frowned, no doubt juggling the terms of the perplexing combination. "Opera. Anthropology. Opera, anthropology?"

"Have you read *Our Inner Ape*?"

"No, haven't heard of it."

"Excellent book by Frans de Waal. I'll lend it to you when I finish."

He chuckled. "I have tons of books on my to-read list. Mostly from estate sales, like this one." He tucked the bird book under his arm. "I'll have a look at it later this evening."

As they wandered from room to room, Mosey, in hopes of gaining his confidence, spoke admiringly of the furniture and other finery, throwing out a comment here and there. They came to a small room between the dining room and library, the shelves and cabinets of which were packed tightly with crockery, paper weights, and pieces of antique glass, some clear, others in shades of iridescent green, turquoise, and gold. Just as they arrived, a cacophony of bells, chimes, and gongs rang out from a dozen or more clocks, some on shelves, others on a lacquered table in the center of the room.

"Looks like we've arrived just at the right moment," he said.

She gazed down at a small porcelain clock designed in the shape of a rose. "I love this one."

"It belonged to my mother, sat on her dressing

table."

She pointed to the only clock on the wall. "That banjo clock…"

"Belonged to my maternal grandfather. He brought it with him from Kentucky in the late eighteen hundreds. It's the best timekeeper of the lot."

Her eyes moved from the banjo clock to the adjacent wall, filled entirely with gun racks. "You collect guns, too. My goodness, you *are* a dedicated collector," she said, bending to examine an antique weapon.

"Why, yes," Raines replied. "That one is one of the finest ever made, or so the maker claimed."

"My grandfather had a shotgun just like that."

"It belonged to my grandfather. He and my father spent many a day afield, but I don't care much for hunting—not anymore."

"But you like guns, obviously."

"Yes, I do. Can't seem to get enough of them." He picked up a long-barreled rifle and held it to his shoulder. He looked through the scope, aiming at the arch that led to the dining room.

"You say you don't hunt?"

He shook his head.

"You must shoot, though."

"Now and then. Couldn't leave all of these firearms collecting dust."

Why not? Everything else was covered in it.

He put the rifle back. "Do you shoot?"

"I used to, a little. My grandfather—"

"I'm teaching Charlotte to handle a gun," he interrupted. "She fancies herself a sportswoman." He picked up a pistol with an embossed handle. "It's an excuse to get out of the house, with all the woods and ponds around."

"I wouldn't think she'd need an excuse."

"Oh, you know. Women tied to the house and all that."

She frowned, surprised to hear there *were* such women in the world. She couldn't think of a one. "Nadia has a falcon—did she tell you?"

"She didn't mention it. You share the interest?"

"She goes with her club, mostly. Mind if I—?"

"Go ahead."

"It isn't loaded, is it?"

Raines laughed. "You aren't suggesting I'd leave a loaded firearm around."

She balanced the shotgun between her palms. "My grandfather hunted with dogs, mainly beagles. But he had an old blue tick, Bachelor, he called him. Used to ride with him in the cab of his truck." She took aim at a white poinsettia on the dining room table. Just then, the butleress came through the arch and stopped with a start. Mosey lowered the gun. "Sorry."

"Mr. Raines, you have a call."

"Can't it wait?"

"It's your broker. He says it's urgent."

"May I leave you alone for a second? This won't take long."

Raines and the butleress left through the arch. Mosey put the shotgun back on the rack and, stepping softly into the library across from the parlor, tiptoed to the only window. It was on the front of the house, all right, but offered a view of the gardens, nothing more. A row of tall junipers blocked the view of Waite House.

At the sound of steps, Mosey resumed her position

in the collection room.

"Sorry to abandon you like that," Raines said.

"There's plenty here to keep a person entertained for hours." She stretched up to peep at a set of gold-rimmed, ruby brandy snifters on a shelf above the banjo clock.

"Can I offer you a drink?" He ushered her toward the parlor. "A glass of wine? A beer?"

"Beer or wine…either would be great."

"Melba," he said, stepping to the door that led into the foyer. "Could you bring us a couple of beers?" Then, turning back to Mosey, "Which do you prefer, dark or light?" he said. "I have a good selection of both."

She rattled off a few of her favorite brews—not entirely sure which were light and which were dark.

"See if I don't have a couple left from that new batch in the refrigerator, please, ma'am," he said to Melba, as he'd called her. Then, turning back to Mosey, he said, smiling, "We share a fondness for hand-crafted beers, I see."

Melba soon returned with a wooden tray filled with mugs, beer, a bowl of mixed nuts, and napkins. She set the tray on the console. "Anything else?"

"Yes, you can ask Mrs. Raines to join us if she'd like."

Melba departed, and Raines offered Mosey a seat. "These chairs," he said, gesturing toward the upholstered pair, "are fairly comfortable."

She sat in the walnut armchair and instinctively rubbed the lush, dark fabric. This was where Raines must have been sitting when he heard the shots—had to be. She could see Waite House perfectly well from there, part of it at least. The parlor…she could see the parlor but not the study. *Not* the study, which was the room where Crump had been murdered. If she craned her neck, she could see a small part of the left side of the house. Yes, she could see the edge of the study window. But *not inside* the window. She could see the window but most definitely not *inside* the room. So why—?

"What do you think of the beer?"

She took a sip. "I like it. I don't think I've tried this brand. You can usually find most of the local craft beers at the liquor store on Lee."

"This one is from Louisiana," he said. "We picked up a case when we were visiting Charlotte's relatives. They live near the brewery."

"You have relatives in Louisiana—so do I, around Lake Providence."

"Charlotte is from Mandeville."

"We were down at Thanksgiving," she said. "My cousins could use a man with your expertise." She took a sip of her beer.

"How's that?"

"Nutria rats," she replied. "They're destroying the Gulf Coast. You've probably heard."

"Yes," he said, wiping the froth from his lips. "But I wouldn't be of any help. I don't shoot animals, gave it up years ago."

"Not even a nutria rat?"

He shook his head. "Not even a nutria rat. Not any other kind of rat, either."

"Not a raccoon or a possum?"

"Well…I've been tempted to reduce the squirrel population. But no, I don't shoot animals."

"My daddy gave it up," she said.

"Oh?"

"My mother hounded him till he stopped. Killed a buck once, and that was the end of it—for Momma."

"Is Frye your maiden or married name?"

"Both. I didn't change my name."

"So your parents' name was Frye." He set his beer on the coffee table.

"That's right."

"Your father was Ellis Frye, I bet."

"That was my daddy." She smiled and sipped her beer.

"He had a law office on Main."

"That's right. Lee Street and Main...with his father, my grandfather."

"Amos Frye?"

"Granddaddy Amos was the one with the gun I was telling you about."

"And your mother was Marie. She was a Moseby, wasn't she?"

"Yes, she was. My middle name is Moseby—Anne Moseby Frye." She sat up straight and placed her beer on the table. She could think of endless ways to prolong the conversation, but she was anxious to get to the point of her visit, and starting down the path of do-you-know-so-and-so could be deadly in Hembree. She opted for a verbal leap. "Mr. Raines."

"Call me Matthew. I'm not so old, you know." He grinned.

"Of course, you aren't old...Matthew." What else could she say? She reached for her beer and took a sip before resting it again on the table. Scooting forward, she looked into his gray eyes. "Matthew, this isn't a pleasant subject but, well—"

He, likewise, moved forward in his chair.

"I can't help thinking—"

"Yes?" Raines said.

"—that Delaney Crump's demise has been a shock, well, for you and Ms. Raines."

All at once, his demeanor, previously carefree, became awkward. He scratched the top of his head, then pulled at his left ear. "Yes, a shock." He got up and strode across the room to the console, picked up a handful of nuts, and held the bowl out to Mosey. "Care for nuts?"

Her directness had evidently ruffled the waters, and, in an attempt to smooth them, she smiled and partook of his offering. "I shouldn't, but I will." She laughed nervously and, meeting him halfway, next to the piano, said, "This piano is gorgeous. Do you play?"

But before he could answer, Ms. Raines descended the stairs. "Matt, dear, I didn't know your guest was a charming young lady. I would have been down sooner."

"Charlotte, this is Ms. Frye...Ms. Mosey Frye. She's the real estate agent for the property across the street."

"Please call me Mosey." She accepted Charlotte's extended hand.

"And you can call me Charlotte," she replied in an accent not unlike Melba's, but the similarity ended there. The look was quite different. Melba's complexion was swarthy—she might be Cajun. Charlotte was quite fair and with sort of a pitiless mien, like a cabaret singer from a bygone era.

Charlotte sat in the chair where her husband had been sitting, and Raines poured a beer for his wife.

"Mosey, would you care for another?"

"Thanks, but, actually, I need to be getting home." Standing, she took her leave as graciously as she could. With Charlotte in the room, she had a feeling her visit was unlikely to render any additional information. And even if Charlotte hadn't come down, Mosey feared she'd bungled her chance to coax anything useful out of Raines. "Thanks so much for your hospitality."

"Wish you wouldn't go," Charlotte said.

"Your home is lovely." Mosey picked up her tote, glancing from wife to husband.

"No need to rush," Raines added. "I'm sure you and Charlotte have much in common."

"You are kind, but my husband's expecting me. I didn't mean to keep you. I didn't intend to stay so long."

"Not at all. Come again."

"Yes, please do," Charlotte echoed. "Did Melba take your coat?"

"No, I left it in my truck. It's warmed up a little today—don't you think?"

"I guess rain will follow," Raines said. "It usually does."

"Hope not. I'm enjoying the sun," Mosey replied.

He showed her out and, after a wave good-bye, she quickened her steps. But once the door closed, she looked back at the grand house—the largest on McAllister—and, pausing, stared up at the second and third stories, then across the street. That's interesting. Not a one of the Queen Anne's windows offered an unobstructed view of Crump's study, which was veiled by the roof of the veranda. "Funny thing about houses," she mumbled. She closed the iron gate. Vantage points, angles, obstructions—like the row of junipers outside the library window—had to be taken into account. Whatever Raines claimed to have seen inside Crump's study was purely imaginary. Or to speak more clearly, a blatant lie. "Plain as day." She got to her truck and pulled out her jacket. Mae Baker's parlor window was in plain sight. The shutters were now open, and the lights were on. Yet, from where Mosey was standing, she couldn't see the interior of the front room.

Mosey, go home. Your husband's waitin' for you.

"Oh, let him wait."

She switched on the ignition. Matthew and Charlotte Raines, some would say December and May. She shifted into first and pulled away from the curb. "Impressive gun collection," she muttered, shifting into second. "He lied. I'd swear it on my grandpa's grave." Not even from the piano bench, which she'd made a point to pass on her way out, could a person see the interior of Crump's study. Matthew had lied, but why? Why on earth would he?

Chapter Six

January 6, 2009
Mosey's House

After a night's sleep, Mosey was refreshed and ready to assemble the facts she'd gathered the day before. The particulars of the case had mysteriously mushroomed overnight, giving rise to shadiness where, in all probability, there wasn't any. She recalled her interview with Mae Baker, in which Mae had referred to Jane Middleton by her maiden name, implying theirs was a long-standing friendship, dating, maybe, from Jane's days at Blanchard. She'd also learned that Hopkins was Crump's mentor and the owner of Waite House before selling it well below market price to his protégé. The professor might have mentioned something about that but hadn't. And Mosey was naturally suspicious of tight-lipped individuals. If they weren't telling, she had to wonder why.

As she stood in front of the mirror, running her fingers through her hair, she reimagined her visit to the big Queen Anne. Her new information was scant, but what she had learned seemed central to the case—Raines was lying through his perfect teeth when he'd said he'd seen something in Crump's study. Her clever discovery, together with Raines's reaction to her mention of the murder, set her focus solidly on him. The atmosphere at the house was a little strained, was it not? An eccentric older man, respected in the community, married to a very attractive, much younger woman. Huh. Was Charlotte pleased with such a match? Not that she'd seen any obvious sign of discontent, but Raines—wouldn't he have felt uneasy with a well-off, good-looking divorcé living right under their noses?

To Mosey, the scenario spelled trouble. Across the street from the perhaps lonely Ms. Raines, she thought, putting on an earring, lived Delaney Crump, young, handsome, *rich*, divorced. Her eyes widened at the idea of it. She leaned into the mirror and brushed a little mascara onto her lashes. If such a scenario existed, mightn't Charlotte—yes, lovely Charlotte—have had a motive as well? Maybe, just maybe the divorced couple had settled their differences. Jane's visit to Delaney might imply a reconciliation. Or, if not, mightn't Charlotte have assumed as much? Seeing Jane at the house, she might have flown into a rage, grabbed a gun from her husband's arsenal, and shot him—ka-pow!— right in the heart. Mosey took a deep breath and gave her shaggy locks a final shake. Then what? She switched off the light and climbed the stairs to the kitchen.

Despite the various possibilities for discontent and violence, neither Raines nor his wife seemed like killers to her. He was a pleasant man, kind of a geek, interested more in games and collectibles than women. And if Charlotte *did* have an affair, would it have driven him to kill? People have affairs all the time. Rarely do the parties involved get smoked for it.

What's more, every time she looked coolly and calmly at Raines, up popped his *inner ape*. She'd pegged him as a bonobo from the start, and, in her mind, he wouldn't do anything a bonobo wouldn't do. She gathered her jacket, tote, and umbrella and headed out the door.

****

"Morning, Saffron." Mosey slipped off her jacket and hung it on the hall tree behind the door. It was the dead of winter, but the room smelled of something citrusy and pungent. "I smell—what's that I smell? Anyone inquire about my listings?"

"Nope." Saffron answered her second question but skipped her first.

Mosey sneezed. "You been buffing again with lemongrass ginger spray?"

"Yep," Saffron said.

"I told you I'm allergic to the stuff." Mosey pulled out a handkerchief and daubed at her nose.

"If I were you, Mosey, I'd put an ad in the paper." She pushed back in her chair, sighed, and got up, ready for a break from whatever it was she was doing.

"It's in the *Star Shopper.* I put it in the *Shopper*— that's where people advertise houses, isn't it?" Mosey backed away from reception, heading toward the coffee niche.

"Nobody reads the *Shopper*," Saffron said. "Put it in the *Gazette*, I'm telling you. Who the heck reads the *Shopper*?"

"I do—well, not that much. Nadia reads it all the time." She pulled a cup from the cabinet. Next to the coffee pot sat a small china tray covered in a pretty linen tea towel, embroidered in pale green leaves and tatted along the edge. She peeked under the cloth. "Oh, my. You're gonna make me fat if it's the last thing you do, aren't you?" The tray was filled with little stacks of biscuits, warm, flaky, and perfectly browned. She slid a biscuit onto a tea napkin and slathered it with butter.

"Make *you* fat. Ha."

Mosey made no response. It was more than established that she was skinny, Saffron was not, and neither was likely to vary more than a pound or two.

"The *Gazette?*" Mosey licked her fingers and picked up her cup and napkin. "Guess I could do that." She smiled at Saffron and walked on to her office.

An ad in the *Gazette*. Huh. She set her cup down and switched on the light. Yeah, an ad in the *Gazette*— could be the thing. And if she delivered the copy in person, she might just get to speak with a reporter— with a little luck, the guy who covered the Crump case. There she went again, trying to kill two birds with one stone. She plopped down at her desk and sat mindlessly shuffling papers, opening envelopes, tossing them into the recycle bin until Saffron appeared at the door, waving a yellow note.

"What?" Mosey said.

"The professor called."

"Professor who?"

"Your ten o'clock appointment. You haven't forgotten your ten o'clock appointment, have you?" She walked to the edge of the desk and, clearing a space, stuck the yellow note on the desk pad calendar.

"What?"

"She *says* can she postpone to next week?" She turned to leave. "You'd better finish that biscuit."

"Where'd you buy these?" Mosey took a bite and licked her fingers again.

Saffron's brow went up. "Uh-uh-uh...*buy* these,

61

she says." And with a swing of her hips, she walked away.

Mosey snickered as she punched in her client's number. "Saffron," she yelled. "I think I'll take advantage of this opening in my schedule to run over to the *Gazette*."

"You do that," Saffron yelled back.

After rescheduling her appointment for the following week, Mosey picked out some attractive shots of Waite House, prepared the copy for the ad, and headed to the office of the *Gazette*, which was just down the street. The sun had gone behind a dark cloud, and rain was coming down in heavy drops against the pavement. She stepped watchfully to avoid the puddles, ruminating as she went over a strategy to use with the crime reporter at the newspaper. What was the guy's name? Tab. Right. What should she say? Nothing direct. She winced, recalling her blunder at the Raines house.

Coming to the entrance, she shook out her shoulders and twisted the knob. "Get it right," she mumbled. "Get it right, girl. You might not have a second chance."

What do you think you're doing, young lady?

"Shush, Daddy! I don't have time for this."

Then you'd better make time, goofball. This is no game, girly. He's a reporter. A reporter! You hear me?

"Watch if you want," she said, wrinkling her nose. "You might learn something." Mosey was getting brazen in her "old age." She sassed her daddy even—something she'd never done when he was alive.

Watch your mouth, young un' or—

"Or what?"

She let the door bang behind her, leaving "him" to contemplate a rejoinder.

She passed reception and stopped at the desk where the business editor usually sat. She laid the manila envelope with the copy and the photographs in a conspicuous spot and, signaling to the nearest gofer, inquired with whom she might speak concerning a police matter. That sounded ominous. Police...why'd she said *police* when she could have said *property*?

A girl dressed in all black removed her oversized readers and scanned a row of metal desks where a half-dozen journalists sat, some busily composing copy, others talking on the phone. "Let me see if Mr. Wilson's free." She approached an untidy desk that bore a striking resemblance to the disheveled man that stood beside it struggling to balance a jumble of folders. The gofer tilted her chin toward Mosey and conferred with the reporter, who now eyed Mosey in a manner neither genial nor unreceptive but somewhere in between.

She recognized the man as Charles Tabbard Wilson, or Tab, as he was called at the Tavernette, where, on Friday nights, Mosey and Robert were regulars for happy hour.

The gofer motioned for Mosey to approach.

Wilson passed the gofer the pile of folders. "File these for me, Josie, if you don't mind." Turning to Mosey, he pointed toward the chair in front of his desk. "Have a seat."

Mosey offered him her hand, which he received with a strained smile. "I'm Mosey Frye. Thanks for seeing me." She twisted to prop her umbrella on the back of the chair. "I'm in a bit of a bind, and I thought you might be able to clarify a couple of things."

"What's this about?" He sat in his swivel chair and stretched back, exposing the front of a wrinkled cotton shirt.

"Here's my card. I'm an agent with Shepherd Realty."

He glanced at it, tucked it under his mouse pad, and silently waited for an explanation.

"The Delaney Crump case—are you familiar with the facts of the case?"

"I covered it," he answered without a blink.

"Good," she replied, glad for an affirmative response. "You must know," she continued, "that when a crime has occurred on a property, disclosure to prospective buyers is required. I'm anticipating an offer on Waite House and wanted to be sure I had all the facts."

"Well, the case has gone cold." Wilson hooked both thumbs over his waistband and rocked back in his chair.

"Yes, so I've heard."

"Crump was found dead, killed by a bullet wound to the chest." He unhooked his thumbs and stretched forward. "Two shots were fired, and, according to a neighbor—"

"Raines?" she interrupted.

"That's right, Matthew Raines."

"I understand only one witness came forward—is that correct?"

"Correct. He lives directly across from the house where Crump was killed, uh, Waite House, some people call it. He spoke to the police the next day."

"Raines reported seeing something, right?" Mosey

said.

"Yes."

She scooted her chair toward the desk and cleared her throat. "If Mr. Raines was sitting in his parlor when he heard the shots—"

Wilson cut in. "The body was found in the study next to the front window, and Raines said he saw Crump sitting next to the window looking out."

She nodded. "That's what the paper said."

"A short time later, he heard the shots."

"Yes, that's what I read, but I'm not sure how that could have happened exactly that way."

"Look," he snapped, "if you want the details, I can give you the details, but I can't solve the crime for you."

Under different circumstances, such effrontery might have caused a person's jaw to drop. But, no, she would not be intimidated. Not by an uncouth so-and-so like Tab Wilson. Instead, she calmly sat back, looped an arm over the back of the chair, and studied his eyes: the lowered brow, the deep circles, the fine lines at the corners.

Mosey, why are you doing that? Wilson isn't a suspect. What's more, there is nothing interesting about his dang eyes!

Her father was right. Wilson's face was all plain—mouth, nose, eyes. His head, on the other hand, had a peculiar shape to it, larger at the bottom than the top. What kind of ape might he be?

"No, of course not," she said. "I didn't mean to suggest you *solve* the case. My goodness, no. It's just that I've been looking for listings in the neighborhood, and Mr. Raines gave me a quick tour of the house."

Wilson's eyes narrowed.

"From the parlor— Raines said he was in the parlor, right? I couldn't see anything at all inside Crump's study, not from the parlor. That's why I'm confused."

The scruffy reporter made a show of ignoring her observation, first jamming his pencil into a beer stein stuffed with writing instruments, then opening the top drawer of his desk and rifling through scraps of paper, note cards, newspaper clippings. Some went into the trash, others landed on the floor, some few remained where they were. He glanced up. "Anything else?"

"No, I guess not." She forced a smile. Eager to depart the muddled workspace, she thanked him and rose to leave.

"Don't forget your umbrella."

"No, I won't." She could have cleared his desk for him in one clean sweep, but resisting, grabbed her umbrella and headed for the door. It had been silly her thinking she could wheedle anything out of Tab Wilson.

Then came the condescending voice.

Mosey, you should have known better. I told you so. You should have listened.

"Not a word, Daddy, not one word."

Chapter Seven

January 6, 2009, 11:20 a.m.
The Tavernette
That might have gone better. She'd approached the reporter hoping to establish some sort of tit-for-tat, but the strategy had flopped. She'd learned nothing more about the murder or Jane and Candice's disappearance. But even if her interview with Wilson had accomplished little, it had prepared her—yes!—for what was next. The police station. She expected to hear grumbling from her daddy, but, so far, nothing.

She checked her phone. It was eleven-twenty. She ought to grab a bite to eat before approaching Hembree's finest. She texted Nadia:

—*Want to meet for lunch at the Tavernette?*—

Nadia texted back:

—*Give me a few minutes to finish up with a customer. Mind swinging by to pick me up? My SUV is full of furniture.*—

—*Fine. Wait for me outside, if you can.*—

The rain was still coming down, and Mosey hurried back to Shepherd Realty for her truck. Shortly thereafter, she and Nadia arrived at the town square and parked near their destination. The Tavernette was a two-story frame building near the corner of Lee Street and Main. Union soldiers had burned it to the ground during the last months of the Civil War, but, some years later, the town had built it back and equipped it with tables, chairs, and booths similar to the original furnishings. Over time, the walls of the squarish first-floor rooms had filled up with photographs of battlegrounds, cemeteries, and veterans. The entrance and the area behind the bar had been turned into a repository of Confederate memorabilia: uniforms, canteens, guns. An old canon loomed reassuringly—or menacingly, as one cared to see it—from behind a massive wooden counter. The upstairs had been made into rooms to accommodate a handful of guests, which was all that was needed, given Hembree's limited draw on tourism.

Popular for its blue-plate special, the Tavernette at rush hour was packed. Professors jabbered in small groups around the bar or pecked away at tablet computers in booths along the back wall. Lawyers from the courthouse flung darts at the dart board mounted between busts of Jeff Davis and Major General Patrick Cleburne, Stonewall of the West. When Blanchard College was in session, students huddled around the foosball table in the back room, putting a little distance between themselves and the adult population.

Mosey and Nadia angled their way through the crowd in the bar and found a booth at the back. With students on winter break, they pretty much had the room to themselves. Mosey slid into the side that offered the best view of the entrance, thinking someone pertinent to her investigation might appear, like Wilson, Raines, or the new head of the police department, Lieutenant Gustavo Olivera. But, instead, it was Mae Baker who showed up, dressed in a blue-gray, open-collared shirt, slim-cut jeans, and a trench coat cinched at the waist.

"Look at that," Mosey remarked. She pointed a thumb in Mae's direction. "Mae Baker...that lady is looking good."

Nadia twisted around. "Mae...I know Mae."

As Mosey summarized for Nadia the goings-on of the previous day, her friend listened without interruption and, judging from her expression, seemed to be wavering between awe and trepidation.

"You dredged up all that in a single afternoon?"

"All that," Mosey said with a smile, "but I'd hoped for something I could sink my teeth in." She dragged the basket of crackers in her direction.

"You say Hopkins was Crump's mentor? Odd he failed to mention the connection."

"Huh. *Odd* for the human race. *Normal* for Hopkins. He make it back for the settee?"

"Not yet."

In describing her encounter with Matthew and Charlotte Raines, Mosey underscored Raines's reaction to her mention of the murder. "We were sitting in the parlor having a beer—a craft beer he'd brought from Louisiana. His wife is from there...Mandeville. She doesn't look Cajun, but her cousin Melba does. Anyway, everything was going fine, he'd given me a tour of the house. Amazing place—have you seen it?"

"Haven't had the pleasure."

"You know about the collections, though."

"What collections?"

"Antique glass. Beautiful pieces. Crockery, clocks, and a whole wall full of old guns."

"Nice. I don't suppose he'd want—"

"I doubt it," Mosey cut in. "But who knows. He

said he'd picked a lot of it up at estate sales."

A pint-sized woman with hair teased high into a poof arrived to take their order.

"Want to split a Tavernette special?" Nadia said.

"Sure. I'm not really that hungry. And bring me a beer, Susie, will you?" Maybe a beer would build her confidence for the afternoon's endeavor. "With extra lime, please, ma'am."

"You want a draft?" Susie said.

"No, bring me a Quarter Moon."

"I'll take the same," Nadia said.

"And a couple of glasses of water?"

"Yes, please, and no ice for me," Nadia added.

"Ice for me."

"I'll be right back with your water and beer."

The waitress scooted away, and Mosey continued her account. "Here's the strange part. The instant I mentioned Crump, the whole thing fell apart."

"What fell apart?"

"I was trying to get Raines to spill the beans, tell me what he knew about the murder."

"Oh."

"Strangest thing," Mosey went on. "He jumps up, crosses the room—"

"That's odd."

"The man was rattled, I'm telling you, completely rattled. But before he does that, he reaches up and scratches the top of his head."

Nadia laughed at her friend's imitation. "You look like a chimpanzee."

"Exactly, and just when I was thinking he was a bonobo—"

"A bonobo—what?"

"Yes," she said firmly. "A bonobo. According to de Waal—the book I'm reading—bonobos are friendly, but chimps can turn dang surly. A chimp will gobble up a baby, if given half a chance."

"Oh, please."

"You don't believe it? Read the book. You see, there're four types of primates, besides us."

"Us!"

"Certainly. Human beings are primates—didn't you know?"

"But we aren't apes."

"No, of course not, silly. There're four species of apes: chimpanzees, bonobos, orangutans, and gorillas."

"Fine. But what's that got to do with anything?"

"Everything. Well, not *everything*, maybe, but *something*, definitely something. You see, personalities differ. Some people are like chimpanzees. Others, like bonobos. Men, in general, are chimpish. Women, not so much."

Nadia wrinkled her brow.

"Raines was friendly as could be—like a bonobo—when he was showing me around the house, but soon as I mentioned the murder, his demeanor completely changed."

"Wonder why."

"Precisely—why?"

Nadia's brown eyes flashed from one side of the booth to the other as if figments of the hairy creatures had materialized in thin air. "So you were thinking Raines was a bonobo and couldn't have committed the murder, but then—"

Susie was back with glasses of water and mugs of beer. "Here's some extra lime, ladies."

"Thanks, Susie." Mosey pulled her mug toward her and took a hearty drink.

"You're going to drink that on an empty stomach?" Nadia said.

"Nope." She popped a cracker in her mouth, then squeezed the last drop of juice out of a lime slice. "But if I get a little tipsy, all the better."

"I think I'd better wait for the burger." Nadia pushed her beer aside and took a sip of water. "Now," she began, "if Raines were involved, it seems to me he'd have shown a bit of caution. I mean, he'd have been watching himself—don't you think?"

"Watching himself," Mosey repeated.

"Yeah, watching what he said, how he reacted."

"If he's smart he would, I suppose."

"So, if he were guilty, he would be trying his darnedest not to *look* guilty."

Mosey nodded in agreement, stuffing another cracker into her mouth.

"So looking guilty," Nadia said, "could mean he's innocent."

Mosey, still chewing, shook her head, then took another sip of beer. "But why carry on like that if he weren't involved? Doesn't make sense."

"No, it doesn't." Nadia stared into her glass for a second, then continued. "He was the one who called the police, right?"

"Yes, said he'd seen Crump sitting near the window. There's *no way* he could have seen him, not with Raines in the parlor and Crump in the study— which we know is true."

Nadia switched water for beer and took a sip. "Why couldn't he have seen him? The houses are right across the street from each other."

"It's the angle. The angle's all wrong." Mosey grabbed a couple of packets of crackers, placed them one across from the other, and slipped a straw in between. "You can't see inside the study from Raines's parlor—not even if you were standing at the window," she explained. "See?" With a couple of toothpicks she indicated the line of sight between Raines's parlor and the crime scene. "You could see the window, but you couldn't see *inside* the window."

"Huh?"

Mosey glanced around the room. "Look over there." She pointed across a row of booths to the floor-to-ceiling windows that looked out on the courthouse. "You can see the courthouse windows, but you can't see inside."

Nadia rose slightly above her seat. "I see what you mean. Maybe Raines was in another room. Maybe he forgot exactly where he was standing."

"I thought about that. The library is the only other first-floor room with a front view, and there's a row of tall junipers right outside the window." She broke off a short piece of toothpick to indicate the position of the shrubs. "You can see a small stretch of the grounds. That's it."

Nadia puckered her brow and took a look at the mock-up.

"Later on," Mosey proceeded, "when I was walking away from the house, I checked the upstairs windows. If Raines had been upstairs, on the second or third story, he *still* couldn't have seen inside the study. The roof's in the way."

"What roof?"

"The roof over the veranda."

"So," Nadia considered, "no matter where a person was standing, he or she could *not* have seen inside the study. Could not. Consequently…Raines must have lied to the police, unless—"

"What?" Mosey said.

"Unless Crump wasn't in the study."

Mosey shook her head. "Of course he was in the study. Raines said he saw Crump *in the study.* The study has a big window and cushions in front of the window. We've sat in there a dozen times—at that very window."

"Well, good grief, who pays attention?"

Susie arrived with their order and two plates. "Can I get you ladies something else, another beer?"

"I'm good," Nadia said.

Mosey held up her half empty mug. "I may want another, but not quite yet."

"Just let me know." She tucked her tray under her arm and headed to another booth where a foursome was signaling for refills.

Nadia divided up the burger, fries, and slaw. "You want the pickle?"

"You can have it."

Nadia snapped off a bite of kosher dill. "They have the best dill pickles. Sure you don't want half?"

Mosey shook her head. "I don't like dill pickles. You know that."

"As I was saying," Nadia continued, "Raines probably said what he *thought* he saw, but maybe what he *really* saw—"

"No, no, no," Mosey interrupted. "He lied. I'm sure of it."

"You can't be sure." Nadia shook her head.

"Okay. Maybe you're right. I can't be *sure* he lied. But I can be dang sure *he didn't tell the truth*." Mosey slathered her half bun, top and bottom, with mayonnaise, sprinkled the patty with pepper, and took a bite. "Yum, this is tasty." She put back the packets of crackers and placed her beer and water next to her plate. "By the way, I dropped by the *Gazette* to talk to the reporter who covered the case. Tab Wilson," she said, pausing to chew, "for all of two minutes." She wiped her mouth.

"And?"

"Nothing. Just what I already knew from reading the paper."

"You're not going to get anything out of Wilson." Nadia finished off the pickle and took a bite of slaw.

"What makes you say that?"

"You've met him, and you have to ask?" She raised a forkful of slaw to her mouth. "Uh-uh-uh, what do they put in this? It is so-o-o good."

"I'm thinking—"

"Thinking what?"

"—I might drop by the police station."

"Oh, oh, oh!"

"What?"

"Mosey, have you lost your feeble mind?"

"Hey," she said with a broad grin. "I forgot all about that. You've been to the police station. What's it like? I've never been."

Nadia, who'd squabbled with a couple of officers concerning a robbery at the shop, was able to describe the station in some detail. "It's like any big office." She put down her fork. "There's a receptionist and, behind her desk, there's a whole bunch of cubicles." She swirled her index finger around the imaginary room. "The walls are covered in bulletin boards, framed documents, that sort of thing."

Mosey eyed the "space" Nadia had created, as if she were actually standing in it.

"People are sitting around in uniforms," Nadia continued, "with guns strapped to their hips."

Mosey recoiled.

Nadia threw back her head and laughed.

"Oh, funny."

"The look on your face…"

Her eyes drifted from Nadia's face to a blank spot on the wall. At the mention of guns, she remembered the collection of munitions she'd seen at the Raines house. "I wonder if the police checked the gun collection."

"What gun collection?"

"At the Raines house. Aren't you listening to me?"

"I'm listening, but you can't expect me to remember every little detail." Nadia picked up a fry and dipped it in the slaw. "Raines is an important man. And besides, they'd have to show probable cause." She blotted her lips with a napkin. "The fries are a bit soggy—don't you think? They used to be nice and crisp here. Aren't you going to eat your fries?"

Mosey, still pensive, ignored Nadia's critique of the fries. "Right. And the lie he told about seeing Crump shortly before the murder, that would constitute probable cause."

Nadia pushed back her plate. "Maybe…but it's a long stretch."

"We'll see." Mosey's voice trailed off as she stood

and looked around for Susie. "I'll be right back."

Mae Baker, still seated at the bar, motioned to Mosey.

"Hey, Mae. You're looking great."

"Thanks, I'm on my way to the Little Rock airport. Going to visit my parents."

"So you're going after all. Your mom get back from Haiti?"

"She cut her trip short. I think she was anxious to get home."

"I hope everything is okay."

"Oh, yes, she's just that way, a homebody, I guess you could say."

"You'll be back, though."

Mae nodded. "Not ready to pull up roots quite yet."

"If you ever do, I hope you'll give me a call," Mosey said, shifting into realtor gear.

"Of course, but I doubt I'll sell the house for at least a year or two."

"Remember us to your parents...Robert and me. Your father won't have forgotten Robert. Unlikely he'll remember me."

"His memory is pretty sharp, and he was very attached to Hembree. I'm not sure he's glad he left."

"Well, you have a good trip."

Mosey paid the check, said good-bye to Mae, and walked back to the booth. "Nadia, you want a ride to the store?"

"I think I'll finish my beer and walk back. Call me," she said. "Don't forget."

"Oh, I won't."

Chapter Eight

Mosey had drunk her beer in vain, for when she reached the police station, which was in sight of the Tavernette, she found that Lieutenant Olivera had "gone fishing" and wouldn't be back for a day or two.

She walked toward the square and, at the corner of Lee and Main, stopped near a familiar door. Beyond it rose a long flight of stairs, worn down to the square nails by the trample of river men: stragglers and gentlemen in white linen suits, some seeking retribution, others, the quiet advice of Amos Frye. Instinctively, she touched the slender gold letters on the translucent door pane. The name of Amos Frye was as faint as a ghost. His son Ellis's name was legible but barely. "Humphrey," on the other hand, was clear and intact, as it should be. Carlotta Humphrey, the only surviving member of Hembree's premier law firm, had taken over the practice at her stepbrother's death.

Mosey had been in awe of her sophisticated step-aunt from the time she'd first caught a glimpse of her, walking arm in arm with her new stepfather at the Napoleon Hunting Club fish fry. But she had to admit that Carlotta had never shown her any particular interest, despite the fact that, at Ellis's death, Mosey had been left without parents or siblings.

She trudged up the long flight of steps and stopped before a second door, solid and plain. She rang the bell and entered.

"Aunt Carlotta around?" She directed her inquiry to a gray-haired woman, as pleasantly smooth and soft as a downy pillow. The woman's fixed stare changed to joy. "Mosey! Come in here, girl. I haven't seen you in, good grief—"

"I know, I know. I always say I'm going to drop by, but you know how it is."

"Uh-huh, uh-huh, I know *just* how it is." The woman Mosey's grandfather had hired as his first paralegal emerged from behind the desk to give her a hug and an affectionate pat on the hand. "Your Aunt Carlotta's not here just now. She'll be back after lunch." She pushed back the sleeve of her dark gray suit coat to check her watch. "Twenty minutes, maybe thirty? She'd love to see you. I know she would. Can't you wait?"

"It's nothing important. I was just wondering about some family stuff."

"Everything's okay, I hope." Dot knitted her brow and stared at Mosey over silver-rimmed, cat-eye readers.

"Oh, yes. I was thinking about something Daddy used to say and thought Carlotta—"

"I doubt she would know anything about that," she said with a wink, "but you can ask." Tugging at Mosey's coat sleeve, she led her to the large leather couch where, from the time Mosey was big enough to wiggle free of her mother's grip, she'd jumped and tumbled without the slightest reproof from Dot Cowsley. Mosey sat, and Dot looked pleased. "Now, then. What was it you wanted to know?" She tapped her foot impatiently against the bare wooden floor.

Mosey, you asked for it.

Mosey glanced at the ceiling—where she imagined her daddy to be—and glowered.

"Can I get you something, a cup of coffee?"

"Don't go to any trouble."

Dot shook her head cheerfully. "It's no trouble, hon. I've just made a pot." She pitter-pattered into the next room and returned with a steamy cup of fresh-brewed coffee. "You want something in that? Sugar substitute, a little half-and-half?"

Mosey smiled and accepted the cup. "Black's fine."

Dot sat beside her. "Now, what was it you wanted to know?" The matronly paralegal couldn't have looked more gripped if she'd been Amos Frye's hound dog Bachelor and Mosey had been a raccoon up a tree.

"Dot, it's nothing. I've just..." She stopped mid-phrase and glanced at the ceiling again.

"What?" Dot scooted a little closer.

"Well, as I said, it's really nothing, but you know Daddy used to tell me not to go running around over at Waite House."

"Waite House."

"You know."

"Of course I know Waite House. Bud and Helen's house."

"So...you don't know what he might have meant by that?"

"Well, okay, I can think of one reason your daddy might not have wanted you hanging around the Waite place."

"You can?"

"It was that youngest girl of theirs, Mona. She and your father were friends in high school. Then, they dated in college—or was it law school?—until Bud caught wind of it." She stopped.

"What?"

Dot's shoulders drooped forward, and her head tilted up, as if she wished she hadn't started down that road. "Well, Mona was—how shall I put it?—a strong-willed girl, sort of like your momma."

"What did Mona do?"

"She got mad one night, had a little too much to drink."

"Go on."

"According to Ellis, she called him up, wanted him to meet her at the Tavernette."

"So?"

"She never showed up."

"Why not?"

"Well, you see, nobody ever knew that."

"Never knew?" Mosey said with a tilt of her head.

"She didn't show up, didn't go home, not that night or the next or the next, until finally, sometime later, her parents got a letter postmarked Los Angeles, I think it was, or San Diego, maybe—I don't remember for sure."

"Goodness." Mosey blew her coffee and carefully sipped.

"As you might guess, her daddy blamed *your* daddy, but, of course, it wasn't *his* fault. It definitely wasn't Ellis's fault."

"So what did Daddy do?"

"He tried his best to find out what had happened to

her. Called half the student body over at Fayetteville. Nobody knew a thing."

"Did anybody ever find out why she left?"

"I don't know. People figured she got sick of her daddy telling her what to do and what not."

"Huh. Did she ever come back?"

"She sure 'nough came back. After your daddy had married your momma."

"So that's all there was to it?"

"Well, as far as was known." She affected a blank look and twisted in her seat.

Mosey sipped her coffee and smiled at Dot. "I appreciate your telling me."

"Course, hon. Glad to help." Dot paused to study Mosey's face. "But now *you* tell *me* something."

I warned you, Mosey.

She picked up the voice clearly enough but held her tongue, not wanting Dot to hear.

"What got you to thinking about that," Dot said, "I mean, what your father used to say?"

"I've listed Waite House."

"Oh, really?"

"I wasn't especially keen on the idea, but John Earle pretty much insisted."

"I see. I'd think you'd stand to make a killing on a place like that."

Unfortunate choice of words, Dot.

Mosey set her cup on the end table. "If it sells."

"Why wouldn't it?"

To start with, it was stigmatized—which was plenty reason in her book. But, not wanting to get into that, Mosey just shrugged and said, "No reason."

"Of course, it'll sell. You just do whatever it is you

realtors do, and you'll sell it before you know it."

"I just put an ad in the *Gazette*. I expect that'll help. I guess I could ask Aunt Carlotta if she knows anybody looking for a big house."

"Now, that's an excellent idea," Dot said. "Carlotta knows half the county."

Mosey, having decided not to wait for her aunt's return, thought now as good a time as any to take her leave. "Maybe you could mention it to her, if you don't mind," she said, standing.

"Don't rush off."

"Dot, you're a sweetheart, but I've taken enough of your time."

"Come by any time you want, and I'll tell Carlotta what you said, just as soon as she gets back. Sure you don't want to wait?"

"No, I need to get going." Mosey reached for her tote.

"Okay, hon, but you call Carlotta in a day or two. She might be able to help you out with the Waite place. And if I hear of anybody looking for a big house..." She hugged Mosey again and let her slip through the door. "You come on back, whenever you want—you hear?"

****

Mosey bided her time and returned not to Frye, Frye, and Humphrey but to the police station as soon as the Chief of Police was back from his fishing trip.

She stopped at the front desk and told a sullen-looking receptionist she'd like to speak with Lieutenant Olivera. The woman made a call, then pointed Mosey toward the far side of the main office. Mosey scanned the room as she went. It was just as Nadia had described: gray walls covered with bulletin boards and framed documents, and metal desks and chairs arranged in rows with partitions in between. A cubicle at the most distant corner of the room was Olivera's office. She came to the glassed-in space, tapped on the open door, and waited.

"Come in," came a low voice. The lieutenant—tall, dark, and handsome, to put it in briefest form—was pulling files from a cabinet in the corner. Undistracted by Mosey's entrance, he continued with what he was doing.

"Hi, I'm Mosey Frye. I'm the agent managing the sale of Waite House." She pulled a card from her pocket and waved it in his direction. "I'm with Shepherd Realty."

"I'm sure you received the standard disclosure report from the attorney. I doubt I have anything to add." Olivera looked up, pushed the file drawer shut, and took a seat in his high-backed Naugahyde executive.

"Yes, I did receive the standard form. It's just that I've been canvassing the neighborhood and came across something—purely by accident—that bothers me a little." She slipped off her gloves and jacket and, in response to his gesture, sat in a folding chair next to his desk.

"Go on," he said.

"I read in the paper, right after Delaney Crump's murder, that it was Matthew Raines who called the police."

"Yes, that's correct."

"He said he'd seen Crump seated at the window, the study window, shortly before the murder. That's what was in the paper."

"Sounds about right."

She propped her elbow on his desk and leaned in. "I think Raines was mistaken."

"Mistaken." He shifted in his chair. "What makes you think that?"

"I was at Mr. Raines's house the other day. I wanted to see if he knew of any properties in the neighborhood. I was canvassing."

"You were looking for listings, you mean."

"Exactly, the housing market, well, I don't need to go into that." She swatted her gloves idly against her knee.

Mosey, get to the point. Just say what you came to say.

"The point is," she said, "I was in the parlor. Well, first, Mr. Raines showed me the house, and then he invited me into the parlor for a beer."

"Go on."

"I was sitting in a chair not far from the windows. I guess I glanced out in the direction of Waite House. It was in plain view, and, if I craned my neck, I could even see the study window. But I couldn't see *inside* the window."

"You couldn't see *inside* the window." He shifted again.

"That's right. I could see the window, but I couldn't see inside. If anybody had been sitting there, on the window seat, I mean, I wouldn't have known it. You see, the angle, the line of vision—"

"I understand," he cut in. "You're saying the angle was wrong." He stared uncomfortably at Mosey.

"The windows line up in such a way—" She

dropped her gloves and used her hands, one behind the other, to indicate the line of sight.

The detective crossed his legs, accidentally kicking the front of the metal desk. Mosey jumped, let out a nervous laugh, and scooted back.

"Let's go over that again, if you don't mind," he suggested. "You were standing at the window, and you determined that a person—"

Mosey shook her head. "No, Lieutenant, I wasn't actually standing *at* the window. I was sitting in a chair, but it's the only place Mr. Raines could have been sitting—he said he was sitting, right?"

"Well, I'd have to check that."

Mosey pulled a folded sheet of paper out of her tote and, unfolding it, placed it on his desk.

"What's this?"

"It's a copy of the story that appeared in the *Gazette*. If you look about halfway down the first column, you'll see—" She stopped talking and waited for him to find the paragraph that summarized Raines's statement.

He read, then looked at Mosey. "You're correct in what you say—well, based on this." He pushed the paper aside. "But reporters don't always get things right. I'd have to check the official report."

"The official report—that's what I was wondering about, if the official report matches what it says here."

"That's quite a bit of information to plow through, Ms. Frye."

Her face fell. "Oh. I thought it might be a matter of pulling out a couple of files."

He grinned and shook his head. "No, ma'am, I'm afraid not."

"So, I guess—"

"Ms. Frye, I don't exactly have time on my hands."
He leaned back and ran his fingers through his hair.

"I know, Lieutenant. I really didn't mean to create
more work for you."

*Don't lie to the man, for God's sake, Mosey. He's a
detective.*

"Yes, I'm sure you didn't." That's what he said,
though, in actual fact, his wrinkled brow seemed to
indicate something else. Like, what the devil was she
doing there? If she'd been a family member—someone
related to Crump or his missing ex-wife—perhaps
then...

Mosey made an effort to look hopeful, despite her
misgivings.

Olivera sat for a minute, tapping his fingers on the
glass desktop. He stopped, looked around. "Springer,"
he yelled.

A burly redhead poked his head in. "Yes, Chief?"

Olivera reached for a notepad and scribbled, then
ripped off the top sheet.

Springer accepted the paper and read. "Right now,
Chief?"

"Right now, Sergeant."

Olivera made signs of getting up.

"One more thing, Lieutenant," Mosey said. "The
murder weapon."

He leaned back. "What about the murder weapon?"

"I believe I read—" She picked up the *Gazette*
article from his desk. "—yes, it says right here: 'A
thorough search of the premises failed—' "

He interrupted. "The weapon hasn't been found, if
that's what you're getting at."

"So this is correct, then."

"Yes." He exhaled noisily.

"Lieutenant Olivera." She stopped, looked over her shoulder, then back at the lieutenant. "Please don't take what I'm about to say the wrong way." She reduced her voice to a whisper and leaned in. "But—"

"But what?"

"If a person were to need a gun, he or she could readily find one at the Raines place. He's got a *gun collection.*"

"A gun collection." He paused. "In Hembree, Ms. Frye, everybody and his brother—"

"I know, I know, Lieutenant." She half covered her eyes with her hand and peeped out. "That was awfully silly of me to think that just because Mr. Raines has a gun collection…" She dropped her hands in her lap. "Wouldn't have any relevance to the Crump case, course it wouldn't." She erased the implication with a sweep of her hand.

Her ramblings had apparently captured his interest. He picked up a pencil and jotted something down. But Mosey, having said what she'd come to say, rose and reached for her tote.

He stood, too. The conversation ended. "Sergeant Springer will show you out." He positioned his head to better yell through the door. "Springer!"

"Yes, Chief?"

"Show Ms. Frye out, would you?"

"Certainly." The sergeant flashed a wide, toothy smile in Mosey's direction and stepped aside. "After you, ma'am."

"I appreciate your taking the time, Lieutenant."

He nodded.

She walked away, Sergeant Springer at her elbow.

****

Days passed. Mosey learned nothing more about the Crump case. Apparently, the information she'd entrusted to the professionals hadn't produced the follow-up she'd hoped for. She decided to give Olivera a call.

"Lieutenant, this is Mosey Frye. Sorry to bother you again. I was just wondering. Do you know if the FBI has found any trace of Jane Middleton?"

"That investigation is out of our hands. The FBI took it over practically from the start."

"But they would have contacted you, had they found something."

"Probably, but not necessarily. Look, Ms. Frye, I'm not in the habit of giving out information to the public."

"I know. I'm sorry. It's just that some of us knew Jane in college, and we're concerned. She's been missing for some seven months now."

"If anything comes up, you can read about it in the *Gazette*—okay?"

"And the baby—he's with Ms. Crump, Delaney's mother?"

"It's my understanding she got temporary custody. Look, I'm pretty busy here."

"Okay, well, thanks for your time."

Having garnered nothing from her conversation, she thought of another possible source: Mae Baker. She wondered if Mae was back from England. She could stop by Waite House and, from there, drop in on Mae.

****

At Waite House, everything looked pretty much

the same. She glanced guardedly at the Queen Anne. One car was parked in the drive, and a light was on in one of the upstairs rooms. The wrought-iron gate was closed, and no one was on the grounds: not Matthew, Charlotte, the gardener, or the insolent butleress.

She parked the truck in front of her listing, crossed the street to the Baker residence. She rang the bell, and Mae came to the door.

"Mosey, hi, won't you come in?"

"No, I don't want to keep you. I was just wondering if you'd heard anything about Jane."

"Not a thing. Why?"

"You might remember Dahlia Qoph and Tom Banks? They were here recently and were asking about Jane. We knew her at Blanchard."

"Yes, you were all there about the same time— weren't you?"

"We graduated together."

"Well, sorry, but I don't know any more than you."

"And I don't suppose you've been in touch with Delaney's mother or sister?"

"No, actually, I just got back in town a few days ago." She took a step back.

"Of course, sorry."

"No problem. Anyone interested in the house?" She glanced toward the house in question.

"Not a soul." Mosey sighed. "At least no one ready to put up any earnest money."

"That's too bad," she said, echoing Mosey's sigh. "Must be frustrating."

"Yes, I'm feeling a bit stymied I guess, waiting for winter to end." She stepped away from the door. The conversation was beginning to seem pointless—like the telephone conversation with Olivera earlier that day. "I've taken enough of your time. You must be tired from your trip."

"Yes, jet lag coming back is always worse than it is going."

"Yeah," she said with a nod. "I've noticed that, too. Get some rest, and thank you again." She was about to give her a hug—she wasn't sure why—but then didn't, remembering that the British weren't big on hugging.

As Mosey crossed the street in the direction of her truck, she couldn't help but look again at the windows of the Queen Anne. The light she'd seen before had been turned off, and the car was missing from the driveway. She leaned against the railing, scanning the front of the house. Then, a sound came from the entrance, and the door opened just a crack. Mosey waited, thinking she'd wave at whoever stepped out. But no one did.

Chapter Nine

January 31, 2009, 8:30 a.m.
Mosey's House
Mosey opened her voice mail. The number was unfamiliar, but it was the voice of Tab Wilson, reporter for the *Gazette*: "Ms. Frye, Tab Wilson here. Meet me at Waite House before ten this morning, if you can. No need to call back."

Robert had already left for an eight o'clock class, and it was a little early to call Nadia. She would text her anyway and ask her to drop by Waite House before she opened the shop.

The phone rang as Mosey was stepping out of the shower. "Hey, I was hoping it was you," she said, patting her short locks with a towel.

"What's up?" Nadia said.

"I got a message from Tab Wilson asking me to meet him at Waite House before ten."

Nadia responded between yawns. "You're kidding."

"No, I'm not kidding. Can you meet me?"

"Why?"

"I'm a bundle of nerves."

"Okay," Nadia muttered. "I'll be there, but pick me up a coffee and a blueberry scone."

Shortly before the appointed hour, Mosey and Nadia were sitting in the cane-back chairs in the parlor of Waite House, having their coffee and pastry. Brushing the crumbs from her hands, Nadia walked to the window. "Looks like Wilson's a no-show."

"He'll be here," Mosey said.

"What do you make of it?"

"Clueless."

"You think he's interested in buying the house?"

"Him?" Mosey frowned.

"It must have to do with the case, then."

"Of course, what else?"

"But you said he didn't give you the time of day."

"He didn't," Mosey said.

"Hey, come here." She beckoned for Mosey to join her at the window.

Two patrol cars had pulled up in front of the Raines property, and three men were getting out—one in street clothes, the other two in uniform. It was Olivera, followed by Springer and another officer. They walked through the gate, up the sidewalk, and onto the veranda. Melba opened the door, just as another car arrived and parked in front of Waite House.

"Must be Wilson," Nadia said.

"Yep, that's Wilson." Mosey moved away from the window, waiting for her visitor's knock. When the light tap came, she opened the French doors and invited him in.

"Well, I guess you can imagine why I wanted you to meet me here." He removed his hat and tapped it against his leg.

"Not entirely, but I'm beginning to get an idea."

"Lieutenant Olivera got a warrant to search the Raines residence."

She inhaled deeply. "Thanks for letting me know."

"Okay, uh, I guess I'd better get over there."

She hurried back to the parlor window.

"Can you believe this?" Nadia exclaimed, searching her friend's face.

"No, I *can't* believe it. Wilson, why would he call me?"

An hour or so passed, and no one arrived, no one came out. Nadia, having agreed to meet an antique dealer at eleven, said good-bye to Mosey and headed to the shop. Mosey stayed behind, waiting for Wilson and the policemen to come out of the house. Eyes glued on the Queen Anne, she tried to imagine the scene in progress within the walls of the stately house. Would Raines be accommodating or resistant? Would Charlotte seclude herself in an upstairs room or stick around to witness the dismantling of her home?

Sometime later, when Olivera exited the house in the company of the officers—Springer carrying a small bag the size of a gun—Mosey intuited that the Crump case was drawing to a close. They must have discovered a weapon capable of firing the shot that had ended the life of Hembree's most eligible bachelor.

What's he to you?

"Nothing, Daddy, I've told you that a dozen times. But come to think of it, what was Mona Waite to you—huh?"

None of your business, young un'.

Mosey paced in front of the parlor window, then returned to the study. De Waal's book lay on the library table. She picked it up and opened it to a dog-eared page. She'd gotten to the final chapter, "The Bipolar Ape." Leafing through the pages, she came to a subheading, "Autist Meets Gorilla." "Autist...never heard that word before," she uttered, then read on. De Waal described the experience of an autistic woman who had found comfort working with gorillas at a zoo. She claimed that while the directness of people made her nervous, the gorillas, by averting their eyes, made her feel more comfortable, less put upon. Most of all, they seemed never to be in a hurry.

Interesting. Maybe there was a lesson in the autist's experience. She'd bear it in mind when doing business with reserved types like Matthew Raines.

An hour passed. She watered the fiddle-leaf fig, picked the dead fronds off the fern, and ran a cloth over the wood furniture, all the while keeping an eye on the house across the street. At last, Wilson emerged and drove away in his old beater. Clearly, the police had discovered something, but they hadn't made any arrests, hadn't even taken anyone in for questioning.

Her phone rang. She put down her dust cloth and reached into her pocket. "Hello."

"It's me," Nadia said. "Where are you?"

"Waite House. Did you see the dealer?"

"Yes, came and went. I'm going over to the Hansbrough estate sale. Want to come with me?"

"Sure. Looks like I'm finished here."

"These things take time. They'll have to analyze whatever they found. And if they found a gun, they'll have to do the ballistics. That could take a day or two."

"You're right. Patience…I need to be patient, like a gorilla."

"What?"

"Chimps, bonobos." Mosey put away her phone and reached again for the book, resolved to finish reading it that day. Patience, no direct stares, no direct questions.

****

The following morning, Mosey was in her attic, searching among shelves and boxes for an item that had belonged to her mother.

"Hey," Robert called out. "What are you doing up there?"

"I'm looking at some stuff."

"You can do that later. Breakfast is ready."

"Okay, okay." She lifted the lid of a small trunk. "Ah ha." Picking up the object of her search, she tucked it under her arm and descended the attic stairs. "I found Grandma Frye's photo album. Look at this," she said, handing Robert a picture of her mother as a child sitting astride a Shetland pony.

"Nice—but right now I want you to sit down and have some breakfast. I made you oatmeal."

"I don't want oatmeal."

"It's good for your cholesterol."

"For Pete's sake, Robert, my cholesterol is fine."

She reluctantly climbed onto the high wicker stool Robert had placed next to the counter. He'd set a bowl on a place mat with a folded newspaper next to the bowl. Just as she picked up the paper, he snatched it out of her hand.

"What are you doing, fool?"

"Your mystery is solved, and I know who did it."

"Give me that."

"No, first you have to guess."

"I'm not amused."

"Guess."

She got down from the stool and poured herself a cup of coffee. "This is easy. The gun—I'm sure that was a gun they found. It belonged to Raines, of course." She spoke as if the mystery surrounding Waite House bored her to tears.

"Right on that score."

"So, I guess that would make *him* the likely suspect. Ho hum." She stepped to the refrigerator and pulled out a carton of cream. "On the other hand…"

"What?"

"I thought he was a chimpanzee at first. But no—I'm sure of it—Raines is a bonobo."

"A bonobo? What do you know about bonobos?"

"More than you might think."

"You've been reading *Our Inner Ape*."

"As a matter of fact, I have. I should have read that before I went into real estate."

Robert smiled. "Raines *is not* the murderer."

"Really? If not Raines—who?"

"Guess again."

"I suppose that leaves *somebody* who had access to the gun."

"Right."

"And that could have been anyone in the house or someone with an occasion to visit." She paused to think of the possibilities. "That neighborhood is *so* inbred. They all know each other. Mae knows Evan; Evan lived at Waite House; Evan was Crump's mentor. The Hopkins and Raines families must have been on speaking terms for decades."

"Cold."

"Cold?"

"Go back to the house."

"Not Charlotte Raines." She grabbed the paper from Robert's hands and read aloud: " 'The murder weapon was a .38-calibre, semi-automatic snub nose, licensed to Matthew Raines, discovered by Sergeant J. T. Springer among a collection of modern and antique firearms displayed in the owner's home. The weapon, the only gun in the collection that smelled of powder residue, matched the bullet removed from the victim's chest. The gun itself had been wiped clean, but the magazine, found in a nearby drawer, bore the fingerprints of Raines's twenty-three-year-old employee, Melba Bujeau, of Mandeville, Louisiana, the cousin of Raines's wife Charlotte.' " Mosey threw down the paper. "I knew it. I swear—I *knew* there was something surly about that woman."

"You *know* Melba Bujeau?"

"No, silly, I don't *know* her, but I did see her briefly when I went to the Raines place. She's his butleress. Came to the door."

"So, in two minutes, you pegged her as surly." Robert's words brimmed with sarcasm.

"In less than that. The way she looked at me when she opened the door." Mosey returned to the story. " 'According to Lieutenant Gustavo Olivera, Bujeau confessed to her involvement in the Crump murder, stating that, though she had grabbed a gun before going to Crump's home on the night of May 23, 2008, her intention had been to threaten her ex-lover, not to kill him.' My word," she exclaimed. "Crump's mistress!"

Wilson's account stated nothing more concerning the confessed killer's motive, but the gaps left by the reporter Mosey filled in with imagined possibilities, which she later shared with Nadia.

"Delaney," she said, "must have patched it up with Jane—you think?"

"Could be," Nadia said.

"And he must have ended his affair with Bujeau."

"Makes sense."

"So Melba must have seen Jane leave the house, got upset, picked up a gun, loaded it…"

"She must have sneaked in through the back."

"The back, huh—why?"

"Because if she'd gone in the front, somebody might have seen her."

Mosey shrugged. "So I'm guessing they argued, and Melba got upset and pressed the trigger by accident—or so she claimed. It was a semi-automatic."

"Still some loose ends here," Nadia said.

"What?"

"The whereabouts of Jane and Candice Middleton, for a start."

Chapter Ten

February 5, 2009
Shepherd Realty
Days passed with no follow-up in the newspaper. Mosey and Nadia phoned back and forth, but neither was able to discover anything more than what had already been reported.

"Why don't you phone Wilson?" Nadia said.

"Nah, it wouldn't do any good."

"You don't know if you don't try."

"If Wilson knew anything, he'd write about it in the paper."

"Guess you're right," Nadia conceded.

"I *could* phone Olivera."

"No, you couldn't."

"Why not?"

"If you ask me, he's a sexist, plain and simple."

"How do you know that?"

"I *know*," Nadia said.

"You're crazy."

"He practically threw me out of the police station," she retorted.

"Oh, I think you might have left *that bit* out before."

"Maybe I did, maybe I didn't, but it's true. Olivera is not one of your...what do you call it—that ape?"

"Bonobo."

"Right, bonobo. He's definitively of the chimpanzee persuasion."

Mosey grinned. "I agree with you on that point. He's definitely more of a chimp."

****

At her wits' end, Mosey was ready to forget the whole matter. But then, one rainy afternoon, as she sat in her office reviewing her listings, a knock came at the door. Not expecting anyone, she was surprised to see Mae Baker and Professor Hopkins looking in through the pane. She motioned for them to come in.

"Sorry to have dropped by without phoning first," Mae apologized.

"Not a problem. I'm glad to see you both. Please, have a seat."

"Okay, but we won't keep you long."

Mae sat, and Hopkins stood near the window looking out.

"So...Professor Hopkins, have you come about the house?"

"Yes, that too," he replied. "You'll understand soon enough."

Mosey sat up straight and looked at Mae.

"I'll get to the point," she began. "We know where Jane Middleton is."

"Really?" Mosey's eyes grew wide.

"We've known all along," Hopkins interjected.

Her brows went up.

"None of us knew what to do. Delaney's death...it all happened so suddenly, and Jane was sure that she'd be the prime suspect. We couldn't think of anyone—"

"Of course, we couldn't." Hopkins approached and sat in the vacant chair. "As far as *we* knew, Delaney didn't have any enemies."

Mosey sat quietly.

"Jane, you see," Mae continued, "came back to the house that night rather late. Delaney had given her his keys, and she was hoping to pick up the baby and be on her way. But when she arrived, the police were there. She panicked and came to my house, entering through the grove at the back of the lot. No one had seen her, and we—the three of us—decided on a course of action."

"I understand," Mosey said, sensing the uneasiness in Mae's voice. "So, you, Professor, came to the open house to…?"

Hopkins looked up at Mosey but said nothing.

"We were wrong," Mae acknowledged, "I suppose we were wrong, but—"

"You were distraught."

"Distraught," she repeated, "confused."

"And you wanted to protect Jane," Mosey said.

"Yes, poor Jane. It was…well, it's hard to describe."

"So, where has she been all this time?" Out of kindness, Mosey directed the conversation away from Mae and Evan's uncomfortable admission of having lied to the police. Obviously, there was a point to their visit—other than to explain their actions on the night of May 23, 2008.

"On that point," Hopkins said, "we'll have to ask for your confidence."

Mosey nodded. "But surely all of this will come out."

"Jane has been staying with Delaney's mother, who took the baby to her home in Colorado."

"Colorado."

"Margaret—that's Delaney's mother—has a ranch in a remote area, and Jane and the little girl were able to stay out of sight fairly easily."

"And the FBI? They never phoned, never went around?" Mosey said.

"Oh, they phoned several times," Mae replied. "But Margaret just kept saying she had no idea where Jane was, and, apparently, they believed her."

"Will Jane be coming back?" Mosey said.

"We're not sure, but just in case she does, Evan has decided to make an offer on the house."

"Hmm. She wouldn't mind living in the place where Delaney was killed?"

"We aren't sure," Hopkins answered, "but the house has been in my family for generations. If Jane doesn't want it, perhaps my son will."

Despite the awkwardness of the occasion, Mosey was pleased. She not only had helped to solve a murder, she was on the verge of selling a house, her first in several months. In fact, not long after, Delaney's relatives agreed to the amount Hopkins offered, and the closing took place within a couple of weeks. Mosey walked away with a more than respectable commission.

There were other questions that remained in her mind. Most of all, she wondered why Matthew Raines had lied about seeing Crump from his parlor window. She assumed the information would never surface but was wrong. Once Melba confessed—waiving her rights to a trial in exchange for a lighter sentence—Raines explained his motive to Lieutenant Olivera.

On a Friday night at the Tavernette, where Mosey and Robert had gone for their usual pitcher, Olivera approached their table.

"Lieutenant, nice to see you," Mosey said. "Robert, do you know Lieutenant Olivera?"

"Gus," the detective corrected.

"Won't you join us?" Robert rose and offered him his chair.

"No, thanks. I'll stay just a minute. I'm meeting a friend."

"You know," she said, turning to Robert, "I spoke to Lieutenant Olivera concerning Waite House."

"Yes," Olivera said, "and that's what I wanted to speak to you about. The lead you gave us… I wanted to thank you."

"No problem. Glad I could help."

"By the way, you'd probably want to know, uh—" He went up on his toes and then back on his heels. "—Raines had no idea of Melba Bujeau's involvement. Knew nothing about the affair *or* the murder. The lie was to provide someone he'd seen near the crime scene with an alibi, in case she needed it."

"Jane Middleton."

Olivera's brow went up and then relaxed. "That's right."

Mosey smiled and thanked him for filling her in.

He said good-bye and moved to the bar to wait for his friend. He shook his head and sipped his beer. "That woman," he muttered, loud enough for Mosey to hear, "I ought to offer her a job."

Robert smiled across the table at his wife. "Satisfied now?"

"One murder down, two to go."

"Two to go?" His face fell.

"Just kidding, but what if during spring break we

take a little ride down to Texas, visit Dahlia and Tommy?"

The Terrace

A Mosey Frye Mystery, Book 2

Chapter One

Warm rain spattered the front window at Abboud's Antiques as Nadia Abboud, in cut-offs and an acid green tee, lifted a photographer's chair and nestled it into a back corner of the display. "N-i-i-i-ce," she drawled, then stepped to one side. "What do you think, Mosey?" She pointed to the new items in the display. "Rosewood occasional table, curio with ceramic birds, wicker photographer's chair."

Mosey Frye had dropped by on her way to Shepherd Realty, figuring Nadia would be changing out the window, putting in some pieces from the Hansbrough estate sale. "Looks good. I love the birds, nice touch for a spring display." She picked up a pretty little bird with an orange chest and brown feathers. His head was down and cocked to one side, as if he were on a high limb, eyeing something on the ground. "What's this one?"

"Carolina wren."

"How much is it?"

"It's marked."

Mosey turned the piece over. "Fifteen. Not bad." She set the bird back on the curio shelf. "Where's the rest of the stuff?"

"In the back."

"Mind if I have a look?"

"Go ahead, but take off those wet boots, please,

ma'am. I've just vacuumed the whole store, front and back."

"You *have* been busy." Mosey shed her boots and set them next to the umbrella stand.

"It's called spring cleaning. You should try it sometime."

Ignoring Nadia's chide, Mosey dodged her way through furniture and boxes to the back room. "I don't know how you vacuumed back here," she yelled, "with all this stuff." She scooted boxes to the left and right, then plopped down cross-legged on the floor. In front of her was a small, dome-topped trunk, edged in highly tooled leather. "Wow, this is pretty," she mumbled. She opened it and lifted out a handful of yellowed papers under which there was a stack of old photographs—not snapshots but large professional prints. She laid them out in front of her on the rug. "Hey, Nadia," she shouted, her eyes fixed on the torn pieces of a large print.

Nadia came to the door. "What?"

"Come here and look." Mosey waved her in. "I just opened this trunk, and see what I found?" She held up the left and right sides of a black-and-white print. "It's been ripped in two."

Nadia cleared a space for herself, and, together, they pored over the print.

It was mounted on black cardboard and matted in a pale shade of cream. The lower right section of the overmat was gone. What remained bore an inscription scrawled in brown ink: "Family Supper, July—."

"Such a wide print," Nadia said. "Must be a panorama, unless it was taken with a wide-angle lens."

"Panorama?" Mosey questioned.

"Well, sure. The photographer would take several exposures, trim off the overlapping parts, then put them together. That was before panoramic cameras came in."

"Really," she said, not entirely convinced her friend knew any more about the fine points of photography than she did. "When did you become such a shutterbug?"

"I read a book," Nadia said.

"Oh."

"But this one's twentieth-century, and it was likely made with a wide-angle lens."

"Sure," Mosey said. "Must be."

"Check out the clothing. I'd say nineteen forties."

"Maybe early forties," Mosey said, "or late thirties."

The focal point, which was on the left, was whole and unspoiled. Three women, two men, and two children posed around an elegantly set outdoor table. The adults, fresh-faced and sophisticated, carried on their repast, while the children, delighted by all appearances to be posing for the photographer, smiled directly into the camera. The picture's only imperfection—the gash down the middle—didn't detract from the diners on the left or the building's entrance on the right—also appealing, with finely-crafted stonework, slender mullioned windows, wide stone steps, and a striped awning that stretched from the terrace up to double doors. On either side of the steps, fluted-column lampposts held up three shimmering globes.

Nadia examined the tear and concluded that a specialist could in all likelihood restore the photograph to its original state. Half heeding Nadia's commentary,

Mosey continued studying the faces of the subjects. She pointed at one of the women, whose face was partially eclipsed by a wide-brimmed hat. "Looks like she's hiding, doesn't it?"

"Huh, maybe she didn't want her picture taken."

"Maybe she's the one who tore up the picture."

"Why would anybody destroy a beautiful print?"

"Indeed. Why would they?" Mosey picked herself up and gathered her jacket, handbag, and keys from among papers and sepia-colored prints.

"You leaving?" Nadia hurriedly cleared a path for Mosey through the contents of the trunk.

"Yep. That's a neat little trunk."

"I thought so. I probably paid twice what it's worth."

"Why'd you do that?"

"I couldn't let Lou Spinks walk off with it."

"The woman from Ebenezer?"

"That's the one. Seems like she and I always end up in a bidding war."

"Mind if I take that with me?" she said, pointing to the torn print.

"If you promise to bring it back. Let me get you a paper bag."

"No need." Mosey opened her tote wide. "I can stick it in here."

"Don't you want some tissue paper?"

"This is fine."

"Okay, but zip that tote. I don't want it to get wet."

"I was thinking of showing it to John Earle. By the way, where'd you get the trunk?"

"The estate sale, silly." Nadia got to her feet. "You helped me tote it out—don't you remember?"

Strangely enough, she didn't. That afternoon back in February had followed close on the heels of a breakthrough in the Crump murder, and she'd spent the better part of the day *woolgathering*—an ever more usual pastime of the incipient sleuth. While Nadia had darted from table to table, separating the items she could afford from the ones she would buy if she had the money, Mosey strolled aimlessly around the perimeter of the great hall mulling over clues. She scarcely registered the impressive array of objects tastefully arranged on tables or the multitude of antique dealers and bargain-seekers who'd come to bid on or simply eye the possessions of the late Thaddeus Hansbrough. Tightfisted as he was, he hadn't managed to take any of it with him.

"Did it belong to Old Man Hansbrough?"

"I'd guess so," Nadia said. "Probably inherited from a relation. It's late nineteenth-century."

"What will you do with the contents?"

"I'll take a look, but it's the trunk I'm interested in." Nadia let the top snap shut. "It's small, but it has the features of a big trunk. It's got the original rollers and lock."

"The original mold, too." Mosey opened her eyes wide, then blinked, sending tears rolling down her cheeks.

"Your allergies bothering you?"

"Oh, gosh, yes. Maybe this rain will clear the air a little."

"You need a tissue?"

"I've got one." She dug into her tote for a tissue and dried her eyes. "I don't guess it would be a doll trunk, would it?"

"Doll trunk?" Nadia shook her head. "No, just small." She ran her fingers along the tooled leather trim. "Look how beautiful the leather is."

"Yeah, and nicely maintained."

Mosey left the store and headed straight to her office, on the off-chance John Earle Shepherd might be in. He'd been selling houses in Hembree longer than anyone else she knew. If anybody could identify the house in the photograph, John Earle could.

On her way in, she stopped to speak to Saffron Smiley, John Earle's personal assistant. "Hey, Saffron. The boss been in?"

Saffron was fiddling with a package of crackers on top of an open magazine. "Not yet. Said he'd be in around three."

"Could you let me know when he gets here?"

"Sure." Saffron looked up and nodded toward the niche off reception. "There's some boysenberry pie left, if you want a piece—and coffee."

Mosey entered the niche, filled a mug with coffee, and headed to her office.

"You passing up my pie?"

"Oh, all right, if you insist."

"Don't put yourself out, missy."

Mosey re-entered the niche and scooped a sliver of pie onto a dessert plate. "Saffron, for Pete's sake. It's March already, and any day now, I'll be trying to squeeze into last year's swimsuit. I got to get rid of this muffin top."

Saffron cackled. "Muffin top—you?" She cackled again.

"Yes, me. I'm not getting any younger, and middle-age spread is just around the corner."

Saffron shook her head. "That'd be one puny little muffin top." She fanned her face with her magazine and went back to opening the crackers.

Mosey entered her office and turned on the desk lamp. She pushed a dusty stack of forms and manuals to one side, a pile of unopened mail to the other, and set the photograph between them. She picked up the phone and punched in her husband's office number. "Robert. I've got a question."

"Shoot, but I'm in a hurry. I've got a three o'clock meeting."

"The new guy in Anthropology—didn't you say he did photographic restoration?"

"Hugh Jessup?"

"That's the one. I need to speak to him."

"What about?"

"I've got this photograph—actually it's Nadia's—but it's torn in two. I wanted to see if he could fix it." She picked up the left side of the picture and ran her fingers along the rough tear.

"Yeah, okay. Call the main office. The secretary can connect you."

Before she could make the call, John Earle, wiping boysenberry from his mouth with a cloth napkin, pushed the door open with his elbow.

"What's up, sista'?"

"John Earle…hey. I want to show you something." She rolled back in her chair, allowing him to get a better look.

"What happened to your picture?"

"Nadia bought an antique trunk at the Hansbrough estate sale, and this photograph was inside. This place look familiar to you?"

He picked up the piece that contained the better shot of the building. "Looks like the Hansbrough house."

"Oh."

He cocked his head, grinned, then chuckled. Mid-fifties, tall, and gawky, John Earle, the wealthiest man in town, was attractive still, especially when he smiled.

"How was I supposed to know?" she demurred. "We only saw the front of the house. This must be the back."

He put down the photograph and, walking around to the window, pushed back the shutters. The gloom was lifting, as big splashes of light broke through steel-gray clouds.

"You think they'll put it up for sale?"

"I imagine they will. None of them lives around here anymore."

"You think we'll get the listing?"

He didn't answer.

"John Earle, would you stop staring out the window and listen to me?" She was well enough acquainted with his inclinations—his penchant for golf in particular—to know the weather forecast meant more to him than the acquisition of any old piece of property. She had an idea her boss wouldn't give a plug nickel for every house in Dent County, not anymore.

"Wouldn't be surprised," he said, still gazing at the sky.

"So what if I went over there and looked around?"

He chuckled and stepped away from the window. "Watch out for rats."

"Rats?"

As soon as he was gone, Mosey left the office and

drove to Nadia's shop. "I'm back," she called, not seeing anyone in the front room. She stopped for a minute to look over the new items in the window. A small bronze frame on top of the curio caught her eye. She picked it up and carried it to the lamp on the counter. The frame held a painting of two blond, brown-eyed boys. "Hey, Nadia, did you see this?"

Nadia emerged from the back room carrying a pair of swan-shaped, crystal vases. "See what?" She set the vases on a mantel attached to the back wall and moved toward the front.

"These boys," Mosey said, "they're the ones in the photograph." She passed the diminutive portrait to Nadia.

"You sure?"

"I'm surprised you didn't notice." Mosey unzipped her tote and took out the left half of the picture. "See for yourself."

She looked back and forth between the smiling boys captured by the photographer and the expressionless twosome portrayed by the artist. "They *are* the same, but they look a little older here." She tapped the portrait. "There's a signature. E. Mordecai. Never heard of him—or her." She flicked a piece of lint off the frame.

Mosey, having made a tolerably comfortable chair of a hooked rug footstool, sat staring up at Nadia. "By the way, when we were at the estate sale, did anybody mention selling the house?"

"Let me think. The woman running the sale, the one sitting at the table in the foyer, that was Hansbrough's granddaughter, I'm pretty sure. I think I saw her talking to Loretta Stark."

"Didn't see them."

She raised her brows in a gesture of wonderment. "You were there, weren't you? I could have *sworn* that was you." She reached for her feather duster.

"Very funny." Mosey crinkled her nose.

"Why don't you give Loretta a call. Maybe they were talking business." She swooshed the dust off a tall china vase.

Mosey sneezed. "Would you get that dang feather duster out of my face?" She sneezed again. "I swear. Either you or Saffron's gonna put me in an early grave—you with all this dusty, moldy stuff, her with her fattening pies."

"Oh, for heaven's sake. Calm down and blow your nose." She held out a box of tissues.

Mosey accepted the box and, moving a safe distance from the feather duster, did as Nadia had suggested. "John Earle thinks if they sell the house they'll list it with us."

"Makes sense."

"I'm thinking of going over there. John Earle says maybe they took the photograph on the back terrace."

"Could be." Nadia pulled back the lid of a Majolica urn and dusted it inside and out.

"Want to come with me?"

"I'll pass. I've got work here. Got to get all this left-over Christmas stuff packed up and stored." She reached down with her free hand to capture a small spider that had emerged from the urn and was getting ready to tat the edge of a linen napkin.

"John Earle told me to watch out for rats."

"Rats?" Nadia deposited the spider in a silent butler ashtray.

"He said to watch out for rats at the Hansbrough estate."

"Rodents or the human kind?"

Mosey sniggered. "Maybe both. By the way, Robert knows a new guy in his department who restores photographs. I'd like to buy it. I'm getting attached. How much would you take for it?"

"Well, it didn't really cost me anything. It's yours for a martini. And let's go to Al's this time."

"Deal." Mosey turned to leave, then turned back. "Sure you don't want to come with me?"

Nadia shook her head and went on with her dusting.

Mosey put the small portrait back on the curio. "Don't sell that portrait."

"You can't afford it."

"Robert can."

On the way to her truck, Mosey called Robert and left a message. "It's me. I haven't called Jessup yet, but, if you see him, tell him about the photograph. I'm driving out to the Hansbrough estate. See you around five-thirty, maybe later." She climbed into her truck and slammed the door.

Mosey, what in the world are you doing?

Her deceased father's words of caution came as no surprise. "What's it look like, huh?"

Mosey—

"Daddy."

Paying him no mind, she took off toward Little Smith en route to the place she and Nadia had visited a few weeks before. It had been February then. Now, early March rains had brought the fields and pastures back to life. But the limbs of the deciduous trees were still bare, and, as Mosey approached the estate, she could make out the house atop a small mound. Trees and undergrowth invaded the sides and back of the property, but the front, taken up by a small pond, was mostly clear. She parked at the gate some thirty yards from the entrance and, grabbing her jacket and a flashlight, stepped down from the cab.

The lock on the gate prevented an easy way in—or out—and she paused to consider the good sense of climbing the fence and entering a posted property. "Hmm," she droned, unsure what to do. She'd told Robert and Nadia she was heading out there. She weighed the embarrassment of losing her nerve—after all, she had a reputation to keep up—against the vexation of being arrested for trespassing. "Okay, I'm going in. I didn't see that posted sign."

Mosey—

"Oh, Daddy, hush."

She placed her right foot on the bottom rail of the rusty fence. Under the weight of her slender frame, it dropped instantly to the ground. She fell back with a thud, landing in wet, muddy gravel. "Dang it!" She raised up on one elbow and felt the back of her head.

I thought you had better sense—

"Would you stop?"

She lay there for a minute, then checked the back of her head for lumps. She checked her fingertips expecting to see blood. There wasn't any, but, be that as it may, the initial mishap had made her think better of her plan.

The sun was going down, and it was cooling off. With a shiver, she got to her feet, and, brushing herself off, headed back to the truck. She climbed in the cab and sat rubbing her head till she was steady enough to drive. The rain had stopped, and the temperature had fallen. Shivering, she cranked the engine and turned on the heat. She grasped the cold steering wheel with both hands and pulled her arms in tight against her sides. Tomorrow was Saturday. She could get Robert to come back with her. She shifted into first and turned the truck around, then crept along through the woodsy entrance to the property. Feeling a little queasy, she rolled the window down a crack. The cra-cra-cra of frogs on the pond—barely audible above the noise of her old engine—rose in the dense air. A raccoon squalled. Squirrels barked, and a pair of doves, one perched on a low hanging limb of a sycamore, the other, below on the ground, tempered the woodland cacophony with appeasing coo-coo-coos.

"Yep," she muttered, "tomorrow, first thing." She clicked open the heat vent and held her hands to the flow of warm air. "Surely Robert or Nadia or somebody…" She shifted into second and rambled down the lane to the main road.

Chapter Two

Mosey pulled into the *porte cochère* and made a beeline for the den, eased into Robert's recliner, and, stretching back, covered her face with the *Gazette*. Head down, feet up, she promptly began to doze until, little more than a powernap later, she was jarred awake. In the hazy distance, somebody was shouting her name.

"Mo-o-se-e-y."

Groggily, she pressed her elbows against the arms of the chair, assumed a vertical position, and yelled back, "I'm in here. Come here, I need you."

"What is it?"

"I fell and hit my head." She raised her hand to the back of her head and felt for the lump.

"What?"

"It's bigger than it was a half-hour ago. Come here and look." Tossing the newspaper onto the floor, she leaned to one side. "Look at my poor head," she groaned, feigning misery.

He pulled up a footstool and sat down beside her. "There's a lump, but it isn't bleeding." He stood up. "What did you do?"

"I was climbing a fence, and it broke. I fell back and hit my head." She watched as the bafflement grew on her husband's face. But, as usual, the more astonishing her revelation, the more indifferent his response.

"Why were you climbing a fence?" he said calmly.

"Are you going to stand there asking questions, or are you going to do something about my head?"

"Do something about your head? If only I could, but short of brain surgery—"

"Very funny," she said, jumping up.

"Steady. I'll get something to clean it." He walked toward the bathroom and returned with a box of cotton and bottle of witch hazel, then began ham-handedly daubing the lump. "You aren't dizzy, are you?"

"Now I'm not. At first, I was so dizzy I could hardly get off the ground. My head was throbbing like crazy. Ouch!" she cried, blocking Robert's hand. "That's enough." She flicked her hair into place.

Robert squelched a yawn. "You feel like going out?"

"Now?"

"I ran into Hugh Jessup and told him we'd meet him for drinks." He rolled his head and massaged the back of his neck.

"Rough day?" She planted both feet on the floor.

"Three classes and a meeting."

"What meeting?"

"Academic Programs."

"Deadly."

Robert walked toward the bedroom, Mosey behind. "Think I'll take a quick shower," he said, emptying his pockets onto the dresser.

Mosey leaned toward the mirror and held a hand mirror to the back of her head. "I guess I can go." She put down the mirror, pulled out a tissue, and blew her nose. "When are we meeting Hugh?"

"Six-thirty."

"Where?"

"Tavernette."

"Hmm…rather go to Al's."

"Fine with me. I'll give him a call."

"And call Nadia."

"What for?"

"I owe her a martini. And hurry up. I need to shower, too."

An hour later, when Mosey and Robert pulled up at Al's Super Club and Lounge, Nadia's SUV was already tucked tightly in between a rusty pick-up and a long, hefty flat-bed. She got out and walked to their car. Mosey rolled down the window. "I didn't realize," she said with a grin, "I'd collect so fast on that photograph."

"Since Robert's buying…"

Robert stepped out of the car and rounded the front toward the passenger side. "Torn photographs, broken fences, bruised heads, martinis. Somebody want to tell me what the devil is going on?"

"Calm down, old man." Nadia patted him on the arm. "I'm trading your wife a ripped photograph for a martini. But broken fences and bruised heads?" She aimed an inquiring look in Mosey's direction. "Can't help you there."

"Forget it. It's nothing." Mosey stepped carefully onto the gravel parking lot. She was wearing her new peep-toe stilettos.

"You looking good, girl," Nadia said, admiring her friend's attire.

"Thank you," Mosey answered with a flirty grin. She'd slipped into her melon sheath, suspecting Nadia would be dressed to the nines. Not that she needed to—

Nadia in a potato sack was a knockout. "Pretty sweater."

They entered the bar and made their way past a gathering of Al's loud-mouthed, backslapping regulars.

"There's Hugh," Robert said. "He's got a table."

The threesome reached the middle of the dimly lighted room, and Mosey and Nadia, smiling at Hugh, wiggled onto raw steel bar stools.

"Hugh Jessup...my wife Mosey, and our friend Nadia Abboud."

"Nice to meet you both."

"You, too," Mosey said.

"What do you guys want?" Robert divested himself of his sports jacket.

"A pomegranate martini," Nadia said.

"Me, too," Mosey said.

"Hugh?"

"I was thinking of getting a beer." Hugh slipped the drink menu back into its holder. "But that sounds good. Make it three."

Robert headed for the bar to order the cocktails, and Mosey took the photograph from her clutch and placed it on the gray glass table in front of Hugh. "Think it can be fixed?"

Hugh picked up the pieces and held them against the light from the nickel and glass mini pendant that hung above the table. "I should be able to fix that. The tear is fairly clean. Mind if I ask what happened?"

"I don't know. I found it this way—in an old trunk Nadia picked up at an estate sale."

"Nice image."

"Is it a panorama?" Nadia leaned toward Hugh.

"I don't think so. In fact, I'm sure it isn't. It wasn't

made with a panoramic camera, either."

"You think it's from the thirties, forties?" Mosey said.

"By the thirties, I think they'd stopped using the older techniques for shots like this." He turned the photograph over. "See this logo?" He pointed to a small, embossed icon. "This paper wasn't used in the thirties. Must be from the forties." He flipped the picture back. "Notice the flatness of the image." He placed the pieces of the print on the table, angling them for Mosey and Nadia to see. "Despite the width, there isn't any distortion. Either the photographer was really good or this shot was taken with a modern lens."

"I see what you mean," Nadia replied. "The entire image is perfectly focused, the left and right same as the center."

"Martini anyone?" Robert interrupted, setting down a tray of cocktails. "So Hugh, you think you can fix it?" He passed glasses of the cold, purplish-pink liquid to Nadia and Mosey.

"I think so. And the new image will look very much like the old one. I'll repair it digitally, make a negative, and print a new picture in the darkroom."

"How much is it going to set me back?"

"Cover the supplies, and I'll throw in the labor for free."

"Sounds good." Robert handed his new colleague a martini.

"Thanks, Robert." Hugh turned to Mosey. "But back to the image itself—what's the attraction?"

"I don't know. I'm not really sure. Everything about it is attractive, exceptional." She ended with a shrug.

"We should warn you," Robert chimed in, arranging his long legs under the table, "Mosey has an abnormally *active* imagination."

"That's not a bad thing—well, not always."

Mosey smiled at Hugh, then frowned at Robert. "My imagination has nothing to do with it."

"So, back to my question. Why the interest?"

"The setting is lovely," she began, happy to expand on her explanation. "The house and the surroundings are quite elegant. Look at the detail. Crystal, china, silver, the white linen tablecloth and napkins. And the diners: attractive, handsomely dressed—even the children. Then there's this tear," she puzzled, "separating the people at the table from the house itself. It's as if—" She stopped mid-sentence, wrinkling her forehead.

"As if what?" Hugh pressed.

Her expression fell. "I don't know."

"What do *you* think it means?" Nadia said, turning to Hugh.

"Could be somebody got mad at the photographer and tore up his picture."

"Or *her* picture," interjected Nadia, the indefatigable feminist.

"Mad at the photographer," Mosey repeated. "Yes, could be. Someone wanted to get back at him or her. I was thinking someone in the picture didn't want to be *in* the picture," she went on. "Or maybe one of the subjects was angry at one of the other subjects."

"It's possible," Robert said. "Or maybe somebody symbolically, so to speak, wanted to separate *these* people from *this* house." He thumped on the left piece, then the right. "Let's say...*from coming into the house,* in the sense of inheriting—"

"Right," Nadia jumped in, turning to Robert. "They wanted them *out* of the picture."

Mosey and Hugh half smiled, half moaned, while Robert and Nadia chuckled, seemingly pleased with themselves.

"Silliness aside," Mosey said, looking askance at Robert and Nadia, "I guess that *is* what I was thinking. Some rift among family members—"

"The really interesting thing about the picture," Hugh cut in, "is the tear—who did it and why?"

Mosey nodded. "But just *any* old torn photograph wouldn't be interesting. There's so much potential here." She looked admiringly at the subjects and their elegant surroundings, then added, "for comfort… happiness."

"And someone comes along and spoils it." Robert sipped his martini.

"If that was the case," Hugh amended.

"That's right," Nadia concurred. "We don't really know what happened to these people. Maybe nothing happened."

Mosey propped her elbows on the table. "Nadia's right. No sense speculating. We know nothing."

"So you're willing to accept there's nothing behind this?" Robert gestured toward the photograph. "It's my guess you won't rest till you've figured it out."

Hugh reached for the right side of the photograph. "Where is this place, anyway?"

"We aren't positive," Nadia said, "but we think it's the back of the Hansbrough estate, not too far from here, actually."

"Are the Hansbroughs still around?"

"The owner died recently, and the younger generation all moved away."

"But his granddaughter was at the estate sale," Mosey added.

"You think the man who recently died is one of these boys?" Hugh glanced at the smiling children.

"Maybe," Nadia said. "Might have been about the right age."

"There're *two* boys," Mosey added. "If one was a Hansbrough, wonder who the other one was."

"Did Old Man Hansbrough have a brother?" Nadia said.

"I've never heard anything about a brother."

"Strange," Hugh said, "that a family of means…in a small place like Hembree would suddenly vanish."

"Yeah, it does seem strange," Robert agreed.

"I think there's a story here." Mosey took a sip of her drink.

"You sure, Mosey, you want to get mixed up in some family dispute—or whatever?" Hugh said.

"Mixed up?" Mosey repeated. "Well—"

"Could be dangerous," he cut in, "getting involved in a family matter you know nothing about—I mean, if there *was* a falling out of some sort."

"When you put it that way." Mosey frowned and stared off in the distance.

"Reminds me of a novel I once read." Hugh paused to sip his drink. "This guy, really nice guy—a priest, in fact—interceded between cousins with the intention of solving a dispute over property. Guess who ended up dead?"

"The priest," Mosey and Nadia said at the same time.

"Yep."

Mosey opened her clutch and slipped in the pieces of the picture, passing over Hugh's worrying remark. "What do you say if we get out of here and go for dinner somewhere? They'll be starting the music soon."

Nadia looked at Mosey. "We haven't finished our drinks. What's the hurry?"

Before Mosey could respond, a strong hand fell on her bare shoulder. "Mosey girl, how 'bout a song?"

Allen Bergeron, proprietor of Al's, was standing behind her, one hand on her shoulder, the other on the table. He was smiling and slowly nodding his head, evidently prepared to counter any sign of resistance.

She surrendered. "Oh, all right. One song, and then we're leaving."

Al straightened up and faced the ensemble. "Start off with a slow one. Mosey's going to sing."

Chapter Three

Mosey opened her eyes and gazed up at the ceiling. In the dim light of the bedroom, she could make out all sorts of shapes. As a kid, she often saw an elephant in one corner, a sheep in another. But this morning, the billowy stain above the chest of drawers didn't look a bit like a sheep—it looked like a pond, the Hansbrough pond.

Eager to find out once and for all if there even was a terrace at the back of the Hansbroughs' place, she reached for the first clothes she could find—a sweatshirt and jeans left dangling from the canopy frame. She slipped them on and sat down on the bed to tie her sneakers. Having seen the house up close only once—and from the front, not the back—she wasn't entirely certain if it *could* be the same house. The one in the torn print was made of pale, gray stone. The house she and Nadia had visited might have been of stone…might have been of brick. As she best recalled, shrubs, neglected by the elderly occupant, had edged their way up and across the façade, hindering a clear view of the walls and windows.

Stepping into the bathroom, she ran a washcloth under a stream of warm water and held it to her face, gently patting her cheeks and lids. She took a bottle of allergy drops from the medicine cabinet and doctored her eyes.

131

"Robert," she called, climbing the stairs. "Want to take a drive?" He'd forgotten to close the door to the stairwell, and the delicious scent of bacon had drifted to the ground floor. But even that wasn't enough to coax her into sitting down and eating a proper breakfast.

"I can't," he said with resolve. "I'm leaving." He got up from the table, crunching the last bite of a buttery piece of sourdough. "How's your head?"

She felt for the lump. "It's gone down some."

"You behave yourself today."

"Come with me to the Hansbrough place, please. This wouldn't have happened if you'd been with me." She opened the refrigerator door and stared in.

"I can't, I told you. I'm playing tennis with Jim." He wiped his mouth and scooted his chair back from the table.

"You'll be sorry," she said, a bottle of almond milk in one hand, a jar of fig preserves in the other.

He stepped over to the hutch and tugged at the top drawer till it popped open, revealing a jumble of change, golf tees, and throat lozenges. He picked through the assortment until he'd found a set of keys.

As Mosey well knew, Robert had his own agenda for Saturday mornings, when he played tennis or golf with his regular partner Jim Bledsoe, the chair of the Anthropology Department. She set the almond milk and preserves next to the toaster and turned to face her husband. "If you won't come with me, I'm calling Hugh."

"So?" He slipped the keys into his pocket. Halfway out the door, he smiled back at Mosey and, in an apparent attempt to amend his brusque departure, raised a vertical hand and gave a slight twist to his wrist.

To which she mumbled, "Who does he think he is, the Queen?"

Tsk, tsk, tsk, girl, you'd better watch that lip—I'm telling you.

In certain places where her father had commonly stood, like her kitchen—which had been *his* kitchen—his presence or absence, she wasn't sure which, was almost palpable. Yet if she reached for it, it vanished like a shot. Ellis Frye, still stalwart and ruddy with health, had gone to his grave too soon. But whatever remained of him resided in his daughter's brain, nowhere else.

Before she had time to lose her nerve, she tapped the number of the local directory and said, "Hugh Jessup." The number dialed automatically, and Hugh, in a drowsy voice, answered. "Who's this?"

"Hugh…it's Mosey. Did I wake you?"

"Honestly?"

"I'm sorry. Thought you'd be up by now. Go back to sleep." She ended the call.

She set the teakettle on the burner, dropped a slice of whole wheat into the toaster, and paced the floor, waiting for the water to boil. Who could she call?—she wondered, brooding a little over her lack of male support. Nadia was the likely choice, but she'd probably be at the store. Desperate, she phoned her anyway. "Hey, girl. You have to work this morning?"

"Afraid so—why?"

"I'm going back to the Hansbrough estate. Hold on a second. I've got a call coming in." She pressed hold. "Hello."

"It's Hugh. Sorry, but I was half asleep when you called before. What was it you wanted?"

133

"Say 'no' if you don't want to, but I was wondering if you'd be interested in driving out to the Hansbrough estate. Robert's playing tennis."

"If you are determined to go out there," he said, pausing to yawn, "I guess I can. You shouldn't go alone. When were you thinking of going?"

"I could pick you up in, say, half an hour?"

"You don't know where I live. I'll pick you up."

"Great, thanks. I was on another line. Got to go." Mosey clicked the hold button and spoke to Nadia again. "Sorry. That was Hugh. He's going with me."

"Hugh, eh? He's a nice guy."

"You interested?"

"In what?"

"Hugh, dummy."

"I just said he was nice, not that I *liked* him."

"He's pretty cute, don't you think?"

"Definitely cute, but what about the rest?"

"I don't know about the rest," Mosey said, "but he does seem concerned about my safety."

"Mosey, you always fall for the protective type."

"I do not. Why would you say that? I'm the most independent woman you know."

"If you say so."

"Water's boiling. Talk to you later."

She put down the phone and turned off the flame under the whistling kettle. She made herself a cup of chai and sat down to read the newspaper. A knock came at the door. She looked up to see John Earle Shepherd peeping through the pane.

"It's open."

He stepped in. "Smells good."

"Want a piece of toast?" She took a bite and licked

her lips. "It's good."

"Thanks. Haven't got time."

"You hitting the links this early?"

He shot her a wry smile. "I just wanted to tell you that Hansbrough's granddaughter dropped by yesterday. She wants us to list the house," he said with a wink.

"Fantastic!"

"Hold on, Dolly. It's not going to bring as much as you think. It's pretty run down."

"Oh."

He grinned.

Mosey didn't give a hoot about the money. She knew it, and John Earle knew it, too. It was that puzzling photograph of hers that had set her on the Hansbrough place like a hound on a fox. "Well, I know it's stupid," she confessed.

"Here're the keys." He placed a set of keys on the counter and stepped back out the door. "Be careful. You could get lost in the underbrush and never be heard from again," he teased.

"You'd come looking for me."

"See ya."

When he was gone, she shrieked. "What luck!" She tossed the keys in the air and caught them. One was a big, old-fashioned key—she assumed it was for the gate. There were some smaller keys, too, likely for the front and back doors. She cleared the table and, sitting back down, picked up the *Gazette* and continued reading.

Not long after, when a second knock came at the door, it was Hugh—taller than she'd remembered, and his hair wasn't brown but red. "Hugh, old man, you're a redhead."

"You night blind?"

"Actually, I am, since birth."

"Ready to go?" He glanced at Mosey's nearly full cup of chai.

"Give me a second to brush my teeth. Want some chai? I could pour you some in a paper cup."

"Sure, I could use a little caffeine."

Filling a cup for Hugh before rushing off to brush her teeth and grab a jacket, she was pleased to begin her investigation of the Hansbrough estate with a six-foot something archeologist—doubtless, the best available substitute for her husband.

"Ready?"

"Sure," she said. "Want to take my truck?" The least she could do was provide a vehicle.

"Not really."

"It's cool," Mosey said.

"Not as cool as my car."

They climbed into Hugh's 1949 ragtop and a quarter of an hour later arrived at their destination. She got out and unlocked the gate, while he parked the car inside the grounds.

"That's a spiffy car you got. Where'd you get it?"

"Box of Cracker Jacks."

"Oh, come on now. Where'd you get it?"

"My grandfather."

"That's wild. I got my truck from my granddaddy. Your granddaddy still alive?"

"Nope," he said, glancing back. "If he were, he'd still be driving that car."

"Yeah, mine, too. He loved that old truck."

The entrance that led to the terrace was also gated, and, after trying several of the small keys, Mosey found one that slipped easily into the padlock.

Passing through the gate, she fell under the spell of the gardens just as she had been captivated by the photograph of the terrace. Though she was hesitant to breathe deeply in sight of anything in bloom, her nostrils filled with the delicious scent of honeysuckle before she could cover her nose.

The gardens stretched all along the back of the stately home—which was built of light gray stone, in fact, and not brick. Overgrown with weeds, wild violets, and honeysuckle, the hardier varieties of cultivated plants had managed to hold their own. Fluffy white hydrangeas dominated the back beds, while along the sides leggy day lilies competed with success against trailing yellow irises.

"It's incredible but not exactly what we saw in the photograph," Hugh said, disturbing her reverie.

"I know." Mosey sighed. "It's very different. Obviously, nature got the last word."

"Well, maybe not the *last* word," Hugh said.

"Of course…you're right. Somebody will buy the house, renovate," which was a common scenario in her experience as a real estate agent—one that rarely yielded improvement, given the bad taste of most people.

Mosey, darlin', you are quite the snob, you know it?

"Honestly, Daddy," she muttered, glancing at Hugh, who hadn't seemed to notice.

"The structures are pretty much the same, don't you think? It's a shame nobody's kept it up."

While Hugh made his way over vines and broken objects to the middle of the terrace, Mosey took a look at the awning, which had collapsed under the weight of leaves and tree limbs. The fluted columns still stood on either side of the steps. Sadly, all but one of the glass globes lay in pieces on the flagstones. The tables and all the chairs were gone, and, apart from the flagstones themselves—mostly intact but covered in soil and moss—little was left of the once lovely setting.

She glanced over at Hugh, who, in a far corner, was on his knees raking debris from a cluster of raised stones.

"Come look at this. There's an inscription here."

"What does it say?" she said, walking toward him.

"Looks like a name and date."

She squatted at his side, and together they scraped the soil from the indentations in the stones.

"Max, 1930-1941."

"A pet cemetery," Mosey deduced.

"Certainly seems like it."

A faint noise, as of something scratching, emerged from beneath the stones.

"Hold on. I think Max is trying to dig his way out."

"What?"

Hugh remained steady. But Mosey, grabbing hold of his shoulder, suddenly stood up, sending her handbag, keys, and Hugh flying backward.

"Whoa!" he yelled, recovering his balance. "Hand me those keys."

"Sorry—what was that?"

"I intend to find out." He took the keys from Mosey and pressed one end of the gate key under the edge of a broken stone. He worked the stone loose and lifted it to reveal a rat's nest snugly positioned inside an earthen container. The rat ran in one direction and

Mosey, in the other. "I guess Robert's never taken you on a dig," he said, apparently amused at her frantic reaction.

"Very funny." She recovered her composure and returned to his side. "Of course he has, plenty of times."

A virtual chortle, not from Hugh but the customary source, sent blood rushing into Mosey's cheeks. "You make me so mad, Daddy."

"You say something?"

"Nope."

The chortle came again, louder. She responded with a silent smirk.

Hugh removed the twigs and mud from the opening, then gently scraped the lip of what appeared to be a ceramic vessel. "Oh, my…what have we here?"

"What is that?" Mosey cocked her head.

"Not sure." He continued to scrape soil from the surface until the shape became apparent. "You see that?"

"What?"

"It's an ear."

"Yeah, I see."

"Usually, practically always, in fact, an indigenous craftsman would paint on the facial features. But not in the case of headpots. See?" He pointed to a perfectly formed ear. "The contours of the pot follow the contours of the human head, and so…" he said, continuing to scrape, "I expect we'll see a nose soon."

"I've heard of headpots. They were effigy masks, sort of, weren't they?"

"Sure were, and the college museum has a couple of these, which is lucky—they're really rare."

"And old, too—aren't they?"

"About 1400 to 1700 C. E."

"So, you think this is a headpot?"

"Could be." He brushed the soil from around it until he'd revealed a large amount of red and white paint as well as a nose. Soon, two starkly painted eyes came into view.

"What a pair of eyes." Mosey shivered. There was something scarily suggestive in the big orbs that looked up from the grave. The artisan or shaman who had painted them—what purpose did he have in mind?

"Hypnotic, aren't they?" Hugh said.

"Why—?" she began but stopped, not sure what to make of them.

"Could be decorative," he said, "or maybe they were meant to tell us something."

"Like what?"

"I don't know." He shrugged. "That the dead can see?"

See, Mosey? said the voice that she alone could hear.

She sighed, ignoring her father but responding to Hugh. "So this is definitely a headpot?"

"Looks like the real thing, but it could be a replica. Doubtful a person, knowing it was real, would have buried it in a dog's grave."

She shifted her attention away from the evocative eyes to the interior of the vessel. "What happened to Max's bones?"

"Good question."

"Is there anything inside?"

He bent over the headpot and looked directly inside. "There *is* something, but I don't think I want to disturb it just yet."

"We should take this over to the lab," she said.

"I suppose so." On hands and knees, he continued to daub around the artifact until he had freed it from the soil. He lifted it up.

"Amazing," she gasped.

"Yes, it is."

"So, how do you think it got into old Max's grave?"

"I'm afraid science can't tell us anything about that." He handed her the headpot and put the stones back in place.

Archeologist and assistant, with their extraordinary find in tow, left the terrace.

"Think I'll call Robert," Mosey said.

"Sure, but don't get his hopes up. We don't know what we've got. If it's a replica, it isn't anything to get excited about."

"You're right. I'll wait."

"You want to look around some more?"

"Not right now." Headpot or replica, she was plenty excited and just dying to see what the pot contained. What a find it was. And not only that, the Hansbrough house was, for sure, the house in the picture. "Seems like enough of a haul for a Saturday morning, don't you think?"

"I'd say so."

Mosey and Hugh, quite pleased with the remarkable unearthing, headed back to Hembree.

Chapter Four

When Hugh drove the car into the driveway, Robert was walking up the kitchen steps. Mosey rolled down the car window and yelled. "Wait till you see what *we've* found." There was triumph in her voice and the smallest touch of I-told-you-so.

Robert waved and called out casually, "Back already?"

She searched for a sign of regret on her husband's face and, seeing none, added, "You should have come with me." But on second thought, maybe it was better he hadn't. It was Hugh who'd gone poking around in Max's grave. Robert wouldn't have been so curious. "Come over here," she insisted, motioning. "You won't believe what we dug up."

They got out of the car, and Hugh opened the trunk and lifted up the ceramic piece. "What do you think?"

"Whoa!" Robert took off his sunglasses and let his tennis gear drop to the ground. "What is *that*?"

"See, I told you," Mosey said.

"Where'd you find it?" He reached for the pot.

"In Max's grave," she said.

"Who the devil is Max?"

"A dog, silly."

Robert shook his head.

"What do you think?" Hugh said. "A replica or the real thing?"

Robert examined the front of the vessel, then the back. "I don't think it's all that old, but you're the expert." He handed it back to Hugh.

"Not really, but you're right—has to be a replica."

"Huh? I thought we had something amazing."

"What are you frowning about? Not an authentic headpot, I'm afraid," Hugh said, "but seems to me you've got a piece of your puzzle."

"How's that?"

"Think about it," Hugh said—as he evidently had been. "Why would anybody bury a headpot—even a replica—in a dog's grave, except expressly to conceal the contents?"

"Hmm." Her expression began to brighten.

"Might as well take a look." Hugh opened the trunk, pulled out a plastic bag, and set the pot inside. "The archeological value is clearly compromised— even if it *were* the real thing."

"So, it's not worth anything—archeologically speaking?"

"A replica?" Robert intervened. "Can't imagine it would be, unless it's worth something as a piece of old ceramic art. It's got some age on it." He picked up his gear, led the way up the steps, and, after unlocking the door, picked up a couple of *Gazettes* from the recycle bin. Inside, he spread the papers over the countertop, while Hugh took three small packages, wrapped in scraps of fabric, out of the pot.

Mosey loosened the wrapping from the first piece and held up some sort of metal container, spherical and with a hole in the lid.

"What *is* that?" Hugh said.

"A brass something or other. I know how to clean

it—lemon juice and sea salt—but couldn't tell you what it's used for. I think we need to call Nadia."

"Why?" Robert said.

"Well, for one thing," she said, batting her eyes in his direction, "she'll know what it is, and I don't—do you?"

How long you gonna make a man pay—?

Mosey cast an icy stare vaguely toward the end of the counter. Who knew where ghosts hung out, but the voice seemed to be coming from that direction. She'd give her daddy a piece of her mind later on, but not now, with Robert and Hugh at her elbows.

Robert unwrapped the second piece, an octagonal gold pendant attached to a chain. "Looks like a locket."

"Sure does," Hugh said, "but that other piece…" he said, puckering his mouth. "The hole in the lid—wonder what that's for."

Mosey took her phone from her jeans' pocket and called Nadia. "Hey," she said, eyes still focused on the brass piece Hugh was turning in his hands, "can you get away for a bit?"

"I suppose I could take a quick lunch break—why?"

"We're at the house—Robert, Hugh, and I. I'll explain when you get here."

Meanwhile, Mosey made some veggie wraps with sprouts and herbs from her spring garden. With Robert in mind—any minute he'd be saying he was famished—she placed a cheeseboard next to the plate of wraps and stacked it with sliced Manchego, a round of goat cheese, and a wedge of Havarti. "I love this Manchego," she said. "Makes my mouth water just to think about it." She bit off the end of a long, thin slice.

"Give me a piece of that," Robert said, wiping his hands.

She passed the cheese board to Robert, then Hugh.

Nadia arrived a short time later and, instead of waiting for an account of the curious items displayed on the kitchen counter, pushed forward with a revelation of her own. "So guess who wants the painting of the two boys," she said to Mosey, shedding her jacket and taking the seat across from Hugh.

"Already?" Mosey said, passing napkins around.

"Already. Mind if I pour myself a glass of water?"

"Keep your seat. I'll get it. So, who?" Mosey opened the freezer door. "You want some ice?"

Nadia extended her glass. "Sure you don't want to guess?"

"Well, let's see…Lizbeth Hansbrough."

"Good guess, and who else?"

"Who else?" Mosey repeated. She filled the glass and handed it back to Nadia. "I thought the Hansbroughs had left town."

"They have, according to Lizbeth."

"I give up—who?"

"Evan Hopkins."

"No." Mosey's eyes widened.

"Yes!" Nadia said with a nod and a smile.

"What in the world…?"

"He's in the portrait—he and Ben. They're first cousins." She took a sip of water, then scooped up some loose sprouts and popped them in her mouth.

"Who are these people," Hugh interrupted, "and what portrait?"

It registered with Mosey that, as a newcomer, Hugh knew hardly anyone outside his department. The names of the local upper crust, like Hansbrough, Waite, and Raines, meant nothing to him. But before she could explain, Robert, self-appointed docent on the topic of all things Hembree, intervened.

"Lizbeth Hansbrough," he said, pausing to chew, "inherited the estate from her father Ben Hansbrough. Evan Hopkins is an Emeritus Professor of Geography, somehow related to the Hansbroughs, apparently."

"Wait a minute," Hugh said. "I thought the man who died was named Thaddeus."

"Yes, he was," Mosey said, "but his son Ben didn't want the place and passed it to his daughter Lizbeth—Thaddeus's granddaughter. If Evan and Ben are the children in the portrait," she said, turning to Nadia, "that solves the mystery of the children in the photograph, doesn't it?"

Nadia swallowed and confirmed with a nod.

"So, what did you tell them?" Mosey said.

Nadia took a sip of water. "That *someone else* had expressed interest in the painting."

"You didn't say it was me?"

"Of course, not."

"So…what?" Mosey passed the cheese board around again. "You guys want a dill pickle? I have some nice koshers."

"I thought you didn't like dill pickles," Nadia said.

"I don't, but you and Robert do."

"I'll take one, but let me get it," Nadia said.

"The pickle fork's in the drawer next to the sink."

"I told them to call back later, and I'd let them know." She set the jar on the table and speared a large dill. "Where'd you get these?"

"Let them know what?" she said, ignoring Nadia's

question.

"Robert, you want one?" Nadia said. "Hugh?" They held out their plates. "I said I'd let them know if the painting was available."

"Oh." Mosey got up and pulled a liter bottle of lager from the refrigerator. "Beer anyone?"

"I'll take some," Hugh said.

"Not me," Nadia said, "I've got to go back to the store. Where'd you get the pickles?"

"Helena...Lost Art—you been there?"

"I've been wanting to go forever."

"You can come with me next time I go."

"I'll take a beer," Robert said, getting up. "Sure you don't want one, Nadia?"

"Wish I could, but I have to get back to work. Mind if I take this pickle with me?"

"Of course, not," Mosey said. "Grab some wax paper. It's in the drawer to the right of the sink."

"So, what's all this stuff?" Nadia said, leaning over the counter.

Mosey gave an abbreviated account of her and Hugh's trip to the estate, the discovery of Max's grave, and the unearthing of the pot. "Obviously this is a locket," Mosey said, pointing to the octagonal ornament, "but what's this?"

"Actually, this *isn't* your typical locket." Nadia opened the elaborately carved piece to reveal a ringlet of red hair. "It's a hair receiver, as is this," she said, lifting the lid off the brass receptacle. "These long strands look like they're from the same head, wouldn't you say?"

"Must be." Mosey reached for the container.

"I wouldn't touch that." Hugh rose in his seat.

"You never know what natural history items might contain."

"What do you mean?" Mosey said, a bit surprised at his intervention.

"Preserved specimens, bones, hair even, sometimes contain toxic substances."

"Like what?" Mosey said.

"Anything—arsenic, cyanide, thallium. You got any rubber gloves?"

She got up and reached under the sink for her gloves.

"Thanks." Nadia slipped them on, then opened the small ivory box. She turned it upside down, and out dropped a folded piece of parchment.

"What's that?" Mosey said.

Nadia unfolded the paper and flattened it out on the counter.

"Looks like a diagram of a human head," Hugh said.

"Yeah, divided into little sections," Mosey said.

"Looks like a phrenology map." Robert cocked his head.

Nadia nodded and smiled. "Very good, Robert."

"Look at that." Mosey pointed to two sections that had been colored in with a red crayon. " 'Tune' and 'Color.' Wonder what that's about."

Nadia tugged at the gloves. "You ought to wash these—better still, get rid of them."

"Just drop them in the sink. I never dreamed there could be so much danger in poking around in old stuff."

"I've never had a problem," Nadia said, "but then I'm not an archeologist." She smiled at Hugh, picked up her keys, and headed for the kitchen door. "What should I tell Hopkins and Lizbeth?"

"Tell them, uh, I'd like to talk to them. No, on second thought, don't tell them anything *yet*."

"Let me know what you decide," Nadia said. "That gold piece, by the way, is worth something."

"But not the brass one?"

"Not to me—I have several at the store."

"Really? I never noticed."

"They're porcelain, but similar. I'll show you next time you're in." Nadia waved goodbye as she started to pull the door shut behind her. "By the way, that replica of a headpot—I'll take it off your hands if you don't want it."

Mosey waved back, then turned to Robert. "See, I told you she would know."

Robert had taken a bag of chips from the cabinet and was searching the refrigerator. "We got any dip?"

"No, but there's some salsa next to the sour cream."

He pulled out the salsa. "You want some?"

"Nope. I'm tired," she said, squelching a yawn.

"Yeah, you didn't sleep so well last night, did you?"

"Not really. See you guys later. I'm gonna lie down for a bit."

Hugh, who was bent over the counter, didn't look up, just went on eyeing the objects someone had buried in a dog's grave.

Chapter Five

Mosey staggered into the kitchen and blinked groggily at the sink brimming with dirty dishes. The counter was covered in old *Gazettes*, and the items from the headpot were still there—dusty and possibly dangerous, according to Hugh. An index card was propped against the ivory box. She picked it up and read: *Gone to the college, be back later. Robert.* "Great," she said with indifference. She slipped on a new pair of rubber gloves and moved the newspapers, headpot, and box to one end of the counter, then spritzed the area with disinfectant and wiped it down. Following Nadia's advice, she tossed the new gloves and the old ones into the trash.

She dragged a tall stool up to the counter and sat down to ponder her next move. Clues were definitely mounting in the case of "Family Supper, July—." She and Nadia had pinpointed the children pretty easily, and now it seemed they were a step away from identifying the adults. Evan Hopkins would probably recall the event, or, if not the event, surely he would recognize the other guests. Ben's daughter Lizbeth was of a younger generation but she, too, ought to be able to pick out a close relative like a grandparent, aunt, or uncle. Then again, Mosey wasn't quite ready to approach either of them, especially Lizbeth. She couldn't imagine broaching a subject of a personal nature with a woman she'd never met.

The phone rang. It was Nadia. "Hey, what's up?"

"I forgot to tell you something."

"What?"

"E. Mordecai," she said, "the man who painted the portrait, remember? 'E' stands for Evan. He's Evan Hopkins's maternal grandfather."

"Maternal grandfather," she repeated. "You mean the professor's grandfather painted the portrait of the boys?"

"Looks like, and I'm thinking if his parents are in the photograph, the father would be a Hopkins of course and the mother, a Mordecai."

"So Hopkins told you his grandfather painted the portrait?"

"He surely did."

"You know it's kind of remarkable," Mosey said. "We've already figured out several of the subjects."

"We? What do you mean *we*?"

"Well, okay, *you* actually." She paced to the end of the counter, turned around and paced back. "I think I know what I need to do."

"What's that?"

"Go to the cemetery."

"Huh? You *never* go to the cemetery."

"I haven't had a reason to go—"

"Well, I don't know about that—"

"—but think about it," she cut in. "What better place to dig into the history of old Hembreeites?"

"Don't you think you've done enough *digging* for today?"

"Oh, Nadia, for Pete's sake, don't be so literal."

"You going all by yourself?"

"Yeah, Robert and Hugh left for the college." She thumped a stray crumb down the counter, and it landed on the parchment. "They took the hair in the hair receivers. Not sure what that's about, but they left some of the stuff here, the containers and the parchment—what'd you say that was?"

"A phrenology map."

"Yeah, I wonder who colored in the sections. Seems like some sort of clue."

"Could be."

"Tune and Color," Mosey said. "Weird clues."

"Look, I need to get back to work, but we can talk later. I just wanted to pass along that information—about the artist."

"Okay, thanks. I'm going to head over to the cemetery. I'll stop by the store on my way back."

"Don't say I didn't warn you."

"I'm just going to stroll around, check out a few graves. I've already got the timeframe and surnames. I imagine I can get the rest from the gravestones. You see that, right? The dates on the graves—"

"Yes," she cut in, "it makes perfect sense but—"

"By the way," Mosey went on, "I suppose there's no point in hanging on to the little portrait of the boys, but hold off if you can. I may need an excuse to speak to Hopkins."

"Mosey, listen to me…"

Nadia's words trailed off as Mosey hung up the phone. Hell-bent on sorting out the Hansbrough-Mordecai connection, she threw on a hoodie, grabbed her keys and sunglasses, and headed out the door.

The day was warm enough for a walk, and the old Hembree cemetery was no more than a mile away. As she strode along the walking path that led to the college, which was only a block from the cemetery, she thought about the professor and the Hansbroughs. Obviously one of his siblings married a Hansbrough. He and Ben were first cousins—she knew that much for sure. "And how else could they be—first cousins, that is?"

How else, Mosey darlin'...yes, indeed—how else?

"Wait—" She squatted to tie a shoelace. "Let me rethink this, Daddy. Evan's father was a Hopkins. His mother must have been a Mordecai—right?—since his grandfather the painter was a Mordecai. Ben's father was a Hansbrough, so his mother must have also been a Mordecai. But let's back up," she continued. "For the sake of argument, let's suppose the unknown sibling *did*, in fact, marry a Hansbrough, Thaddeus to be precise. That sibling would be female...well, not necessarily, not now...but back then." She slipped her hand in her pocket, felt for her pad and pen, and sat down on a bench off the path. She sketched a quick diagram of what she assumed to be the Evan-Ben connection: two circles for the cousins, then, four more for their parents. The names of the fathers were obvious, Hopkins and Hansbrough. And, if the new evidence from Nadia was accurate—that the boys' maternal grandfather was Evan Mordecai—then the siblings in question were the mothers, both of whom must have been Mordecais before marriage. Hard evidence, though, that's what she needed. Without it, working out the kinships among the different families was a crap shoot. Too many possibilities. She printed across the top of the diagram: *Names and dates of the mothers—Ben's and Evan's.* Getting up from the bench, she stretched out her hamstrings, shook out her arms, and resumed her trek, quickening her pace to a slow jog. She felt confident the respective family plots would provide the evidence she needed.

Coming to the campus, she crossed the quad in front of the library and soon got to the cemetery gate. A funeral was in progress, and two gravediggers, one middle-aged, the other young, stood at a respectful distance from the burial site. Good, she thought, she wouldn't have to search the entire cemetery. The gravediggers would be able to direct her to the plots she was looking for. She quietly made her way to the spot where they were standing, a good distance from the burial site. "Nathan?" She lowered her voice. "Is that you?"

"Mrs. Ellison?"

"Actually, it's Frye. I didn't change my name. You're one of Robert's students, aren't you?"

"Yes, ma'am. I believe we met at convocation."

"That's what I was thinking. Tell me," she said, "are you acquainted with the general layout of the cemetery—the family plots, I mean?"

"I wouldn't know much about that, ma'am, but my grandfather would."

The older man tipped his hat.

"Mosey Frye...nice to meet you, sir." She extended a hand.

The man dug in his pocket for a handkerchief and, after rubbing it over both hands, responded to Mosey's gesture. "Boyd Granger." He rolled the handkerchief into a ball and stuffed it into the pocket of his coveralls.

"I'm trying to locate the graves of some family

members for an out-of-town client," she explained, fabricating an excuse for her mission. "Would you by any chance know where the Hansbrough plot is? I kind of think I remember it—the one with the big statue?"

"Ma'am," Granger said, pointing a finger toward an area enclosed by a short fence, "that's the Hansbrough plot over there. See that big oak?"

She looked in the direction he was pointing. About fifty feet away stood a large live oak, as wide as it was tall, with branches long and full enough to shade the graves of generations of Hansbroughs. "That's the Hansbrough plot?"

"Yes, ma'am."

"What about the Mordecais and the Hopkinses?"

"The Mordecais are to the left of the Hansbroughs," he said, motioning, "over yonder. Both families have lived around here for a long time, uh, since the 1800s."

"And the Hopkins family?"

"Hopkins, uh, that's more complicated. The name Hopkins is common in these parts. You know which one you're looking for?"

"Actually, I'm not sure of the given names."

"There's a good-sized plot over there. Belongs to Professor Evan Hopkins's family. Reckon that's it?"

"Could be," she answered. She thanked them for their help and headed for the largest and nearest of the plots. Quietly opening the gate, she stepped cautiously among the graves; she'd always feared stepping on a grave but wasn't sure why. Probably wasn't any harm in it. Just a matter of respect. Toward the back of the plot, a statue of a knight loomed high above the final resting place of the patriarch Lucien Hansbrough. His dates, in Gothic script, were carved into the marker. "June 3, 1893...December 13, 1953." Pad and pencil in hand, she turned to a fresh page, and scribbled down his name and dates.

Lucien's wife, Lillian Dubois Hansbrough, May 9, 1896 to February 20, 1940, was buried on his right. To the left of him lay his two sons, the recently deceased Thaddeus and his brother Edward, a few years his junior. Edward had preceded his brother in death by twenty-odd years. The older brother's grave, still fresh, bore only a birth date, July 10, 1915. "July." She thought back to the inscription on the photograph, then printed across the top of the page: *Important Clue. Family Supper, July...very likely Thaddeus's birthday dinner*. And, following that line of thinking, she listed the family members likely to have attended. Thaddeus...his wife...his brother and his wife—if Edward had a wife. Her eyes wandered to a headstone to the left of Thaddeus's grave. The material was the same, but it was more delicately engraved. There was a heart of flowers below the deceased's name: Lydia M. Hansbrough, born May 3, 1919, deceased January 6, 1959. Lydia M.—surely, M stood for Mordecai. Lydia must have been the sister of Evan Hopkins's mother. She stepped back from the graves. "That's it...has to be." She flipped to the diagram and scribbled "Lydia M." in the circle next to "Thaddeus" and above "Ben."

That'd be a hell of a case to make, girl. Supposition, pure supposition. Lydia might have been his second wife or his third—or who knows?

"Daddy, if you make this too dang complicated, I'll never figure it out, so just hush."

A cough somewhere in the distance caught her

attention, and she looked up as the Grangers disappeared behind a clump of redbud trees just in bloom. The mourners were taking their leave. One, then the next, then the next approached an older gentleman in a dark suit. Some shook his hand, while others gave him an affectionate embrace.

Before she left the family plot, she looked again at the dark granite statue of the medieval knight, erected in memory of Lucien Hansbrough. It wasn't a prayerful or solemn figure, but bold and brave. The sword was drawn, the shield was clutched close to the heart. Had Lucien been that kind of man, ready to do battle for his loved ones or his business? She knew little about him, other than what was said. A tight old man, tight as Dick's hatband.

Mosey, that's not what that means. Tight, like tight around the waist—not tightfisted.

Mosey giggled. "I know, Daddy."

She jotted down the rest of the names and dates, then headed for the Mordecai plot some twenty feet away where a stately figure in robes stared out above the final resting place of the Mordecais. She walked around the statue. Must be Biblical. The beard was long and full. A robe hung in deeply carved folds from the figure's broad shoulders. "Of course…Mordecai." She stared up at the vacant eyes, halfway expecting the statue to answer. "Mordecai, of the house of Benjamin," she said, "the adoptive father of Esther." She wasn't especially religious, but she did know her Bible.

She surveyed the formidable sculpture from all sides and, with fingertips, traced the folds of the robe. Minute vegetation had pitted the surface and colored the crevices a light greenish gray. Sandaled feet protruded from beneath the robe, and the toes of the left foot extended slightly beyond the pedestal. The sculptor, or perhaps the stone cutter, had spaced the letters of the surname across the full width of the marble platform. There was something very impressive—or daunting—about a name carved in stone. The letters were spaced apart, as if to say, this was a man to be reckoned with…to be remembered.

She assumed the statue had been erected in memory of Evan Mordecai, whose grave was in closest proximity. His headstone, no larger or more elaborate than the others, bore his name and dates, March 31, 1890-November 4, 1962. But unlike the other headstones, it carried an inscription: "One who sat in the king's gate."

She read the phrase aloud several times, and then, settling upon "king" as the truly puzzling element, rolled the phrase over in her mind. *King's* gate…*king's* gate. Seemed like an ambiguous bit of language for an epitaph.

She jotted it down, then moved on to the headstone that marked the grave of his wife, Estelle J. Mordecai, April 30, 1895-April 14, 1943. The graves of two of the three Mordecai daughters flanked the graves of their parents. Next to the father lay the eldest, Ruth M. Hopkins, October 10, 1913-May 5, 1969. Alongside the mother, lay the youngest, Fanny Mordecai, September 1, 1924-August 7, 1946. One of the three sisters was missing. Lydia, yes, Lydia. They had buried her in the Hansbrough plot where, a good many years later, her husband Thaddeus would be buried. He'd lost his wife young and would never marry again.

Standing now before the grave of the girl who had died *very* young—younger than her sister Lydia—Mosey faintly mumbled, "Twenty-two...no, not quite." She would have been, if she'd lived a few weeks longer. Had *she* been the other young woman at the family supper? It seemed plausible, even likely. Why not Fanny, if her sisters had attended?

Given the three sisters' birth dates—1913, 1919, 1924—she surmised that the two visible faces in the photograph were Lydia's and Fanny's, while the face hidden behind the wide-brimmed hat was Ruth's. She looked back at her grave. "What made you turn away, Ruth, just as the photographer snapped the picture?"

She stepped back from the grave, and glancing around, realized the mourners and gravediggers had departed. She was alone in the cemetery, and the light was beginning to fade. She still had the Hopkins plot to go but decided to leave it for another day.

The towering Biblical figure caught her eye again, then the inscription on Evan's headstone: "One who sat in the king's gate."

Be careful, Mosey.

She didn't respond but gazed past the statue to a plot a short distance from where she was standing, an unassuming plot without statues or anything elaborate to commemorate the dead. Her eyes rested for a moment on a stretch of soft, green Zoysia and the modest headstones of Amos and Evelyn Frye, their son Ellis, and his wife Marie.

"Of course, Daddy, of course," she said, the words catching in her throat. "I'll be careful. I always am. You know I am."

Chapter Six

On her way home, Mosey stopped by the antique shop to share her findings with Nadia. Entering the store, she noticed that the small portrait of Evan and Ben had been moved from its former location to a shelf behind the cash register. "Hey, Nadia, you moved the portrait," she said with a frown.

"I figure it's sold, right?"

"You're *selling* it to them?" She leaned on the counter and peered over at the portrait.

"Yep, for the amount I paid for it. Seemed like the right thing to do."

"What about the photograph? Think they'll want it, too?"

"Maybe, but it's yours now—isn't it?"

"I think I'll give the original to Hopkins and keep the one Hugh's making," she said, relaxing into a dark red leather wing chair.

"Hold on a minute." Nadia stuck her head out to check on a couple who'd stopped to look at a bistro table on the patio beyond the storefront. "Can I help you?" They shook their heads and walked on along.

"Interested?" Mosey said.

"Nope." She closed the door. "Just looking."

"I'm thinking I may know a few things about the Hopkins family that even *he* doesn't know."

"*He* who?"

"Hopkins." Mosey scooted to the edge of her chair and picked up a toy soldier from the display on the coffee table. A whole troop was doing battle near a painted riverbank dotted with absurdly tall cypresses.

"And, knowing you, I imagine you want to know more." Nadia sat in the matching wing chair across from Mosey.

"I haven't quite put it together, but I found out a ton of stuff at the cemetery." She pulled out her pad and turned to the list. "The names I've underlined are the ones in the photograph." She passed it to Nadia.

"Thaddeus Hansbrough," Nadia said, sliding her finger from name to name. "Edward Hansbrough." She flipped to the next page. "Lydia, Ruth, and Fanny Mordecai." She flipped back to the Hansbrough page. "So, the one who died recently, Thaddeus, had a brother named Edward?" She looked up at Mosey.

Mosey nodded.

"And they're the men in the photograph?" She looked up again.

"Seems likely," Mosey said. "Lydia Mordecai was married to Thaddeus, and their son Ben is the younger of the two boys in the portrait."

"You sure?"

"No, but that's what I'm thinking."

"And the women are the Mordecai sisters?" Nadia said.

"You got it." Mosey smiled. "Lydia, Ruth, and Fanny, Fanny being the youngest, Ruth the oldest."

"Then, Ruth," Nadia said, "who married a Hopkins, is the professor's mother?"

"Uh-huh, Ruth Mordecai Hopkins."

"If Hugh was right, and the photograph is from the

Kay Pritchett

early forties, that would put the adults in their twenties
or thirties, more or less." Nadia laid the pad on the table
and reached for a handful of soldiers. "Lydia...Ruth...
Fanny." After arranging them around a small
rectangular brass tray, she picked up four more.
"Thaddeus, Edward, and the two boys."

"I'm guessing Ruth," Mosey said, "is the one with
the hat."

"Right...the one who didn't want to be in the
picture." Nadia turned one of the soldiers around so that
it faced away from the tray.

"And the youngest," Mosey said, "must be Fanny,
the pretty one with the curly hair."

Nadia picked up Mosey's pad and opened it to the
Mordecai page. "Fanny...she died *really* young. What
was she—twenty-two?"

"Close to it."

"I wonder what happened."

"Hopkins might know," Mosey said, "but he was
still a child. Must have been eight or nine. He may not
remember."

"True, but he *might*. I was barely seven when my
grandmother died, but I remember everything, the
funeral..."

"I don't see me asking Hopkins about his aunt's
death," Mosey said.

Nadia shrugged and, picking up the two smallest
soldiers, placed them in the foreground. "That's better.
They're facing the photographer."

Mosey pulled the mock-up toward her.

"Hold on," Nadia said. "Someone's missing,"

"Who's missing?" Mosey cocked her head.

Nadia counted. "Two men, three women, two

162

children. That's seven…but there were *eight* chairs, *eight* place settings."

"Are you sure?"

She nodded. "We've been assuming the picture was taken by a professional photographer, but what if *he* or *she*—"

"—was one of the guests?"

"Or the host," Nadia added. "Who do you suppose hosted the supper?"

"Well, that's easy." She reached for a toy general and set him at a short distance from the make-believe table. "The owner of the house."

"Of course…Lucien," Nadia said. "So, wonder where Lucien's wife was? If both she and Lucien were there, that would put *nine* at the table."

"Hum." Mosey checked her notes. "Lillian died in 1940." She sat back, eyeing the curious diners. "So Lucien, the recently widowed host, was the photographer and eighth diner."

"Yeah, that works out perfectly." She gathered the soldiers in both hands and returned them to the field of battle.

"I've got to get going." Mosey rose from her chair. "By the way, if Robert takes me out to dinner, you want to join us? We could invite Hugh."

Nadia looked at Mosey. "Hugh, eh?"

"Yeah, I thought it might be fun. You like Hugh, right?" Mosey grinned.

"I don't *know* Hugh."

"He seems your type."

Nadia scrunched her nose, as if she didn't give much credit to that idea. "And what would that be?"

"Tall…handsome…smart."

"And probably seeing someone."

Mosey shook her head. "I don't think so."

"I'll think about it—dinner, not Hugh," she replied, with a toggle of her head.

"Yes, you *think* about it," Mosey mocked, as she walked out the door. "See you later."

Mosey trekked back to her house and, reaching the top of the kitchen steps, peeped in the open door. "Hey, what's going on?"

"We've been cleaning." Robert moved his bucket from one spot to another.

"I already cleaned."

"Maybe not enough," Hugh said.

"Explain, please," she persisted, slipping off her sneakers.

"You'd better sit down first and, here," Robert said, taking a tall goblet from the cabinet and setting it on the counter, "pour yourself a glass of wine."

She filled the goblet halfway and, scanning her radiant surroundings, tiptoed to the other side of the room. "What, for heaven's sake, prompted you to clean on a Saturday afternoon?" She sipped the Beaujolais and waited for an answer.

Robert removed his rubber gloves, stepped into the dining room, and returned with two envelopes. "Take a look." He handed her the envelopes.

"What's this?"

"Go ahead. Open them."

From the larger of the two, she pulled out the pieces of "Family Supper, July—" along with Hugh's copy, identical to the original except for the tear. "Good job, Hugh."

"Thanks. I think it turned out okay." He sat down

across from Mosey.

She opened the other envelope. "Printouts?"

"Charts," Hugh said, "composite profiles of the substances we found in the hair specimens. We put them through the GC."

"The what?"

"The gas chromatograph…it detects substances, breaks the specimen into parts. Linked to the MS—"

"What?" Mosey interrupted.

"The mass spectrometer."

"Please, spare me the details." She tossed the charts on the table. "What do they *mean*?"

"What they mean," Robert said, "is we ought to call the police."

"The police?"

"The long strands of hair contained large amounts of 'inheritance powder.' "

"Plain English, please."

"Arsenic."

"Holy Mary!" she gulped.

"The ringlet," Hugh added, "released considerable amounts of formaldehyde and methanol—in addition to a smaller amount of arsenic."

"You're saying somebody was *poisoned*?" Her eyes widened.

"Looks like it," Robert said.

"What's odd," Hugh mused, "is that the long strands and the short ringlet contain different poisons. Formaldehyde and methanol are used in embalming. What could have happened—and this is just a theory— is that the red-haired individual was poisoned with arsenic, which is what the hair collected in the brass hair receiver suggests." He turned to Robert. "Could you pour me a glass of that?"

Robert picked up the bottle but paused to add his suppositions to Hugh's. "The ringlet must have been snipped *after* the body was embalmed."

Hugh held out his glass. "Which would explain the large amounts of formaldehyde and methanol and the smaller amount of arsenic."

"I don't get it," said Mosey. "If this person—he or she—was poisoned, why would the ringlet contain *less* arsenic?"

"Simple," Hugh said. "A ringlet cut from the end of the hair would typically contain less arsenic than the hair close to the root."

"Plus, embalming fluid would partially mask the arsenic," Robert said, opening a box of wheat crackers. "Anybody hungry?" He poured half the box onto a large cutting board, then tore open a package of cheese and stacked the slices next to the crackers. "Hugh, care for cheese?"

"Thanks, don't mind if I do."

"I was hoping we might go out to dinner," said Mosey, "but I think I've lost my appetite." She got up and, ignoring the damp floor, walked to the sink and poured herself a glass of water.

"It's not like we've got a corpse." Robert twisted in his chair.

"No corpse, just an *insinuated* corpse." Mosey drank and set her glass next to the sink.

"No need to get emotionally involved," Robert said. "But we do need to inform the police—right, Hugh?"

"I think we must."

"Can we put that off a bit? I need to call John Earle

first."

"John Earle?"

"The owner and general manager of Shepherd Realty," she said. "He listed the estate."

"Oh, I see." Hugh reached for a cracker.

"My gosh," she said, tapping her forehead with the heel of her hand. "What about Nadia? She bought a ton of stuff at the estate sale. You suppose it might—?"

"I wouldn't think so," Hugh cut in, "unless there was significant contact between the object and the victim."

"The problem is," Robert said, "we don't know where the poisoning occurred or when."

"Or *who*," Hugh added.

Mosey's face was all frown. She slumped down in the chair across from Hugh. "No *who* or *where* or *when*. Only a headpot full of baffling clues and, dadgummit, another stigmatized property."

Chapter Seven

Lost in thought, Mosey sat twisting a strand of linguini around her fork. The foursome had arrived at Fontana's Ristorante around eight o'clock and ordered promptly. It was now approaching eight-forty, and Mosey had barely touched her food.

"It's not the muddle you think it is." Hugh passed her a basket of Italian bread.

She accepted the basket and set it in front of Nadia.

Robert leaned toward his wife. "Not hungry?"

She shrugged.

"As I was saying," Hugh began again, "it's not the muddle you think it is. Look at the salient facts."

"Let's hear it," Nadia said.

"Here's what we're certain of," Hugh said, "unless the entire business is *staged*."

"Staged," Nadia repeated. "Interesting angle."

"But let's rule that out for the time being and assume that there is, in fact, a victim."

"Go on." Mosey laid down her fork.

She—and apparently the others, too—wanted to hear Hugh's "salient facts." Nadia seemed especially intent, having pushed her plate back and tucked her hair behind her ears.

"First," Hugh said, "the victim is likely a female. Men, even men with long hair, didn't collect their hair in hair receivers, did they?"

"I agree with that," Nadia said.

"We don't know the exact time frame," Hugh continued, "but we *do* know hair receivers had little purpose after—what, the forties?"

"How you figure?" Robert brushed his napkin across his mouth.

Nadia had the answer. "Women stopped using rats about then, well, most women…"

Robert gawked. "What?"

"R-a-t," Nadia said. "They made a rat out of their hair and used it to punch up their hairdos."

"If you say so." He took another bite of ravioli.

"We might also assume," Hugh said, "that the victim was linked to the Hansbrough estate. The clues certainly point in that direction."

"Also, we can eliminate the people who didn't have red, curly hair." Mosey broke a piece of bread and dipped it in olive oil. "Lydia the middle sister had dark, straight hair."

"Of the potential victims, then—i. e., the ones with a Hansbrough connection—that leaves Fanny Mordecai and Ruth Hopkins."

"If, indeed, Fanny and Ruth *are* the women in the picture," Mosey clarified. "That's an inference, pure and simple."

"True, but even if they weren't present at the supper, there's still a connection." Hugh took a sip of wine.

"Yes, of course, you're right." She moved a tomato from one side of her salad plate to the other.

"Now," he said, "let's take the date on Max's grave as a starting point. He died in 1941. A person looking for a hiding place for clues—ones he wanted to hide for the time being but to come to light at some future date—might have removed the dog's bones and put the headpot in the grave. Right?"

"I don't know." Nadia frowned. "Who goes around digging up dog graves?"

"Good point," Hugh said, "and maybe that's why they buried him on the terrace in the first place. Maybe they figured it would be refurbished at some point. Maybe they even *knew* that was the plan. At any rate, if they lived there or went there often, they might have had some control over the eventual exposure of the clues."

"Makes sense," Robert said. "So, who died after 1941?"

Mosey reached in her clutch for her notepad. "Fanny died in 1946; Lydia—who we've eliminated as the victim—in 1959, and Ruth, in 1969."

"I'd say Fanny's the victim," Nadia stated with assurance.

"How you figure that?" Robert said.

"I seriously doubt that Ruth Hopkins, as late as 1969, would have been saving her hair in a hair receiver. Not in the late sixties." Nadia batted her eyes at Robert, but not in a flirty way.

"Well, how was I supposed to know?" He blotted his mouth and shifted in his seat.

"Hair styles had totally changed by the sixties, hon." Mosey patted him on the hand. "Women's liberation and all that. And besides," she turned to Nadia, "wouldn't she have been gray? How old was she?"

"When was she born?" Nadia said.

Mosey checked her notepad again. "In 1913, so she

would have been...fifty-six when she died. Unlikely she would have still had her red hair—if she ever had red hair." Mosey picked up a piece of lettuce and nibbled the edge.

"Yeah," Hugh said, "Fanny's the victim."

Mosey pushed back in her chair. "I don't know how you can be so sure. Everything we *say* we know is little more than conjecture."

"Investigations often begin that way." Hugh refilled Nadia's glass, then his.

"With suppositions, you mean," Robert said.

"Yes, suppositions, suspicions—"

"That's right," Nadia put in. "Suspects. The police always have their suspects."

"And a corpse," Mosey added.

"Not always," Hugh corrected. "Want some wine?" He motioned with the bottle toward Mosey, then Robert.

In one move, Mosey emptied her wine glass and rose from her chair. "When I get back from calling John Earle," she announced, "let's change the subject. I'm tired of thinking about victims, suspects, hair."

Robert watched his wife as she crossed the dining room into the foyer. He let out a sigh and shook his head. "She's projected herself entirely into that house."

"Realtors do that, don't they?" Hugh said.

"Not like Mosey," Nadia said. "But this time, it's not the house, it's the *victim*."

"Well, whatever it is, she needs to take a step back, let the cops figure it out." He scooped up a spoonful of clam sauce from Mosey's bowl. "Um, this is pretty good."

Hugh looked at his watch. "It's not quite nine.

Maybe we should call the station."

"Yeah, call Olivera." Nadia dipped a bread stick into the clam sauce. "Ask for Lieutenant Gustavo Olivera."

"We're on a first name basis with the police, are we?" he said with a grin.

Nadia rolled her eyes. "It's Mosey who knows him, not I."

Hugh chuckled. "So, which one of us is going to call?"

"Why don't *you* call?" Robert looked at Hugh.

"It's Mosey's listing and her mystery," he said.

"But you found the arsenic, old man," Robert said.

"Oops," Nadia said, "here she comes."

Robert stood and pulled out Mosey's chair. "What'd he say?"

"He said to call the police." She sat, looked down at her plate, then at Robert. "Hey, what happened to my clam sauce?"

He reacted to her question with a blank stare. "Good, we all agree for once. Time to call Olivera."

"John Earle's calling Lizbeth Hansbrough."

"Oh, dear," Nadia said.

"What's the matter?"

"I hate to think of Lizbeth being mixed up in this, and I guess I am, too."

"Why?"

"Everything I bought—furniture, accessories—"

"I'd say we *all* are, except for Robert," Mosey said.

Hugh looked at his colleague. "Wait till Jim Bledsoe hears we've been doing crime work in his lab."

Robert choked.

"Take some water." Mosey offered him her glass.

"You know there's one thing we haven't talked about," Hugh went on, passing over Robert's distress. "Motive."

"It's not called 'inheritance powder' for nothing," Nadia observed.

"But if Fanny is the victim," Mosey said, "what money did *she* have?"

"The one with the money was Lucien Hansbrough," Nadia said.

"Right," Hugh confirmed. "So what if—"

"That's it!" Mosey interrupted, clutching Hugh's arm.

"What?"

Mosey placed her notepad next to Hugh's plate. "Think about it." She leaned forward, hunching over the pad. "Lucien's wife died in 1940. What if, a year later, he set his eye on Fanny Mordecai—young, beautiful, available. But his sons didn't want their rich, old daddy marrying a sweet young thing about *their* age." Suddenly hungry, Mosey scooped up a spoonful of linguini and stuffed it in her mouth. "So, they decided to take action." She paused to chew. "They *poisoned* Fanny...I'm sure of it...to keep her from getting the old man's money." She daubed her lips. Her eyes shifted from Robert to Nadia to Hugh.

Hugh smiled. "That makes perfect sense."

"Who knows?—they might have administered the first dose at the family supper," she said excitedly.

"Too bad," Nadia said, "you can't detect arsenic in a picture."

"But you *can* in hair." Hugh paused to rescue a strand of Nadia's hair that had swept perilously close to the floating wick of a cresset lamp.

She tucked the strand behind her ear and glanced uncomfortably at Hugh.

"And the person," he continued, "who filled two hair receivers with the victim's hair and then buried them, must have known that."

"Why didn't he just pick up the phone and call the cops?" Robert pondered.

"Maybe he or she was afraid," Mosey said.

"She?" Hugh questioned.

"Or uncertain," Nadia said.

"So, who was our mole?" Hugh said.

"Ruth Mordecai." Mosey stretched her shoulders and sighed.

"Ruth," Nadia said, "she probably didn't want any part of the whole hideous mess, and that's why she hid behind her hat."

"Wonder what else Ruth suspected?" Hugh queried.

"Good question." Robert said, folding his napkin and placing it next to his empty plate.

"More to the point," Mosey added, "what does Ruth's *son* know?"

"Maybe it wasn't Ruth at all," Robert said. "Maybe it was Lydia who knew. She was married to Thaddeus, wasn't she?"

"Maybe they *both* knew," Hugh said.

"But they're dead now," Mosey said, a bit deflated, "except for the professor and Ben Hansbrough." She flopped back against her chair, jostling the table. The oil in the cresset lamp sloshed, and the flame went out.

Chapter Eight

On Monday morning at ten o'clock, Lieutenant Olivera entered Abboud's Antiques and asked to speak to the owner.

"I'm the owner." Nadia stepped down from a ladder. "Can I help you?"

"Lieutenant Olivera," he said, removing his hat. "I'm investigating a possible homicide. I'm sure your friend, uh, Ms. Frye, has filled you in."

Nadia detected a hint of sarcasm in the detective's voice. She lifted the ladder and set it behind the counter, then cleared a path for her unwanted visitor. "Yes, I know about that," she responded uneasily.

"So it seems, uh, she found a photograph in a box of papers...one *you* purchased at the Hansbrough estate sale."

"That's right."

"I'd like to take a look at it, if you don't mind."

"Would it make any difference if I did?" She'd watched enough detective stories to know about search warrants.

"I can get a warrant easily enough," he replied, propping his right foot on a beaded Victorian footstool.

She eyed the stool. "I suppose there's no harm in showing you the box. It's in the back."

They walked to the back of the store, and she pointed to the box in question. It was where Mosey had left it, on a small Duncan Fife table surrounded by a half-dozen mahogany ladder-backs.

"That's it," she said, shoving a chair to one side. "I haven't had a chance to examine the contents."

Olivera leaned against the doorframe as Nadia opened the top flaps to reveal stacks of photographs and papers. She lifted a bundle of letters by the ribbon they were tied with and blew lightly to remove the dust.

"If you don't mind," he said, "I'll just take the whole box back to the station."

She continued lifting bundles until she had reached the bottom. "Nothing much in here but a bunch of old cards, letters, and photographs."

"Ms. Abboud, uh—"

"Okay, okay," she said, dropping the last bundle, "but I'll need a receipt."

He slipped on a pair of latex gloves before refilling the box, then walked back toward the front of the store.

"My receipt, Lieutenant."

He pulled out his notepad and scribbled, saying aloud, "One box from Hansbrough estate...taken from Abboud's Antiques, March 25, 2009." He ripped out the sheet, handed it to Nadia, and, picking up the box, headed for the door.

"Let me get that for you." She grasped the knob. "Will I get the box back?"

"Yes, unless it contains evidence." He balanced the box on one arm, adjusted his hat and, with a quick nod, left the shop.

As soon as he'd gone, she reached for the phone. "Mosey, it's me."

"What's up?"

"Olivera was just here."

"I'm not surprised. I told him about the photograph and the box."

"He took the box."

"We never looked through the papers," Mosey said.

"I know. I wonder if there was anything of interest."

"Wonder if he will tell us if he finds something."

"I seriously doubt it—why would he?"

"What are you doing?" Mosey said.

"Working."

"I have to show a house at eleven. You want to meet later at the Tavernette, grab a bite of lunch?"

"What time?"

"It'll be around twelve, twelve-thirty."

Hearing the door open, she ended the conversation and turned to see Evan Hopkins entering the store.

"Professor, you're back," she said, managing a smile.

"I came to check on the painting. I guess you don't know anything yet." He removed his hat.

"I spoke to the potential buyer, and she's willing to let you take it."

"Good. I have very little of my grandfather's work."

"I'll get it for you. I put it back in the display." She stepped inside the window and, agile as a cat, made her way to the curio. "I picked up some very nice pieces at the estate sale."

Hopkins glanced around the store at the collection of objects atop tables, chest-of-drawers, and sideboards. "I see you did." He picked up a crystal jelly dish and held it up to the light. "I imagine my cousin Ben would be interested in seeing what you have."

"Ben Hansbrough, you mean. Wasn't he here for the sale?"

He put down the jelly dish and, brows raised, eyelids half closed, assumed a posture of stiff reluctance. "No, he wasn't here for the sale."

That's new information, Nadia thought, registering the professor's words. "Some of the items are here in the showcase. That curio"—she pointed—"and the ceramic birds, the occasional table, and the photographer's chair in the corner."

He craned his neck. "How much do you want for the chair?"

"Let's see," said Nadia. She handed the painting out to Hopkins and then looked for the price tag on the chair. "Eight hundred and forty-nine."

"I see." He lifted his brows.

"A wicker photographer's chair that's in excellent condition, as is this one, is a high-priced item."

"And the portrait, how much do you want for it?"

"Since you're one of the subjects, I thought I'd let you have it at cost." She stepped down from the window. "I paid seventy-five for it."

"I'll take the portrait now. I'll have to think about the chair." He tugged one ear.

"I could probably give you a discount, since—"

"It's not for me," he cut in, "it's for Ben. That was his grandfather Lucien's photographer's chair."

"Lucien Hansbrough was a photographer?"

"Yes, an exceptional photographer," he crowed.

"And your grandfather was a painter."

"Yes, my mother's father, Evan Mordecai. I said that the other day."

"I know," she said with emphasis. "I remember your mentioning that." Hopkins was one of those people who expected others to remember their every word. She went behind the counter and ripped a large piece of brown paper off a roll. "I'll wrap that for you," she offered, managing, with effort, another smile.

"Thanks." He handed her the painting and reached inside his lapel pocket for his checkbook. "You said seventy-five."

"Yes, plus tax." She added the tax and handed him the bill. Then, choosing her words guardedly, she said, "I wonder if the print I have...it's fairly wide, like a panorama...I wonder if Lucien Hansbrough was the photographer. I believe you and your cousin are in the picture."

"What photograph?"

"It was torn in two. A friend of mine is making a copy."

"Torn in two?"

"Yes, that's what I said, torn—"

"When will you get it back?"

"Soon, I suppose."

"I'll call back." He handed her the check. "Thanks for the discount."

"You're welcome. See you later, then."

After Hopkins left and she'd resumed her cleaning, the phone rang. "Abboud's Antiques."

"Olivera here."

"Lieutenant, didn't expect to hear from you again today." She put down her cloth.

"I'm meeting Ms. Hansbrough this afternoon at her late grandfather's home."

"At the Hansbrough estate, you mean."

"That's right, around four, four-thirty. Could you be there?"

"Not sure why you want *me* there. Besides, I would have to close the store."

"Could you make it by four-thirty? It's *your* store. Closing early can't be a serious impediment, surely."

She glanced at her agenda. "I suppose I could, if it's important."

"Good. Uh, I need to send some officers back to the store, looks like."

"Look, Lieutenant, I've got a business to run."

Undaunted, apparently, he continued. "As I was saying, we need to get a list of everything you purchased. There might be more evidence."

"When will the officers be here?"

"Actually, they're on their way."

"Fine...I'll be here." She hung up the phone and immediately called Mosey, got no answer, and called Robert. "Robert, glad you answered."

"Nadia?"

"Olivera was at the store, and now some officers are coming to look for *more* evidence."

"Is that a problem?"

"Of course, it's a problem. I don't want policemen rummaging around my store, good grief."

"Well—"

"He says he's meeting with Lizbeth Hansbrough later today at the estate. He wants *me* there."

"Yeah, he called us, too."

"Does Mosey know?"

"Nope, she's out showing a house."

"I'm seeing her for lunch. I'll tell her."

"It's okay, you know. Nothing to worry about," he

soothed.

"Nothing to worry about," she mumbled under her breath, hanging up the phone.

She walked to the back room, where, squeezed in among items singled out for repair, stood a compact refrigerator with a small microwave oven on top. She dropped a teabag into a flowered teacup, filled it with water, set it in the microwave, and pushed the minute button. Then, perching on a wobbly bar stool, she peered over a tall stack of faded table linens at a painting of a handsome Confederate soldier, who sat astride a rampant Appaloosa stallion. The young man's hazel eyes, sad or maybe solemn, seemed to be staring back at her. "Cup of tea...or something stronger?" she said with a wink. She reached for a tarnished silver flask, but just as she was swirling it in front of the painting, a jingle brought her chitchat to a halt. She put down the flask and went to see who had entered the shop.

"Mosey...glad it's you."

"Who'd you think it was?"

"The police! Olivera's already been here—he took the box. Hopkins was here, too. And now some officers are coming...to gather evidence, *more* evidence." The slightest accusatory tone entered her voice.

"*Ah ciel*," Mosey exclaimed.

"You can say that again." Nadia turned and headed toward the back. "Want some tea? I was about to have a cup."

Mosey checked her watch. "Sure. I've got a couple of minutes to burn."

Nadia took her cup out of the microwave. "Black or green?"

"Either's fine." Moving the springs from an old cushion onto the floor, Mosey sat on a backless chair.

"There's a meeting," Nadia said, "four-thirty at the estate." She placed another cup in the microwave.

"What meeting?" Mosey robotically plucked at the springs.

"You, me, Robert and Hugh, Lizbeth Hansbrough. Not sure who else."

Mosey stopped her plucking and frowned. "Olivera has called a meeting?"

"Indeed, he has. I just spoke with Robert. Olivera had already phoned him and Hugh."

Mosey checked her cell phone. "Yep, looks like I missed his call."

"Did he leave a message?"

"Nope." She glanced down at her watch. "When are the officers coming?"

"Any minute."

"I have to meet Clive Anderson over on Main at eleven." She looked closely at her friend.

"It's okay. I'm fine."

"There's nothing here, right? You gave Olivera the box?"

"Yeah, there's stuff here—the curio, the table, the trunk." The microwave binged, and Nadia passed Mosey her cup. "Hopkins was here again, by the way. He came back for the portrait."

"Already?" responded Mosey, heading back toward the front.

The doorbell jingled, the door flew back, and two uniformed officers walked in, one carrying a forensic kit and the other, evidence bags. "Ma'am," said the officer with the kit, "I'm going to have to place a crime scene cone outside, just while we're here." He set the kit on the counter and reached for his ID.

Nadia's face was all apprehension. "Fine." She looked over at Mosey, who was fumbling in her satchel.

The second officer set his bags down and went back for the cone, while the other pressed back the flaps on his kit and lifted out two small jars, a brush, a utility knife, and a stack of 3 x 5 printed cards. "Could you show me the items, please?"

"Nadia," Mosey interrupted in a whisper, "sorry, but I've got to get going." She set her cup on the counter. "Sorry about the tea. See you this afternoon. I'll swing by for you, okay?"

Nadia nodded.

Mosey put on her sunglasses and, tiptoeing past the officer, left the shop.

Chapter Nine

Around four-thirty, Mosey's truck entered the gate of the Hansbrough estate and moved slowly along the drive, stopping short of a row of crime scene cubes some few yards from the entrance. She and Nadia remained in the truck until Robert and Hugh pulled in behind them. Mosey turned off the engine, and she and Nadia got out and walked toward the entrance.

"Where's the stuff?" Mosey called back to Robert.

"You mean the charts? Olivera has them."

"Yeah, same here," Nadia said. "He picked up the box this morning, then sent around a couple of uniforms." Nadia snapped her fingers, as she often did upon suddenly remembering something that had slipped her mind. "I can't believe it," she exclaimed.

"What?"

"I forgot to tell you."

"Tell me what?"

"Lucien Hansbrough was a photographer. The chair I picked up at the estate sale belonged to him."

"How do you know that?" Mosey looked askance at Nadia.

"Hopkins came back for the portrait, and, when he saw the photographer's chair, he said Ben might want it because it was his grandfather Lucien's photographer's chair."

"The police—did they find anything?" Hugh said,

catching up with the women.

"I don't know. They went over everything with a fine-tooth comb and took some samples."

"Of what?" Robert said.

"Dust? How should I know?"

The four of them passed through stone-trimmed arches to the main entrance.

"Lucien, a photographer," Mosey said to Nadia. "You were right. Lucien must have been the host, and *he* took the picture."

Robert grasped the iron knocker in the middle of the dark paneled door and let it fall with a clang. A uniformed office, one of the men who had scrutinized Nadia's acquisitions earlier that day, opened the door and asked to see their identification. He checked their driver's licenses, then ushered them into the parlor through a foyer with elegant casings that mimicked the exterior archway. The furnishings had been removed, and all that remained of the once lavish living quarters were velvet drapes, worn and dusty at the hem, a stone mantel with a deftly carved lintel and surrounds, a deeply fringed Victorian floor lamp, and an ostentatious chandelier, the spear-shaped crystals of which splayed colorful lights across the east wall.

A second officer was lighting tapers on the mantelpiece, and a third was setting up a row of folding chairs in front of a long, metal table. Lizbeth Hansbrough and Evan Hopkins sat in silence near the table. The professor stood up when Mosey and Nadia entered the room. His cousin, a slender woman, mid-thirties, wore her dark hair pulled back in a simple coif. Her eyes, outlined in dark lashes, dominated her face, oval and soft.

"Ms. Frye…Ms. Abboud, we meet again," Hopkins said.

Nadia, the only member of the gathering acquainted with everyone present, introduced the group to Lizbeth Hansbrough, who nodded at the mention of her name.

"Professor Hopkins," Robert said, extending his hand, "we've met before. I know your son Brad."

"Yes, I remember." Hopkins gave Robert's hand a perfunctory shake.

Given to small talk, Robert would have gladly rambled on, mentioning that he himself now taught at Blanchard College, as did Hugh, or, on another note, that Brad, in fact, had been married to his cousin—none of which would have interested the professor in the least. Olivera's timely entrance halted the conversation, mercifully sparing Robert the slight.

"The sergeant tells me everyone is here," Olivera said as he entered briskly from the foyer. "Shall we get started?"

"Perhaps you could begin, Lieutenant, by telling us what this is all about," Hopkins suggested.

Olivera cast a mistrustful eye in the professor's direction. "Of course, and perhaps you, Professor, will be able to answer some of *my* questions as well."

"I don't know what you think we know," Hopkins lobbed back, then took a seat.

Olivera approached the table where the headpot and other objects were scattered from end to end. "I will be as brief as possible. These items were discovered on this property—under a flagstone on the back terrace, to be exact. It was Ms. Frye, who works for Shepherd Realty—" Olivera paused, turning toward

Hopkins's cousin. "Ms. Hansbrough, you've listed the house with Shepherd Realty, correct?"

The heiress to the Hansbrough estate confirmed Olivera's statement with a dip of her chin.

He continued. "Ms. Frye and her friend Professor Jessup made the discovery Saturday morning." He glanced at Mosey and Hugh, who, nodding, confirmed his statement.

"And it was Professors Jessup and Ellison who discovered later that day that strands of hair from two hair receivers...these hair receivers," he said, pointing to the objects, "found inside this replica of an Indian headpot..." He paused again. "Professor Hopkins, Ms. Hansbrough, do either of you recognize any of these items?"

Lizbeth rose from her chair and went up to the table. "I believe I have seen this locket," she said, bending over the elaborately carved piece.

"How is that possible? This locket has probably been in the ground since before you were born."

"I haven't *seen* it, you're right," she clarified, "but I think I've seen it in a portrait. It belonged to my great-grandmother."

"That would be Lucien Hansbrough's wife."

"Yes, my great-grandmother Lillian."

"Do you have the portrait?"

"No, it belongs to my father."

"Ben Hansbrough that would be. And where is it now?"

"He must have it."

Hopkins twisted in his chair, apparently impatient with the lieutenant's line of questioning. He stood and approached the table.

"Professor Hopkins, perhaps you have seen the locket as well."

He slipped his glasses off and took a close look. "Yes, I would say so."

"Have you seen the *actual* object?"

"Whether I've seen it or not, I can't be certain, but I believe I know something about it."

"Go on."

"Just as Ms. Hansbrough has said, it belonged to Lillian Dubois, Ben Hansbrough's grandmother. But after she died, it was given to my aunt, Fanny Mordecai."

"And how do you know that?"

"My mother, Ruth Mordecai Hopkins, had a photograph of her sister wearing that same locket."

Mosey glanced guardedly at her friend.

Hopkins and Lizbeth returned to their seats, and Olivera rounded the table and paused immediately in front of the professor.

"Professor Hopkins, could you describe your aunt for us?"

"Physically, you mean?"

"Yes, physically."

"Well, I don't know—she was an attractive woman, I suppose, and very young, the youngest of the Mordecai girls. She was a redhead. I'm sure of that."

Olivera removed a clear plastic container from a cardboard box and placed it next to the hair receivers. "Could this be her hair?"

Hopkins, expressionless, leaned forward. "Yes, I guess it could be."

"Did any other members of the Mordecai family have red hair?"

"No, just she. Actually—" Hopkins looked away from the table and glanced toward the large windows that ran along the front of the great hall. He tugged at his ear, a gesture that, had he been a gambler, would have been his tell, given that his facial features revealed nothing he didn't want them to reveal.

"Go on, anything you know would be helpful."

"Fanny was adopted. It wasn't spoken about, but my mother told me that her youngest sister had been adopted."

"Adopted." Olivera scratched his head. He walked hesitantly along the table, lightly tapping the rim at intervals. "Your aunt—adoptive aunt, I suppose I should say—Fanny Mordecai, uh, died young, I believe."

"Yes."

"You were very young yourself when she died."

"I was."

"She died in 1946, at the age of twenty-one."

"That's about right. I was ten years younger than my aunt. I must have been ten or eleven."

"You must remember the circumstances of her death, then."

"She died after a long illness."

"Did you hear anyone mention the exact cause of death?"

"I would think that would have been recorded on the death certificate." Hopkins tugged at his ear.

Oliver pulled an envelope from his lapel pocket and, taking out the certificate in question, placed it on the table next to the plastic container. "According to the death certificate, she died of diabetes."

Hopkins said nothing.

"We now have reason to believe that the death certificate is in error. These specimens," he explained, pointing to the victim's hair, "contain significant amounts of poisonous substances. Isn't that the case, Professor Jessup?"

Hugh cleared his throat. "Yes, that's correct. We—Professor Ellison and I—ran the samples through the gas chromatograph in the forensic anthropology lab at the college and found arsenic in both. The ringlet also contains formaldehyde and methanol."

The Hansbrough cousins fastened their eyes on Hugh and Robert. Lizbeth Hansbrough, who had remained wooden throughout the proceedings, went a little pale.

"Explain, please." Olivera, although he had directed his question to Hugh, was now looking quite intently at Hopkins.

"Well," Hugh said, "we can't be sure, but it would seem that the longer strands were collected in the last months of the victim's life when the poison was being administered. The shorter lock, the piece containing formaldehyde and methanol—which are found in embalming fluid, by the way—was cut from the victim's hair after death."

"And you are convinced"—Olivera turned toward Hugh—"that this theory of yours is plausible?"

"We have little to go on, but given the evidence, I would say yes, most definitely."

"And Professor Ellison, you share your colleague's certainty, I suppose?"

"Yes, I agree with Jessup."

Olivera looked drolly at Evan Hopkins. "Do you have anything to add to what you said before about the death of Fanny Mordecai?"

Hopkins sat stiffly in his chair. "I have nothing to add."

"Ms. Hansbrough, another question if you don't mind." Olivera walked over to the mantel and, picking up one of the lit candles, placed it on the table next to the ivory box. He took out the parchment and unfolded it. "Have you seen this before?"

"Why, yes...my father had something like that. It's a phrenology map."

"That's interesting," Olivera said. "Did your father ever say anything about this, uh, phrenology map, as you called it?"

"Yes," she responded. "I heard him say once that his grandfather Lucien was interested in phrenology. It was a hobby of his."

"Did he attempt to *map*, so to speak, any of the family members—as far as you know?"

"The diagram my father had was of *his* father's head."

"Thaddeus Hansbrough, you mean."

"Yes."

"And one more question. It is my understanding that you inherited your grandfather's estate. Shouldn't it have gone to Thaddeus's son?"

Lizbeth cleared her throat. "My father wasn't on the best of terms with his father."

"Was any explanation ever offered?"

"Not to me."

"I see." Olivera walked back to the center of the table and, without so much as a glimpse at the gathering seated before him, called to the officer who'd remained in the foyer. "Springer!"

Striding steps against the stone floor broke the silence of the hall. "Yes, Chief."

Mosey glanced back to see the burly figure of the officer framed within the archway.

"Let's pack these things up and take them back to the station."

"Now, Chief?"

"Yes, now."

Hopkins, a befuddled look on his face, stood and turned to his cousin. "I suppose we can leave now."

"Huh...I suppose we can," Mosey said, echoing his assumption. "Lieutenant Olivera." She walked to where he was standing.

"Yes, Ms. Frye."

"Is that all?"

"For today."

"You mean—?"

"That's all for today, Ms. Frye."

Plenty remained to be said, indeed, there was new information to be shuffled into the mix, questions to be posed, suppositions to be made. Be that as it may, little more than inquiring looks passed among Mosey, Nadia, Robert, and Hugh as they walked hurriedly toward their respective vehicles. Hopkins and Lizbeth, a few paces ahead of them, bustled into his gray sedan and sped out of the gate.

Chapter Ten

Mosey opened the bottom drawer of the breakfront. On top was a tablecloth that had belonged to Grandma Frye—a dingy white cotton square dotted with watermelon wedges. She gave it a good shake and floated it over the breakfast table, then smoothed out the wrinkles with her hands.

Robert shuffled into the kitchen, still in his pajamas and slides. "Why'd you bring out that old thing?"

"I love this old cloth." She set out dishes and flatware, while he poured the coffee and placed a platter of hot biscuits and link sausages on the table.

"That phrase, 'One who sat in the king's gate,' " Mosey said. She placed her grandmother's Bible on the table next to her plate. "It's from the book of Esther."

"What did you say?" Robert sat down and forked a sausage.

"Evan Mordecai's tomb stone."

"What about it?"

"That's the epitaph: 'One who sat in the king's gate.' "

"From Esther, you said." He split open a biscuit and, folding it around the sausage, took a bite.

"Esther, the Jewish queen. Her story is the basis for Purim. You've heard of Esther, haven't you?"

"Of course, I've heard of Esther. So, what does it mean—the epitaph?"

"Mordecai adopted his cousin—Hadassah was her name. But he changed it to Esther. When Mordecai heard Xerxes was looking for a new wife, he brought Esther to the palace, and she was taken into the harem."

"Nasty custom." Robert took another bite of his biscuit sandwich.

"Oh, please. You know you'd love one."

"If any of them could cook, maybe."

"Hey!"

"Just kidding." He slathered a biscuit in peach jam and handed it to Mosey.

"Thanks." She laid the biscuit down and continued. "So, as soon as Xerxes saw her, he was smitten and made her his queen. But Mordecai, to protect his adopted daughter, 'sat in the king's gate.' It's all right here," she said, opening to a marked page.

"I suppose you think Fanny is Esther," Robert said.

Mosey's brow went up. Instead of shooing her off the subject, he had apparently taken an interest.

He stirred his coffee and continued, "—which would make Evan, Fanny's adoptive father, Mordecai—the biblical Mordecai."

"Right, which would make Lucien, Xerxes. Evan had already married one daughter to a future 'king.'"

"Thaddeus, you mean."

Mosey nodded. "So, when Lillian died, he figured, well, why not bump up the family fortune some more? Lucien was only forty-seven when Lillian died."

"That's quite an age difference—I mean between Lucien and Fanny."

"I know. Fanny was only twenty-one, but that was not so unusual for then."

"According to your source there"—he gestured

toward the Bible with his knife—"Evan Mordecai placed Fanny in Lucien's sight, which was easy enough since his daughter Lydia was already married to Lucien's son."

"And then," she said, excitement in her voice, "Lucien fell in love."

"And who wanted that?" Robert shrugged. "Not his sons, for sure."

"Well, think what they stood to lose if their father remarried."

"Which gives them a motive, I suppose."

She stood and carried her dish to the sink. "Dare I call Gus Olivera?"

"Better him than Evan Hopkins."

"Actually, I have an excuse to call Evan."

"Come back here. You've hardly eaten a bite."

"Not very hungry," she replied. "I've got to get out of here. I've got work to do."

"*Real* work?"

He might have suspected otherwise, if he'd seen her slip the envelope with the photograph into her tote. She was on a roll, and it would have taken more than biscuits and sausages to slow her down. She was determined to link up the bits and pieces of "Family Supper, July——." If she could do that, she might be able to figure out who poisoned Fanny. If left up to Olivera, the whole matter, she feared, was destined for the cold case files. That "mole"—Hugh's word for the person who'd stashed the clues in Max's grave—she couldn't stop thinking about the mole. Hiding clues in a dog's grave seemed like something a child might do, but it was highly unlikely a child would have suspected that Fanny had been poisoned. Hopkins thought she died of diabetes, so maybe he and Cousin Ben didn't know. But maybe later on...

Mosey kissed Robert on the cheek and stepped out onto the landing. "Nice day."

"You be careful, you hear?"

"Robert, you sound like my daddy." She pushed the door closed and waved through the pane.

With no clear purpose other than the desire to think in a quiet place, Mosey drove out to the Hansbrough estate. Maybe something at the crime scene—if, indeed, it was a crime scene—would pique her awareness of some detail she'd failed to notice before. She drove through the open gate, parked close to the house, and, using her key, entered the foyer. Light streaming through the tall windows illuminated the backdrop of the previous day's event. Like props in an abandoned theater, the folding table and chairs stood in the same place next to the fireplace. Half-burned candles sat atop the mantel. One candle—the one Olivera had placed next to the phrenology map—was still on the table.

Although the mole had apparently considered the phrenology map an important clue, no one had attempted to decipher its message. Just as modern science gave little credence to phrenology, no one had paid much attention to the parchment diagram of someone's head—Thaddeus's, according to Lizbeth. The highlighted portions of the cranium, the ones that someone had colored in red, were pretty much ignored. 'Tune' and 'Color,' she thought, recalling the words that labeled the colored sections. If she had a computer, she probably could find out what that meant. Impatient for an answer yet unready to depart the deserted stage, she pulled her cell phone from her pocket and called

Nadia. "You got a customer in the store?"

"No, why?"

"I need you to look something up for me—you mind?"

"Can't you look it up yourself? I'm busy."

"I'm at the Hansbrough estate."

"For Pete's sake, why?"

"I'll explain later. Look up 'phrenology map' on the computer—would you, please?"

"Fine. Hold on a second."

She paced along the table, remembering the other clues that had been there the day before: the hair receivers, the headpot, and the ivory box that had held the peculiar map.

"Okay," Nadia said, "phrenology map. I've got it. What do you want to know?"

"Find 'Tune' and 'Color,' " she instructed.

"Okay. What now?"

"Does it give an explanation?"

"Color...that's the twenty-eighth organ, in case you're interested."

"That doesn't tell me anything. What bearing does it have on a person's brain, personality, whatever?"

"Well, it's all about perception of color...or not."

"Huh?"

"It says here, 'Organ twenty-eight determines an individual's aptitude for color perception with regard to art, décor,' and so on. 'The adverse is also a possibility. He or she may lack interest in color and, in extreme cases, be unable to distinguish one color from another.' "

"Color blindness," Mosey said. "*That* could be it."

"What?"

"Finish. What does it say for 'Tune'?"

" 'The thirty-fourth organ pertains to all things musical including an aptitude for composition or performance, or, likewise, a deficiency.' "

"Tone deafness," Mosey broke in.

"Is that all?" Nadia said. "Someone just came in."

"Yes, and thanks. I'll drop by later."

Mosey put her phone away and glanced around the perimeter of the vacant room. Being in the house where all the "actors" had come together hadn't helped. If only she were a medium. Hey! That was an idea...a medium. Unfortunately, she didn't know of any in Hembree. The mole wasn't coming forth with anything other than what he—or she—had already revealed. Which was quite a bit, come to think of it: the victim, the method, and likely the killer or killers: Tune and Color. Too bad the mole's clues were apparently destined for someone who *knew* the perpetrator or perpetrators of the crime. Deficiencies like tone deafness, color blindness might easily have singled them out.

Having absorbed what information she could from the abandoned house, she headed out, leaving the gate open, as she had found it. Taking the main road back to town, she soon arrived at Abboud's Antiques and parked, leaving the engine idling.

Nadia poked her head out. "Hey."

Mosey switched off the engine and got out.

"That isn't the scene of the crime, *this* is," she said, entering the shop.

"Huh?" Nadia, befuddled, might have taken offense if she'd had the slightest clue as to what she was talking about.

"The Hansbrough estate...it didn't start there. It started here, *right here*, with the photograph."

"Well, to you, maybe." Nadia at her heels, Mosey walked to the back room and stopped at the spot where the small trunk had stood. Mouth agape, she turned to Nadia. "The trunk—what happened to the trunk?"

"Hopkins came back for it this morning."

"Did he take anything else?"

"Well, he'd already taken the portrait—why?"

"He said he wanted to see the photograph."

"He did," said Nadia, "but he didn't mention it this morning."

Mosey pulled the envelope from her purse and handed it to Nadia. "Take it, he can have it." Eyes fixed on the empty spot, she continued. "If Evan Mordecai had been a vigilant man—as he was thought to be—he should have known Fanny was in danger."

"I'm not following you."

"The epitaph on Evan's marker..." Mosey stood stock-still, as if waiting for a smidgen of truth to manifest—drop from the ceiling, drift up from the floor—and once established, to crowd out the countless possibilities vying for legitimacy. She glanced at the tidy stack of photographs and papers fastidious Nadia had placed on the shelves of a Victorian étagère. "Are those from the trunk?"

"Olivera took all that. I told you, didn't I?"

"No, you didn't tell me."

"That's right. I guess I told Robert. You were showing a house."

Mosey pulled out a ladder-back chair and sat. She retrieved the tablet from her tote and turned to the page where she'd recopied the names and dates of the

Hansbroughs and Mordecais. "Look, here's all the names and dates." She circled the year of Fanny's death, and then began checking off names.

"What are you doing?" Nadia peeked over her shoulder.

"Checking off the ones who died after 1946. Trying to narrow this thing down."

"People don't always *see* things, you know," Nadia said, "even when they witness a crime."

"Yes, exactly," she said. "So what blinded the victim's father?"

"Blinded? I wouldn't say blinded," Nadia said. "It's human nature—that's all." She reached for a cloth and wiped the rungs of the chairs. "Who knows? Could have been a lot of things, like...his friendship with Lucien Hansbrough."

"I don't think so." She continued to examine the list. "I think there was one thing in particular."

"Like what?"

Mosey paused, tapping the tablet against the chair arm. "Ambition."

"Ambition, right." Nadia coughed. "Could be ambition." She coughed again.

"What's wrong?"

"Dust. I'm surprised you didn't notice."

So immersed was she in the morass of information relating to Fanny Mordecai's murder—*murder*, there, she'd thought it—that she'd been oblivious to the specks of dust emerging from beneath the chairs. "Good grief, Nadia. Can't you wait till I'm out of here?" She got up from the table and crossed the room. "He wanted Fanny to marry 'the king.' "

"What king?" Nadia cast a puzzled look at Mosey.

"Lucien Hansbrough, of course." She ruminated for a moment. "Call Hopkins."

"Why?"

"Just call him, please."

"I might," she said, "if you give me a good reason."

"You could say you have the photograph and—"

"Fine, I'll call him." She tossed the cloth onto the marble top of a horn and wood occasional table and walked toward the front.

Just as Nadia had hung up the phone, Mosey emerged from the back and headed toward the door. "Is he coming?"

"Yes, he said he'd drop by directly."

"I've got to run."

"Slow down, would you?"

"Show him the photograph," she instructed, rushing past Nadia. "Tell him it's his. I have the copy."

Just then, the lower hook of a bamboo coat rack caught the sleeve of Mosey's jacket and went teetering to the floor. "Sorry," she said, wincing and returning the rack to an upright position. "Got a text from John Earle. He's waiting for me at the office. He says it's urgent."

"What about Hopkins?"

Not looking quite as diffident as she might, given her unceremonious departure, Mosey waved good-bye as she pushed through the door. "Give him the photograph, and ask him if Ben wants the photographer's chair."

"I am *not* your—"

Nadia's objection went unfinished. Mosey had left, leaving the door open behind her. She kicked the door closed with her foot and, stretching her brows upward, groaned and went back to her cleaning. She dampened her cloth with lemon oil and, taking her annoyance out on the horn and wood table, slapped at the crisscrossed legs. "You are, indeed, an ugly cuss. Yes, you are—and expensive. Why'd I buy you—huh?"

Meanwhile, Mosey was in her truck on her way to Shepherd Realty. When she reached the drive, John Earle was getting out of his car.

She rolled down the window. "Got your text, but you didn't say what it's about."

"Ben Hansbrough and his wife."

"They're here?" she said with surprise.

"They sure are."

"I didn't know Ben Hansbrough *had* a wife." She pulled into her parking place and, catching up with John Earle, slipped through the door ahead of him, smoothing her hair and reaching for a lipstick in her tote.

"Hey, Saffron," John said. "I guess our appointment hasn't arrived."

She dropped a half-eaten bonbon into a drawer and swiveled around. "Nope, but he called."

"He leave a message?"

She pulled a sticky note off her desk pad and waved it in the air. "Said he'd rather meet you at the estate."

"Did he say when?"

She glanced at the wall clock. "About now."

"Guess we'd better get going," John Earle said to Mosey.

In the ten to fifteen minutes it took to drive out to the Hansbrough place, Mosey attempted to fill in the blanks of Ben and wife's unexpected appearance. "When did they call?"

"This morning."

"So, when did they get here?"

"I'm not sure. I guess either late last night or this morning." On the corner of Old Ebenezer and Little Smith, he stepped on the brake, barely missing a tractor with an extra-wide row planter hitched to the back.

"They're planting already?" Mosey said.

"Looks like it."

Though she'd grown up three miles from a cotton patch, she hadn't a clue about plowing, planting, picking, ginning—none of the steps necessary to get in a crop of so-called white gold of the Delta.

"You from around here?" John Earle said dryly.

She rolled her eyes.

He waited for the tractor to pass and turned onto Little Smith.

"So," she continued, "what do they want to speak to us about? His daughter inherited the estate, didn't she? I don't understand."

"Does seem odd. But I reckon it wouldn't be the first time I've been called in to sort out a sale between relations. You know old—?"

"What?"

"Better not get into that."

"Hmph."

Minutes later, they entered the gate and drove along the drive leading to the main entrance. The yellow cubes Olivera's crew had put near the front door were still there. John Earle pulled up next to an expensive looking SUV, presumably the one that had brought Ben Hansbrough and his wife to his former home.

"Shepherd," a voice yelled out, "over here." Ben Hansbrough was standing by the gate to the terrace.

John Earle smiled and waved, and on reaching the gate, shook hands with the man who, under different circumstances, would have inherited the land they were standing on.

"Ben, this is Mosey Frye. She's handling the sale of the property, and she's a mighty fine agent, if I say so myself."

Delighted with the compliment, Mosey dropped her eyes before stretching a hand toward her new client.

"Nice to meet you, Miss Frye—or is it Mrs. Frye? Ben Hansbrough."

"Hi—happy to meet you too, Mr. Hansbrough. You can call me Mosey."

"And this is my wife Annie."

Hansbrough's wife faced her new acquaintances, and Mosey found herself looking straight into the eyes of Fanny Mordecai. Her lips, parted to utter a warm greeting, were unable to get out a single syllable. Taking a step backward, she waited for someone to fill the space created by her awkward silence.

Annie moved toward her and, taking hold of her hand, said, "Ms. Frye, you're the one who offered to give up the portrait of Ben and Evan. Thank you for doing that."

"Oh...sure," she stammered. "I was happy to let them have it."

"We do appreciate that," Hansbrough said. "Evan's giving it to me as a homecoming gift." He chuckled.

"You're thinking of moving back to Hembree, are you?" John Earle said.

"Yes, and that's why I wanted you to meet us here. We're buying the property. We've already spoken to Lizbeth. We've come to an agreement. And we'd like you to help us out with the paperwork."

"Why, certainly." John Earle placed a hand on the older gentleman's shoulder. "We'd be glad to help you with whatever you need. Mosey can have the papers drawn up right away—can't you, Mosey?"

"Yes, of course, I'd be happy to."

"And maybe now," Hansbrough looked from one to the other, "you could show us around a little, since Annie has never seen the place."

The two women passed through the gate and walked toward the main entrance, followed by the men.

"Please forgive, uh, my saying so," Mosey began, addressing Annie Hansbrough with hesitancy, "but you look familiar. I thought you might be from around here."

"I've never been to Hembree before, but I guess it's okay to tell you this—I see no reason not to. Fanny Mordecai's half-sister was my mother. You've seen Fanny's photograph, I understand."

"Yes, that's right," she said. "I found a family photograph among some things my friend Nadia Abboud purchased at the estate sale." Mosey, relieved to know the connection, was still unclear how Fanny's niece had come to marry Lydia Hansbrough's son. But she wasn't about to ask that directly.

"We've spoken to Evan and Lizbeth. We know all about this unpleasant business," she said, her expression turning a bit sour. "The headpot, the police and all."

Mosey, suddenly feeling a little ashamed, could

feel her daddy's eyes on the back of her neck—even though she didn't hear a sound—as she accompanied Annie into her soon-to-be home. It seemed that, only in the last day, Annie had learned that Fanny, her late aunt, had been murdered, possibly by a member of her husband's family, his father or perhaps his uncle—who knew?

Apparently sensing Mosey's discomfort, Annie continued, "You should know that none of this is entirely new to us. It was Ben's suspicions…years ago…that drove a wedge between him and his father." Her eyes fell on the slate sidewalk in front of her, as did Mosey's.

"I guess I suspected that." Mosey's answer was short and simple, given she and Annie had reached the door where John Earle and Ben were waiting.

If Ellis Frye had been around—in whatever form the dead are capable of manifesting themselves—it's likely he would have kept his mouth shut. His meddlesome daughter seemed suitably remorseful for having poked her nose into business that was private and ultimately distressing for others—Ben and Annie Hansbrough in particular, who seemed like decent people. But if he *had* been around that day, likely he'd have said what he'd said so often it rolled right off his tongue. *Mosey, what'd I tell you about nosing around in things that don't concern you? See? You see?* And she would have answered as always, "I don't know what got into me, Daddy. I didn't mean to offend anybody, I promise."

Chapter Eleven

"Don't think you're getting away from here so easy, Mosey." Nadia picked up the last of the laundered napkins, sprinkled it, and passed the iron quickly from seam to seam. The scent of fresh linen drifted across the room.

"Okay," Mosey agreed, "but let's go somewhere. I'm thirsty."

"Where to?"

"The Tavernette?"

"Fine. I'll lock up and meet you there."

The Tavernette was nearby, and the two women pulled up within a half-minute of each other.

"Get a booth," Mosey yelled from her truck window. "I'm giving Robert a call."

Nadia entered the bar and found a booth near the back. A young waiter with a shaved head and full beard approached the table.

"Hi, I'd like a pitcher of margaritas, two glasses, and some chips."

"Very good, miss," he said, making a note on his pad and slipping it into his apron pocket.

As the waiter turned to leave, Mosey slid into the booth across from Nadia. "Who's that?" She scrunched up her nose. "Robert's coming, by the way."

"Waiter," Nadia called. "Sorry, but would you make that three glasses?"

"Certainly, miss."

"He's bringing Hugh," Mosey said.

"Sorry, there'll be four of us."

"Anything else?" He scratched through the number of glasses for the second time.

"Salt, please, on one of the glasses."

"Two of the glasses."

"Something more?"

"No," said Nadia, "that'll hold us for an hour, half an hour, quarter of an hour." They let out a snicker.

"And if two tall guys come in," Mosey said, "— one with red hair—tell them we're back here, if you don't mind." She watched as the young man disappeared into the adjoining bar, then said, "Who's that?"

"Never saw him before in my life. You can bet he's not from Ebenezer."

"Or Hickahala."

They snickered again. "So tell me," Nadia began.

"No, you tell me. Did Hopkins show up?"

"Of course, he did."

"What'd he say about the photograph?"

Nadia raised her brows and closed her eyelids halfway, mocking the professor's formality. "He said, 'Thank you, Ms. Abboud,' and left."

Mosey chortled. "Did you ask him if his cousin wanted the photographer's chair?"

"Yes."

"And?"

"He said he'd ask him."

"So he never mentioned Ben Hansbrough's being in Hembree?"

"What?"

"You heard me."

"No, he didn't say anything about Hansbrough being in Hembree. What are you talking about?"

"Well, it wasn't just Hansbrough, was it? His wife was with him."

"His wife?"

"Yes, and she could be Fanny Mordecai's twin."

"No-o-o."

"They wanted to buy the house."

"From Lizbeth?"

Mosey nodded. "Hold on. There's Robert," she said, waving. "We're over here."

Just then, the waiter arrived with a tray of glasses, a large pitcher of margaritas, an ample serving of chips, and a quartered lime.

"Perfect," Mosey said to the waiter. "The others just got here."

"Shall I pour the drinks, miss?" He placed frosty, salt-rimmed glasses on the table.

"Yes, please."

He nodded, poured the drinks, and walked away twirling the empty tray.

Nadia lifted her glass. "Cheers." She took a sip. "Good margarita, a little strong, though."

Robert and Hugh squeezed through the crowded bar to the booth. "Good, you ordered." Robert slid in next to Mosey.

"Hey, Hugh," Mosey said, "glad you came."

"Margaritas?" He glanced at the drinks. "I thought you were a martini girl."

"We have Nadia to thank for this common fare."

"Oh, please." Nadia squeezed a lime slice into her drink.

"Try one." Mosey placed glasses in front of Hugh and Robert. "Lime?"

"Sure, I'll take a slice," Robert said.

"So what's the occasion?" Hugh said

"I sold the Hansbrough estate to its *rightful* owner."

"Get out," Robert exclaimed, reaching for a chip.

"You think I'm lying?"

"*I* think you're lying," Hugh said.

Robert dipped the chip in salsa and stuffed it into his wife's open mouth.

"Hey, watch it," Mosey sputtered. "I'm not lying. I sold the estate to Ben and Annie Hansbrough this very afternoon. The papers aren't drawn up yet, but it'll close in a week or two."

Robert shook his head. "This just gets crazier and crazier."

"Get this," Nadia began, evidently eager to verbalize her version of the afternoon's events. "Mosey comes into the shop, tells me—no, *orders* me—to call Evan Hopkins and tell him I've got the photograph. Then, pretty as you please, she jumps up, says she's got to meet John Earle, and runs out, leaving me there on my own."

"What was I supposed to do?" Mosey grumbled. "I got a text from John Earle telling me to get over to the office in nothing flat."

"And Hansbrough and his wife appeared?" Robert surmised.

"No, we had to drive out to the estate."

"And so you met them…Ben and his wife," Hugh interjected, satisfying his hunger for another chip.

"Yes," Mosey said, "and they were nice, really

nice, and Ben's wife—Annie by name—is Fanny Mordecai's niece, half-niece, whatever, and she looks *exactly* like her, except older."

"No-o-o," Robert said.

"Yes."

"Crazy."

Mosey squinted at Robert.

"Robert's right," Hugh said. "This doesn't make a damn bit of sense."

"Maybe it does," Nadia put in. "Maybe, now that old Thaddeus is dead, Ben's ready to come back and take over the estate."

"But he's *not* the legal heir," Robert corrected. "His *daughter* is."

"But he *would have been* the heir," Mosey said, "if he hadn't accused his father of murder."

"What?" Robert exclaimed.

"So, was Ben the mole?" Hugh probed, pursuing his favorite angle.

"Couldn't have been," Mosey snapped back. "He was a kid."

"Not really," Hugh corrected. "He was a kid when Fanny died, but he wasn't when he left Hembree. Somebody could have passed along their suspicions to Ben, maybe his mother or his Aunt Ruth, and then—"

"Then what?" Mosey said. "He just happens to run across some of his long-deceased aunt's hair, collected before and after her death, stuffs it into a couple of hair receivers—"

"Stop." Hugh waved his hands in front of his face. "I surrender. Ben's not the mole."

"I think the mole is Ruth," Nadia said, "or maybe Ruth and Lydia. They were with her when she died.

211

They must have known better than anyone what was going on between her and Lucien. They'd have known what her symptoms were when she became ill—"

"—and they'd have cared about Fanny more than anyone," Mosey added.

"Except maybe her father," Hugh put in.

It was Robert who followed up with a question. "But could Evan Mordecai have buried the headpot in Lucien Hansbrough's backyard?"

"Terrace," Mosey said.

"Right, terrace. Opportunity…that's important."

Mosey looked at her husband. "So you think it was Lydia."

"Yes, I think it was Lydia, with Ruth's help, and besides that, I think one of them told Ben about her—or their—suspicions."

"Robert's right," Nadia added. "Where's your list?" She turned to Mosey. "When did they die…Lydia and Ruth?"

Mosey pulled out her pad. "Lydia died in 1959 and Ruth in 1969."

"And when was Ben born?"

"In 1938."

"So when Lydia died, Ben was twenty-one, and when Ruth died, he was thirty-one."

"Had to have been Lydia, then," Mosey quickly affirmed, practiced at juggling figures in her head. "Ben was long gone from Hembree before he was thirty-one."

"How do you know that?" Nadia said.

"Because Annie said she'd never been to Hembree, never seen the house."

"He could have married late."

"Not that late. His daughter's a good ten, fifteen years older than we are. You saw her."

"Saw who?" Robert said.

"Lizbeth...Ben's daughter," she explained.

"Pour me some of that would you?" Robert passed his glass to Mosey. "All this math is making my head spin."

"Steady, bud, you're driving," Hugh cautioned.

Nadia squeezed a slice of lime into what remained of her drink and glanced over at Mosey. "I'm wondering how Ben came to know his dead Aunt Fanny's half-sister's child. Fanny was adopted. How would he have known about her biological family?— well, normally one wouldn't."

"Okay," said Hugh, waving a chip in the air. "This is far-fetched, but let's say that when Fanny died, her adoptive parents contacted her biological mother."

"That's not far-fetched," Nadia said. "That's, well, normal. Could be normal."

"Maybe, maybe not," Hugh said. "But let's say that the biological mother came to the funeral. I can imagine that happening."

"By the way," Nadia interrupted, looking at Mosey. "What was Fanny's real mother's name?"

"Hmm...I don't know. Annie didn't say."

"Wait a minute," Robert said. "I'm confused again. Who is Annie?"

"Fanny's niece, her honest-to-goodness blood niece. The Mordecais were Fanny's *adoptive* family— get it?"

"Yes, I think so."

"As I was saying," Hugh said, pressing forward with his theory, "she—this woman whose name we

213

don't know, Fanny's mom—she wanted to go to the funeral but didn't want to go alone, so she took Annie—still a young girl—with her."

"I can see that," Nadia commented.

"But why take Annie, why not take her daughter?" Mosey said.

"Maybe she did," Hugh said. "Maybe she took both of them."

"Okay," Mosey agreed, going along with Hugh's revised scenario.

"But you're assuming," Robert said, "that the Mordecais *knew* who the mother was."

"Yes," Hugh said, "I guess I am."

Mosey rested her cheek on her fist and gazed at Hugh. She was beginning to see his point. "If you think about it, that's a pretty safe assumption. How *else* would Ben have met Fanny's niece? Someone had to know who the mother was."

"And who better than the father?" Hugh added.

"I think I see where you're going with this." Nadia turned to Hugh. "You think Evan Mordecai was Fanny's biological father."

Hugh smiled. "As I said before, this is a little far-fetched—"

"But not entirely improbable." Nadia finished his sentence.

"Well, it's just a theory," Hugh said. "But, you see, I know another case similar to this. This friend of my father's got a young woman pregnant. He was already married with children of his own. So, to avoid having the baby given up for adoption, he adopted it himself. The mother was young, and it seemed like a way out of the dilemma."

"Good grief," Mosey said. "And the wife was okay with that?"

"Well, I imagine she was not happy about it at first, but babies have a way of—"

"Yeah," Mosey cut in, "I reckon they do."

"Emotions aside," Robert said, "it kind of makes sense. At least for then, maybe not now."

"It would explain a lot," Nadia agreed.

"But wouldn't that make Ben and Annie blood kin?" Robert probed.

Hugh thought for a second. "No, because Annie wasn't related to any of them, the Mordecais or the Hansbroughs. The birth mother—whose name we don't know—must have married and had another child. That child was Annie's mother. So," Hugh paused, "she wasn't a Hansbrough or a Mordecai."

"That's right," Mosey said, relieved at the exclusion of incest.

"That still leaves a lot to fill in," Nadia pointed out.

"Yes, like how Ben and Annie met, fell in love, married," Mosey appended. This time it was she who proposed a scenario. "Okay." She set down her glass. "Let's say that Lydia, Thaddeus's wife, is dying. She tells her son Ben about her suspicions concerning the death of her young sister Fanny. She also tells him that he is to contact Fanny's biological mother. So Ben, maybe after his mother's death, visits Fanny's mother, who would have been in her forties, more or less. He meets the mother, Fanny's half-sister, and Annie—who is the half-sister's child."

"And he and Annie like each other," Nadia added.

"Of course!" Hugh plunked his glass on the table. "*That's* what cemented the feud between Thaddeus and his son. Ben's engagement to Annie."

"Here, here." Robert lifted his glass to his colleague. "That's a rather bizarre admonishment, don't you think? Almost biblical."

"Exactly." Hugh clicked his glass. "The son of the magnate Thaddeus marries Annie, whose family his father had robbed of their part of the estate—well, if Fanny and Lucien had married."

"Which, to old Thaddeus's way of thinking, was a dressing-down he couldn't stomach," Robert added.

Nadia's eyes widened. "Poetic justice."

Hugh scraped the last bit of salsa onto a chip. "Makes for a nice story."

****

It was the end of May—two months after the closing—when Mosey and Nadia, along with Robert and Hugh, entered the Hansbrough mansion, walked through the restored and redecorated rooms, and eventually came to the door that led to the terrace. Mosey passed a roving gaze over the renovated area. The awning—new but exactly like the old one— extended from the back entrance to the bottom of the steps. The glass globes atop the fluted columns lit up the dining area, revealing a clean and repaired flagstone terrace furnished with wrought-iron tables and chairs. About a dozen guests were expected for dinner, and each of the tables was set for six.

"My, my," said Robert, who was the first to speak upon seeing what closely approximated a reenactment of "Family Supper, July—."

"You sit over here." It was Annie speaking to Mosey. "We want you to sit with us." She pointed to the table closest to the steps.

"We'd be honored," Mosey replied.

They took their seats at the table indicated. Lizbeth Hansbrough, Evan Hopkins, John Earle Shepherd and his wife, and a couple Mosey didn't know sat at the second table.

"So, Mosey, what do you say about this?" Hugh said. He hadn't seen the terrace since his discovery of Max's grave.

"I'm floored," she whispered, noticing that their host and hostess were looking in their direction.

"Me, too," Nadia whispered back.

A server approached the table and filled the glasses with wine. Ben and Annie, who hadn't yet taken their seats, stood at the bottom of the steps. When the server had finished pouring, Evan Hopkins stood and raised his glass.

"I would like to propose a toast to Ben and Annie. Ben," he turned toward his cousin, "welcome home. For me, Hembree's a much nicer place with you here."

The other guests lifted their glasses and drank to Ben.

"And Annie," Hopkins went on, "welcome to Hembree and your new home. The house is as lovely as it once was, thanks to you."

"To Annie." Ben looked admiringly at the woman at his side.

After a superb meal, Annie rose and addressed the group. "Thanks to all of you for joining us tonight for supper. We hope to see you often in our home. Please remain here on the terrace, if you'd like…for as long as you'd care to. But for those who might be interested, I'd be happy to offer a tour of the house."

"Anyone up for a tour?" Robert stood and offered

to help Mosey with her chair.

"Are you kidding?" Mosey whispered. "I wouldn't miss this—"

"Nor would I," Nadia joined in, getting out of her chair with help from Hugh.

"What do you say, Hugh?" Robert said.

"Not much for house tours. I'd rather have a taste of that scotch." He gestured in the direction of a server carrying a tray with a decanter and glasses. At his side, a second server held an ice bucket and tongs.

"Looks like you ladies are on your own," Robert said to Mosey and Nadia.

Mosey, Nadia, and Lizbeth followed Annie up the steps of the terrace. Robert and Hugh remained at the table with Ben, and after a round of scotch, it was the conversation of the three men that turned to matters pertinent to the mysterious "Family Supper, July—."

"You've done a remarkable job restoring the terrace," Hugh said. "It's identical to the photograph."

"Thanks, Hugh. That photograph was actually very helpful. It was Annie's idea to put it all back exactly as it was."

The server had left the tray and ice bucket next to Ben, who lifted the decanter and offered Robert and Hugh a drink.

"Don't mind if I do." Robert took the decanter from Ben.

"You could top off my glass." Hugh passed his glass to Robert.

"Well, that's not entirely true—I mean about the terrace," Ben said.

"Looks the same to me," Hugh said, scanning the area.

"It wouldn't…if you took a closer look," Ben said.

"What's different?" Robert said.

"That corner over there—Hugh knows the one."

"I suppose," Hugh said, "you're referring to Max's grave."

"Yes, the grave. The stone is gone. Too ghastly, the whole business." His sad eyes turned briefly toward Hugh.

Hugh glanced down at his glass, then ventured to mention something that had roused his curiosity. "The headpot we unearthed—you know for a minute or two I thought it might have been the real thing."

"My mother made that," Ben said. "She was an artist, had a good eye for design and color. Nothing like my father, who had no taste at all. He was color blind, in fact."

"Really," Hugh said, failing to mask his interest.

Ben sipped his whisky, then continued. "Difficult to imagine how those two got together."

"Your mom and dad, you mean?" Robert said.

"Yes, Thaddeus and Lydia, my mother and father. May they rest in peace." Ben lifted his glass again, as if to toast to his deceased parents.

Robert and Hugh remained silent.

"Well, as much as I hate to say it," Robert said, as he pushed back in his chair, "I'm afraid we're going to have to make an early evening of it."

"Right." Hugh followed suit.

"I have to give an exam at seven-thirty. Finals."

"Yes, I understand," Ben said. "Annie mentioned that you might have to leave early. That's fine. We'll get together again, this summer, maybe. You guys like to fish?"

Robert answered that question rapidly. "Whenever I get a chance."

"Never fished much," Hugh said, "but I'd give it a try."

"The pond in front—is it stocked?" Robert said.

"With the nicest bass and bream you'll ever catch around here."

"Well, then. Let us know when you're up for company." Robert beamed, apparently delighted at the prospect of a new place to put in his fishing pole.

Ben showed Robert and Hugh through the house and out the front, picking up Mosey and Nadia as they went.

From the entrance, Annie waved good-bye. "Y'all come back soon."

They thanked her and strolled back toward Robert's hatchback.

"You'd better drive." Robert tossed the car keys to Mosey.

"Why? You and Hugh fill up on whisky?"

"One and a smidgen each, that's all." Hugh opened the back door for Nadia.

As Mosey pulled through the gate, she glanced back at the house. Ben stood by the terrace gate, watching his guests drive away.

"That's a sad man," Hugh remarked, also catching sight of Ben.

"Why—did he say something?" Mosey said.

"Not exactly, but it's pretty clear he wasn't a fan of his father—who was color blind, by the way."

"Color blind." Nadia turned abruptly to face Hugh. "How did *that* come up?"

"Ben told us. He said his mother was an artist,

made the headpot, and that his father was a tasteless jerk."

"Well, not exactly *that*," Robert corrected, looking back at Hugh. "He said he didn't understand how his mother and father got together, her being an artist and him, color blind. You ladies find out anything?"

"Nothing," Mosey said, "not a dadgum thing."

"There was one thing," Nadia said.

"What?" Mosey glanced at Nadia in the rear-view mirror.

"A small portrait of Fanny Mordecai—it was on the dresser in one of the bedrooms, with the hair receiver right next to it."

"The brass one, you mean?"

"The brass one," Nadia said. "And I suppose none of you noticed."

"Noticed what?" Hugh said.

"Annie was wearing her aunt's gold locket."

Just as they reached the end of the drive, a sudden wind blew up. A live oak—as tall, maybe taller, than the highest gable of the beautifully restored house—swayed dangerously, as if to break off at the root.

Peculiar, thought Mosey. It *was* peculiar indeed for the Arkansas Delta, where, by the end of May, it could be hot and sticky, even in early evening.

"So, if Thaddeus was color blind," Nadia pondered, "who was tone deaf?"

"His brother Edward, of course," Mosey said. Not at all sure *how* she knew—she rarely was—she knew all the same.

221

The House with a Corner Door

A Mosey Frye Mystery, Book 3

Chapter One

At four on a blistering July afternoon, the Lost Dog Saloon was filling up with locals and, during that particular week, anthropologists, like Hugh Jessup, who'd come to town for the Southwest Regional Meeting of the American Anthropological Society.

Outside the saloon, a row of bikers, bare-armed and tattooed, leaned indifferently against the plate glass window. Inside, Hugh, back from a dig, rocked back and forth on a wooden stool, tilting noticeably in the barmaid's direction. "Selena, another draft when you can."

She stood at the sink, methodically stuffing a scrub brush into one glass after the next. She paused to fill Hugh's mug, then glimpsed up. "Yesterday, I think it was, I was talking to a woman sitting with that Mexican friend of yours—"

"Fernando?" Hugh said, wiping the froth from his lips.

"Yeah, Fernando. One of you anthropologists." Her turned-down mouth shifted into a slight smile.

"You find us amusing, do you?" Hugh said.

A request from a threesome engaged in an earnest game of pool brought Selena's story to a halt. "Round of pale ale over here, please, ma'am."

Selena popped open three bottles, served them, and returned to the sink. "At first, she—Eleanor was her name—just looked at me but then went on talking to Fernando. About half an hour later, he took off. She stayed behind, finished her Chardonnay, and ordered another. And, soon as I set it in front of her, she started talking, telling me a story about a breakdown."

"Huh? How'd she get into that?"

"I asked her what sort of work she did—just making small talk—and she said she was a publicist. At one time she'd worked for a big company, Ingot, I think she said."

"Ingot," Hugh repeated. "I've heard of it, yeah—a big Midwestern firm."

Selena rinsed the last of the glasses and set it on a marble shelf above the sink. "She said she'd gotten along well with management, the people who'd hired her. But then the Ingot folks showed up, pushed them out." She dried her hands and pulled a cigarette from her apron pocket.

"Sounds like a takeover," Hugh said.

"Must've been." She lit the cigarette and blew a plume of smoke toward the open door. "Eleanor fell apart."

"Wow, probably couldn't adjust."

"So, then she said, 'People who see a psychiatrist, they don't say anything at all, keep it hidden. Either that or they tell you the whole story.' " She set her cigarette on the edge of the sink and lifted her chestnut hair off her neck, twisted it into a ponytail and let it fall.

Hugh glanced at his watch.

"Am I boring you?"

Hugh laughed. "No, not at all. I'm supposed to meet some friends here. They're late."

Selena picked up a glass and started polishing. "So,

this Eleanor, the publicist—they carted her off in a straitjacket."

"Good lord! What was the problem exactly?"

"I don't know. She kept saying she was crazy out of her mind."

"Well, but—"

"She *did* say one thing." Selena set the glass on the shelf and stepped closer to Hugh. "She said she *thought* she'd underpaid her taxes—she *thought* she had—and kept sending money to the government. Then she came to her senses and hired a lawyer to get her money back. Thousands of dollars she'd overpaid."

"Crazy."

"She looked me straight in the eye and said, 'If I'd met you a year ago, I'd have told you—and would have believed it—that you were going to die.' "

"What?"

"Just that, like I'm telling you. 'I'd have said you were going to die.' And *then* she said, 'And *I would have known it was my fault.*' "

"*Her* fault?"

"That's what she said."

"Sweet Jesus!"

"She told people the same thing for months—they were going to die, and it was her fault." She took a drag off her cigarette and stubbed it out half smoked in the sink. "Then she got well."

Hugh cocked his head in disbelief. "You believed her?"

"Yes, I believed her. But I'd have to say she gave off sort of an I-am-a-nut vibe."

"Hold that thought," he said, fumbling for his cell phone. He headed for the front, away from the noise of the pool tables. "Robert, where are you?"

"Just pulled up at the Velvet Arms."

"What took you so long?"

"Ran into a hailstorm a little past Fort Worth."

"I'm at the Lost Dog. You coming over?"

"We'll be there in a few minutes, soon as we get checked in."

Heading back to his seat, Hugh passed Selena walking toward the entrance. A biker was standing at the threshold, waiting to see her, apparently. Hugh sat on the stool and, from there, watched the developing scene, conveniently reflected in the mirror behind the bar. It seemed like an ordinary exchange. She spoke to the biker, accepted a cigarette. He propped himself against the doorframe, took off his sunglasses, lit the cigarette, and uttered a few words.

From across the room, a customer yelled out. "Selena, tab, when you can."

"Hold on," she called. "I'll be right there."

While Selena attended to the customer, the biker sauntered to the back and entered the men's room. A few minutes later, he emerged, approached Selena, and, as Hugh could best tell, tucked a folded bill in her apron pocket. Shortly after, he left the bar, straddled his bike, and, with an extra loud *vroom-vroom*, took off.

Hugh didn't think much of the encounter yet could hardly help wondering what the folded bill was about. Didn't seem like a tip. The biker hadn't drunk anything.

A short while later, Selena leaned out the open door and looked up and down First.

Hugh twisted around. "Selena, come finish your story."

She returned to her spot at the bar. "Where was I?"

"You were saying—"

"Oh, yeah," she cut in. "Eleanor...she said she never worked after that." She smoothed her hair and tucked it behind her ears. Slender topaz crystals dangled from her earlobes. "So...if she got well—like she said she did—why didn't she go back to work?"

"Good question." He thought for a moment. "Maybe the company blacklisted her."

"Could be, I guess." She reached under the bar for a cloth and wiped up the splatter from the sink. "Wonder what she's doing at this conference of yours?"

"A retired publicist at an anthropology conference, huh." Hugh tumbled that idea around. "Does seem odd."

"If you find out, let me know, would you?"

"Sure."

"Strange chick." Selena shook her head and moved along the bar gathering bottles.

He was sorely tempted to toss out a query about her biker friend but decided to hold his tongue. After all, what could he say? "Who's the guy who slipped a bill in your apron pocket?" Or, "Who the hell are those bikers? They've been out there the whole blooming day. Don't they work?"

The pool players behind him suddenly became silent, and he looked around just in time to see a ball smash headlong into another, knocking both into a side pocket. Whistles, groans, and then laughter.

Hugh polished off his ale, took a twenty from his billfold, and slipped it under his empty mug. "Catch you later, Selena. Looks like my friends are a no-show."

Chapter Two

The following morning, Mosey came out of room 314, locked the door with a large, flat key, and moved along the dimly lit corridor toward the staircase. No one was in the hall, and no noise was coming from the dozen or so third-floor rooms. They must have hustled to make the eight o'clock session. "Academics," she muttered with dismay, unable to fathom the brutal schedules conference attendees set for themselves.

She descended the stairs and, reaching the ground floor, glanced around the lobby before handing the key to the clerk. A spray of wildflowers in a silver urn stood atop the reception desk, a bulky Spanish colonial bureau. She leaned in and sniffed the blue flax nestled among paintbrush, bird vetch, and Rocky Mountain bee balm. Voicing her opinion to no one in particular, "Umm," she said, "smells good."

The Velvet Arms, built in the 1890s, possessed the dark leanness of a modest Western hotel. To Mosey's satisfaction, successive custodians had managed to rectify the effects of time without destroying the character of the building. Even the original crystal light fixtures glared down from the tin ceiling. The décor, in fact, looked as convincingly Victorian as it must have once been—and for that she was glad.

She drew a facial tissue from her handbag and patted her forehead, cheeks, and chin. "No air conditioning?" she inquired of the desk clerk.

"No air conditioning."

From that single spoken phrase, she registered traces of an accent reminiscent of the American Southwest—California, Arizona, New Mexico, west Texas—where those whose perfect Spanish implied they might be from elsewhere, would invariably answer "From here," when she said "Where are you from?"

"No elevator, either?"

"No elevator."

The receptionist, who was checking in a drooping octogenarian, accepted Mosey's key and slipped it into a cubbyhole. The recently arrived guest glanced sideways at Mosey, tipped the brim of his Australian slouch hat—the breadth of which accentuated the thin strait between torso and cranium—and said cheerily, "How do you do?"

"How do you do?" she replied with a half-smile and then turned again to the clerk. "Should my husband Robert Ellison want to know, I'll be back around lunchtime."

"Certainly, ma'am. I'll let him know if he asks." The clerk scribbled a note, folded it, and slipped it under the key.

Again, she sniffed the blue flax.

"Careful," said the man in the slouch hat. "Blue flowers can be dangerous."

She cast a sharp look in his direction. "I'm aware of that." She nodded at the curious man and left through the glass doors.

She lingered outside the Velvet Arms. "Silver," she said, checking her map. "This is Silver." She swiveled from left to right to left, and, deciding to go left, followed Silver toward First. Her plan was to stop at a café she'd noticed the night before, which, if she'd remembered correctly, was near the intersection of the two main streets. She soon came to her destination, the Carcajou Internet Café. But, to her annoyance, a group of goths were lined up along the sidewalk on either side of the door. "That's odd," she mused, as she strode across to the opposite side. She'd seen plenty of goths. Hembree was full of them *still*, even if the heyday of pasty complexions and black clothing, piercings and pink hair, had long passed. She glanced back to confirm that she'd seen what she'd seen. Indeed, some of them were wearing gas masks, and the two positioned at the entrance had on shiny black PVC doctors masks—what the heck?

With an hour to kill before her walking tour, she set off for the Square, halting here, there, and yon to examine rustic furnishings and handspun yarns. She cupped her hands over her eyes and inspected the bounty of native crafts. "Nadia would die here," she muttered. Then, her eyes fell on a display of hand-knitted sweaters in colors as bright and warm as a desert sunset. A tag peeked timidly out of a cuff, partially revealing the price of a cardigan with a cowl collar: $4—. "No, no, no," she groaned. "I am *not* spending four hundred dollars on a sweater."

At the next shop down, a pretty little bronze-skinned girl squatted next to the window. When Mosey waved and tapped on the pane, the girl pressed her nose, mouth, and hands against the glass and made a funny face. Mosey placed her hands over the child's and stretched her eyebrows up high. The child giggled and backed away.

Coming to the Square, she chose Engels Bakery from among several cafés and restaurants, ordered an iced coffee and slice of lemon-thyme pound cake, and took a seat well-removed from the busiest corner, where a dozen customers sat engaged in lively conversation. The Parcheesi yellow umbrellas that shaded the tables contrasted agreeably with the purple flowers sprouted from the clay soil. A garden of the Southwest variety, covered in gravel and planted with succulents, encircled a Mexican coquina stone fountain. At the edge of the fountain, a cactus lifted a prickly arm as if to salute its likeness reflected in the water. She relaxed into a barrel-shaped chair and, for a minute or two, fancied herself a Westford resident, a regular at the Square. She pinched off a piece of cake, a tasty mélange of tart and aromatic flavors, sipped her coffee, and observed the people seated across the way. A man in the group stood up to leave. He was wearing a long, cotton coat, an old-fashioned frock coat, looked like. He threw on a bowler hat—to his companions' delight. Then, tucking a brown leather case into the curl of his arm, he passed through the arch onto First and proceeded along the street in the direction from which Mosey had just come.

Minutes later, she popped the last lemony crumb in her mouth and left the Square. Arriving back at the Velvet Arms in time to grab a hat and bottle of water, she said to the desk clerk in passing, "That man who was here before, I can't help thinking I know him."

"Ha," the clerk replied, "he said the same about you, ma'am."

"I guess you couldn't tell me his name."

"Sorry, we can't give out information—"

233

"—about guests," Mosey said.

"Right," he said. "Sorry."

After arming herself with water and a brimmed hat for the hot day ahead, she left for the museum, which was on Silver, only a few yards from the Velvet Arms. No one was on the porch or in the garden, and she went inside to inquire. "The tour of downtown begins here, right?" she said to the museum volunteer at the desk.

"They should be along shortly. It's not quite ten." She nodded toward an antique clock on the wall.

"Who's leading the tour—do you know?"

"Arnold Schulte—Dr. Schulte he calls himself. Teaches at Elmore College."

"I guess I'll wait on the porch."

Several women had arrived and seated themselves on the railing. "You ladies here for the tour?" Mosey said. "I'm Mosey Frye...Robert Ellison's wife."

"Yes, I remember you," a gray-haired lady replied. "I'm Anne Howard, and this is my daughter Shelly." The girl, tall and gangly, was a feminine double of a man she and Robert had met the year before.

"Howard," Mosey repeated. "I think I may have met your husband."

"And I'm sure I've met yours. Most of us are old-timers."

"This is my third conference," Mosey said.

"I've lost count." The woman laughed.

"Have you seen our guide?" Mosey said.

"It's the gentleman over there."

It was the man from the Square. "Yes, of course. I saw him earlier and wondered about the costume."

"He likes to assume the personality of a relevant historic figure," Anne said with a shrug.

"Interesting." Mosey gazed warily in his direction.

The guide began shepherding the tour participants, all women, toward the garden, where a row of benches circled a large willow. "I think we'll be comfortable over there." He signaled with his water bottle. "The railing here is delicate," he warned. His body language was brusque, more like a lifeguard's than a tour guide's.

"I fear it's going to be a long day," Mosey muttered to Anne.

Mosey, you are a catty little cuss, if I do say so myself.

Even detached from its natural habitat, her late father's voice rang clear. She hoped she'd left it in Hembree, but no. It had followed her to Westford, apparently ready to nit and pick at every little thing however small or unimportant.

"Daddy..." She heaved a sigh and then, doing as Schulte had told them, abandoned the porch railing and moved to the benches along with the others, where, shifting and squeezing, they all managed to find a spot.

"I'm Dr. Schulte," he began, "but my character is Palmer Shoemaker. When I have on my hat, I'm Palmer, and I will answer questions as Palmer." He rested the bowler hat on his balding head. "When my hat is off, I will speak as Dr. Schulte," he said, aiming a closed-mouth smile at his small "brood."

A woman, from whose neck dangled a camera, lifted it to snap Schulte-Shoemaker's picture.

"Please, no pictures," countered the startled tour guide. He whipped his head to the side and pulled the bowler down tight over his ears. For a split second, he wasn't Schulte *or* Shoemaker, but, rather, a familiar

Western figure, a sort of Bat Masterson look-alike, sadly morphed into late middle age. "I have a stalker."

"Poor thing," Mosey mumbled under her breath.

Mosey—

The surprised woman let the camera drop, and Schulte-Shoemaker went on with his remarks. Speaking as Shoemaker, he recounted "his" life before and after moving to Westford in the 1870s. At his father's death, he told them, he'd assumed control of the family construction firm and, for the rest of his days, built streets, businesses, and houses throughout the downtown area. As the tour progressed up a street parallel to First, Shoemaker—i.e., Schulte with his hat on—pointed out street markers that bore the distinctive Shoemaker horseshoe. Then, turning onto a street perpendicular to First, he led them up the steps of a church, where he (Shoemaker)—and now he (Schulte)—was a member. They all stopped to admire the bronze-plated doors that depicted local events of historical importance before following him onto First, then past First to the original Main Street, where Shoemaker's home stood, a three-story Victorian with a corner door. At the turn of the century, he explained, flash floods terrifyingly brought to life the riverbed where Westford settlers had foolishly constructed the main street of town. "This street," he said, waving an arm toward what wasn't a street at all, "was once dotted with businesses and homes. Then, poof! The rains turned it into a gorge." They all ogled the gorge, deep and wide. "This house," he said, with a twist of his head, "was the only one that withstood the flood. I managed to save it with the help of my wife's sewing circle. All the other buildings were carried off by the raging waters."

"How'd you manage that?" said a voice from behind Mosey.

"Well, you see, we hastily stitched bags, hundreds. And some of our workers at the sand pit filled them and stacked them around the house."

"And the corner door?" called out a voice from the back of the group.

"Glad you asked. It was an unusual architectural feature back then," he said, "sort of a badge of prosperity and privilege. No one could afford it but a well-heeled minority," he beamed.

"Harrumph," Mosey said.

"You say something to me?" Anne said.

"Me? Oh, no. Just clearing my throat."

"You want some water?"

"I've got some, thank you." Mosey pulled out her bottle and took a long drink to quench her feigned thirst.

"Shoemaker," the guide, said waving his bowler in front of his face, "coming home from a late-night event, lost his footing, tumbled down a considerable stretch, and lay all night next to the boulder that stopped his fall. The next day, some workers from a nearby mine tossed down ropes and pulled him up. In no time, he recovered and led an active life until mid-century, when he died at the age of ninety." Schulte took a bow, then thrust his bowler toward the crowd with a gentle shake.

"We're supposed to tip him?" Mosey said to Anne.

"I usually toss in a dollar. The conference doesn't pay much."

"Oh, okay." Mosey dug into her tote.

The tour ended and, after dropping a bill into

Schulte's hat, she walked away. What she really wanted to do—but didn't—was to strike up a conversation with the man, pursue his intriguing comment about the stalker. Instead, she decided to go back to the Velvet Arms and wait for Robert and Hugh. Still, the notion continued to swell in her mind that, regardless of age and aspect, Schulte was vulnerable to something— what, she couldn't imagine.

She'd come to the corner of First and Prospect, a good twenty yards from the gorge, when a desperate cry rose up. She rapidly retraced her tracks and, very near the spot where she and the others had been standing, several women—Anne and Shelly among them—were leaning over the metal railing and waving at something down below.

"What's the matter, Anne?" she shouted.

Anne pushed herself upright. "There's someone down there!"

"It's a woman…over there." Shelly pointed to a spot a considerable way down. A dark figure lay motionless on a ledge. The face was hidden by undergrowth, but the torso appeared to be that of a woman.

Mosey's first thought was to scramble down the steep incline to see if she was alive. But seeing the difficulty of the climb—and if she got to her, how would she get her out?—she pulled out her cell phone and dialed 911.

As she was calling, a man came hastening along the sidewalk. "Has she moved?" Mosey said. "Did you see her move?"

He shook his head.

"Anne!" She waved her hands high. "Help is on the

way."

A small crowd was gathering along the sides of the gorge, and before long, sirens broke the stillness as a police SUV arrived followed by an ambulance and a fire truck. The crowd was pushed back, and Mosey, Anne, and Shelly moved down the path along the edge of the embankment. From there, they watched the rescue, as firemen with picks and ropes lowered themselves into the shadowy chasm. They soon reached the victim, a young woman. One of the firemen knelt at her side, felt for a pulse, then stood and shook his head.

"She's dead?" Shelly said.

Mosey answered with a nod.

Chapter Three

At the Silver Star Barbecue and Lounge, Mosey passed through the bar into the dining area and found a table in a secluded spot at the back. She sat, fluffed her bangs and, reaching into her handbag for a lipstick, coated her lips with a soothing mauve balm. She took a peek at herself in a small mirror, and with a tissue, daubed off a smudge of mascara. Cosseted from the pockets of bystanders collecting along First Street, she sat staring into the bachelor-button wallpaper that extended up the wall from the chair rail to the tin ceiling. She glanced from time to time over the half-wall that separated bar and restaurant. "Not the way I expected the day to go," she mumbled.

"Can I get you something to drink?" A young man dressed in black trousers, white shirt, and black tie flipped open his ticket pad and pulled a pencil from behind his ear.

"Yes, a glass of wine, please, a Pinot Grigio or Sauvignon Blanc. Something light."

"Certainly."

"I'm expecting my husband and a friend."

"Fine, I'll check back."

Soon after, Robert and Hugh entered the restaurant and stopped at the bar. She rose and waved to Robert, who moved promptly in her direction.

"How *are* you?" Robert said.

She stood, and he gave her a firm hug. Hugh, behind Robert, followed suit.

"I'm okay," she said unconvincingly.

"Quite a morning you've had," Hugh said.

"Do they have any idea who she was or what happened?" Robert said.

"They wouldn't let us get close enough to find out."

The waiter was back to serve her wine and take Hugh's and Robert's orders.

"Bring me a draft—a Blue Rocket, if you have it," Hugh said.

"Same for me," Robert added.

"Would anyone like to see a menu?" the waiter said.

"Just bring me a salad," Mosey replied, "blue cheese dressing on the side."

"And you, sir?"

"I'll take the house burger," Robert said. "Hold the mustard, extra lettuce and pickles—and chips."

"Bring me one of those, too, with mustard—and a side of fries," Hugh said.

The waiter walked away, opening a narrow path through conference participants on break between sessions.

"You see that guy over there, the one in the gray hoodie?" Hugh was staring at a middle-aged man but youngish, wearing a hoodie and shorts. Having found a table, the man beckoned to someone at the bar. "The one in the hoodie—that's Fernando," Hugh said. "You met him last year."

"Looks familiar," Robert responded.

"And that woman," Hugh paused, stealing a look at

the woman who was joining his friend, "that's Eleanor, I'm pretty sure."

"Eleanor who?" Robert looked up from the package of saltines he was opening.

"The one I was telling you about, the publicist—retired publicist. I don't know her last name."

"Who are you talking about?" Mosey looked toward the table where the man and woman in question were sitting.

"Fernando Law," Hugh repeated, then stopped to acknowledge the waiter who'd brought their beers. "He teaches at a university in Mexico, not sure which. And that woman with him, I think she's the publicist the waitress at the Lost Dog was telling me about. Selena—you remember her. Craziest story." He took a sip of his beer. "This woman, Eleanor, lost it—result of a takeover, supposedly. Couldn't adjust to new management. They committed her to a hospital, treated her, and eventually let her go home."

"Not so unusual," Robert observed.

"True, but that's not all. She went around telling people they were going to *die* and it was *her* fault."

"Obsessive compulsive disorder, sounds like," Mosey interjected.

Hugh looked at Mosey. "I hadn't thought of that."

"She's a psych major." Robert sipped his beer.

"Of course. I forgot."

"It's not uncommon for people with OCD," Mosey said, continuing her diagnosis, "to have fears about causing harm—to themselves or other people."

"And get this," Hugh added. "She overpaid her taxes by thousands of dollars."

"Uh-huh," Mosey said, "another compulsion. Fits

the pattern."

"So…does a person get over an illness like that?"

"Of course, with medication and treatment."

"Apparently, Eleanor has never worked again."

"Then she probably isn't symptom free."

"Sounds to me," Robert said, "like her *story* is her new obsession."

The waiter arrived with a tray of food.

"Could I get a glass of water, please?" Robert said. "Mosey, want another glass of—what's that you're drinking?"

"Pinot Grigio, but I'm fine."

"Hugh?"

"No, thanks." Hugh opened his burger and reached for the pepper shaker. "You're right. The story or actually the telling of the story again and again to anyone who'll listen—that could be a symptom. So, she's still crazy, then."

"I wouldn't say *crazy*," Mosey opposed. "Maybe obsessive-compulsive."

"There's a difference?" Hugh said.

"She could be perfectly rational otherwise."

"Right." Hugh looked again at Fernando, who was chatting amicably with Eleanor.

"The professor who led the tour this morning, Arnold Schulte," Mosey said, "he has a stalker, turns out."

"How strange is that?" Robert bit into his burger and chewed.

"I thought so, too," she replied, filching a chip from his plate. "I can't imagine a middle-aged academic having a stalker."

"How did you come by that piece of information?"

Hugh said.

"He told us—the whole group. He was in costume, pretending to be Palmer Shoemaker, and a woman in the group raised a camera to take his picture. Schulte stopped her in her tracks, said he had a stalker."

"Must be something in the water," Hugh said.

"What do you mean?" Robert said.

"This town," Hugh replied.

"Nothing wrong with Westford," Robert rejoined.

"I don't know," Mosey said.

"How would you?" Robert said. "You've been here—what, twenty hours?"

"Exactly, and in twenty hours, I've—"

Before she could finish, the approach of Hugh's friend diverted her attention.

"Sorry to interrupt," said the man in the hoodie.

"Not a bit." Hugh stood. "You've met Fernando Law, haven't you, Mosey?"

"Yes, I'm sure we've met." She shifted her eyes upward.

"Pretty *señorita*." Law winked at Mosey before turning his dark brown eyes on Hugh. "Could I speak to you for a second?"

"Certainly." Hugh accompanied Fernando to a spot a few yards from the table.

"Well, how do like that?" Robert frowned.

"What?"

"The nerve of the guy."

Mosey shrugged and shook her head. "Nothing to worry about. He's a bonobo."

"You're still on that?"

Mosey rolled her eyes and filched another chip.

Robert lightly swatted his wife's hand, then

motioned with his head toward Hugh. "Wonder what that's about?"

"Don't know." Mosey looked from Fernando to his lady friend, who'd been left alone to finish her lunch. "You know Fernando?" She popped a slice of green pepper into her mouth.

"Not well. He's a little aloof, if you ask me."

"A snob?"

"Reserved, not a snob."

"Reserved, huh. He's got a little bit of a macho thing going, if you ask me."

"He's a Communist."

"Oh. Not many of those around." She chomped a carrot, then placed a couple of sticks on Robert's plate.

"You'd be surprised."

"You're right, I would be."

She glanced at Hugh. He was nervously rubbing his chin, then his arm. "Must be something wrong," she said.

"What?"

"Look at Hugh."

"Hmm. I hope it's not something to do with the conference. I should step over there, maybe."

"I wouldn't."

"Why not?"

"Hugh will tell us if he wants us to know."

Hugh and Fernando returned to their respective tables.

"Everything okay?" Robert said.

"I don't know."

"Something happen?" Mosey said.

"Selena didn't come to work today."

"So?"

"They're saying over at the Lost Dog she might be the one they found in the gorge."

"Surely not," Robert said.

"A little staggering." Hugh lifted his mug.

"Why do they think that?" Mosey said.

"Well, there was something else besides her not showing up for work. They found a motorcycle wrecked and spattered in blood. One of her friends rides the same model."

"Where'd they find it?" Robert said.

"Near the cliff dwellings. Fernando and Eleanor were coming back from over there, saw the cops, and stopped to see what was going on."

"So, where's the guy?"

"They don't know."

"I expect the police will know something soon," Mosey suggested.

"Yeah," Hugh confirmed. "I guess we'll know soon enough."

Robert and Hugh finished their meal and took off for the conference hall. Mosey stayed behind, sipping an espresso and glancing now and then at Fernando and Eleanor. If she strained her ears, she could pick up some of the conversation. He wanted to head back to the conference. She was more interested in exploring an old Masonic cemetery.

"Cemetery, conference papers, cemetery," she said as she disassembled a wildflower from a slender cut-glass vase of wilted specimens. She was the lucky one, she thought. She didn't have to go to either. Bead Magic, just down the street, sounded like a more pleasant place to dally away a hot afternoon. Or she could wander around First, go back to the Square, eavesdrop on word-of-mouth accounts of the morning's unsettling discovery. None seemed especially alluring, though any one of them would qualify as a tolerable distraction—better than yawning her way through academic papers or stumbling around a graveyard in 100-degree heat.

The waiter came to remove the empty dishes. "Would you care for another espresso?"

"Well…okay, why not?" she said, not entirely ready to venture off.

As soon as he left, she realized that, while she'd been speaking with the waiter, Fernando had departed and Eleanor had stayed behind. After a mutual exchange of glances and awkward smiles, Eleanor rose from her chair and motioned to Mosey. "Mind if I join you?" she mouthed.

Mosey waved her over.

"Sure you don't mind?"

"Of course, not." Mosey stood and pulled out a chair for Eleanor. "I was just sitting here wondering what a person does in Westford on a Thursday afternoon."

"Well, I can't help you there. I'm Eleanor French, by the way."

"Nice to meet you. I'm Mosey Frye."

"I know," Eleanor said. "Fernando was filling me in. He knows Hugh Jessup. I guess Hugh mentioned he was waiting for you and your husband to get here yesterday afternoon."

"Hugh flew out, but Robert and I drove from Arkansas." Mosey sipped her coffee. "Where are you from, by the way?"

"South Texas, but Portland, originally," she said,

casting her crystal green eyes in all directions except Mosey's.

"That's a lovely place I've heard."

"It is. I get back there whenever I can," Eleanor said, reaching for the salt and pepper shakers, though she had nothing to season. "So you know Portland?"

"Not really. I was there once with Robert at an anthropology conference."

"Speaking of which, I'm not an anthropologist." She wiped the tops of the shakers with a paper napkin, then set them in the middle of the table, side by side.

"Yes, Hugh mentioned that."

"Really?" She glanced at Mosey.

"You're a publicist, right?"

"Yes…used to be. I haven't worked, well, it's been a few years since I held a steady job."

While engaging in a few minutes of effortless conversation, Mosey noted, one, that Eleanor had essentially reset the table, and, two, that she'd tugged at the outer corner of her left eye a dozen times. Her perfunctory diagnosis had been correct. Obsessive compulsive, yes—well, if not firmly "yes," at least "in all probability."

The instant Eleanor mentioned work, Mosey was sure her *story* was soon to trail. Would she hear it, or would she channel the discussion into another vein? "Eleanor, you wouldn't mind if I asked your opinion about something? It isn't personal, but—"

"What?" Eleanor was curious.

"I understand this isn't your first trip to Westford."

"That's right, I've been here a few times."

"As my husband reminded me at lunch, I've only been here twenty or so hours, but Westford is a strange town, if you ask me." The waiter returned with her espresso. She tore open a packet of raw sugar and poured it in.

"Okay, I can see why a person would think that."

"You can?"

"Sure."

"When I left the hotel this morning—we're staying at the Velvet Arms—this man—I'm not sure…maybe I've seen him before—says to me, 'Blue flowers can be dangerous.' There was a bouquet of wildflowers on the reception desk, and I'd sniffed them, the blue flax in particular."

"Odd thing to say to a stranger." Eleanor tugged at her eye.

Odd thing to *repeat* to a stranger, thought Mosey. Nonetheless, she had opted for a meandering route to her goal. "I'm glad you agree. I thought it very odd. So, I left the hotel and rounded the corner, hoping to get something to eat at the Carcajou Internet Café—over there, across the street." She pointed. "But a legion of goths—yes, that's right, a *legion*—and the weirdest goths I've ever seen, had stationed themselves on either side of the door. I didn't go in. I *couldn't* go in, so instead I walked down to the Square."

"Goths, right. I've seen them. Hard to miss. They're always there." Eleanor stared vacantly out the window. "Like the bikers at the Lost Dog."

Mosey babbled on. "Then, after I'd grabbed a bite to eat at the Square, I joined the walking tour of the downtown area. Our guide, Dr. Arnold Schulte, reacted very strangely when a woman tried to take his picture. He said he had a stalker." Did she dare tap Eleanor's arm? Sure, why not?

Eleanor shrank back. "Really?"

"Yes, I can't imagine."

"That's rather unsettling."

"I thought so. But the climax of it all," Mosey said, forging ahead, her eyes opening wider as she approached the finale, "yes, the *climax* was this." She scooted forward, and Eleanor scooted back. "The tour ended. Everyone was gone but Anne Howard, her daughter, and a couple of other women. So, I decided to leave, too, thinking I'd go back to the Velvet Arms. But just as I got to First, I heard a scream and ran back to the gorge. Some of the women, bent over the railing, were waving."

"I know. I heard. Dreadful business." She looked out the window.

"It really was. I was the one who called 911." She looked out, too, to see what Eleanor was staring at. There was nothing, only the odd sightseer.

"So you saw the body?" Eleanor said. "Must have been horrible."

It had been a shock seeing the body, but Mosey was determined to be resilient for the moment and press forward, wheedle whatever she could out of Eleanor. She had a strong hunch she knew something. "Your friend Fernando told Hugh that the barwoman at the Lost Dog might be the victim." She watched for some reaction.

"Yes…Selena Billings—do you know her?"

Mosey shook her head. "No, I've never met her, but Hugh has. Did you know her?"

"Yes, I did…no, I *do* know Selena. I don't want to think it was her."

"I think Hugh is fond of her."

"I'm fond of her, too. Reminds me of a girl—" Eleanor broke off mid-sentence.

"What was that?"

"Nothing," Eleanor answered.

"How could a person like that, young, well-liked, have enemies?"

"Everyone has enemies. We all have enemies."

"Oh, surely not." She countered Eleanor's cynicism with a buoyancy she herself could not quite support, not after the morning she'd had.

"*I* could be an enemy," Eleanor told her.

"You?"

"Me."

Mosey responded with a nervous laugh. "In that case," she added quickly, knowing that, if Eleanor took the lead, she would steer the conversation away from the matter at hand and into the drift of her personal obsession. "Hurry, Mosey," her inner voice nudged. "Say something quick."

Too late.

"I've hurt a lot of people," Eleanor said. "I didn't mean to, but I did. At least I thought I did."

"Oh, well, I'm sure we've all hurt people when we didn't mean to. That's not quite the same as being, well, an enemy."

"Yeah…enemy is a strong word. Are you sure she had an enemy? The dead woman, I mean. Maybe she just fell."

She felt a little uncomfortable. Eleanor, supposedly deranged, had come to a conclusion more sensible than her own. "Sure, maybe it was an accident. I guess the police will figure it out."

The conversation with Eleanor was going nowhere,

becoming a little tedious, in fact. Mosey was ready to get out of there, go for a stroll, do something. She sat up straight and looked around for the waiter.

"Are you leaving?" Eleanor said.

"I thought I might go for a walk. You're welcome to join me. Did your friend leave?"

"He went back to the conference. I didn't want to."

The waiter arrived.

"How much do I owe you for the second espresso?"

"Nothing, ma'am. It was on the house."

After she'd thanked him and left a tip, she and Eleanor walked through the bar and onto Westford's main thoroughfare. From the Silver Star, they could see the edge of the gorge, but a row of buildings blocked their view of the area where the body was found.

"Want to take a look?" Mosey said. "We could walk along the path next to the gorge."

"Oh...I don't know. I'm not sure I want to go there."

"Scared of heights?" Mosey laughed.

"Are you kidding—I'm a mountain climber, used to be a mountain climber."

"Yes, actually I *was* kidding."

"Right." Eleanor nervously pulled at her cuff.

"The truth is, as ghastly as this business is, my curiosity is getting the best of me. I'm wondering if the police have found something."

"You go ahead," Eleanor said. "I think I'll go back to the hotel. I need to call my husband."

"Oh, okay. Well, maybe we'll see each other later. At the banquet, perhaps?"

"Okay, well...be careful."

Eleanor headed toward the Velvet Arms, and Mosey walked around the corner to the sidewalk behind the buildings. Eleanor didn't seem like a bad sort to her. She liked her, in fact. A little fragile, but pleasant. Their conversation, however, had been sort of a waste of time. If anything, she'd learned the woman couldn't harm a fly. As usual, Mosey had let her imagination run away with her. Eleanor was probably right, and the dead woman had simply stumbled into the gorge. But before she put the mystery entirely to rest, she had to find out who the victim was. That, if nothing more.

Chapter Four

Mosey was one of scores of curiosity-seekers in Westford. The sidewalk along the so-called Gap, deserted earlier in the day, was crowded with men, women, and children. Some stared into the gorge, while others craned their necks to see to the opposite end, where the police had launched a search for evidence.

Mosey called out to Anne and Shelly Howard, who were standing a few yards down the walk.

"Mosey...hi," Anne called back.

"Hear anything?"

"No, we've just gotten back from lunch. You?"

"Nothing certain but, according to rumor," Mosey said, lowering her voice as she approached, "it might be Selena Billings, the bartender at the Lost Dog."

"They aren't sure?" Anne knitted her brow.

Mosey shook her head. "That's what we heard at the Silver Star."

"Lots of excitement for a conference," Anne said.

"Hadn't thought of it that way, but you're right. This is the least boring conference I've ever attended."

Anne and Shelly laughed.

"By the way," Mosey said, "what did you make of that stalker comment earlier?"

"Not entirely surprising," Anne said.

"Really?"

"Arnold Schulte...I don't know him well, but

Lionel says he's had problems at the college."

"Elmore, you mean?"

Anne nodded.

"Like what?"

"He's been known to date his students."

"Isn't he a little old for that?"

"Most definitely."

"So the stalker might be a student?" Mosey inferred.

"I wouldn't be surprised," Anne responded.

"That makes sense, I guess," Mosey added, putting two and two together. "But if the stalker was a student, wouldn't they know where to find him?"

"Good point."

"So maybe…" Mosey paused.

Shelly piped up. "Just because he *says* he has a stalker doesn't mean he has one."

"That's true," Mosey concurred, delighted to see Anne's daughter open her mouth. "But why would he say he had a stalker if he didn't?"

"He's in hiding," Shelly said. "Seems obvious to me."

"So…Shelly," Mosey probed gently, "sounds to me like you know something."

"Just what the other students say." She looked out vacantly across the gorge.

"What do they say?" Anne said.

"They say he was caught selling drugs."

"What?" Evidently, Anne, a mere wife, was less acquainted with college twaddle than her daughter, an Elmore senior.

"Not at Elmore, Mother. At his last job."

"I've never heard anything about that," Anne said.

255

"What kind of drugs?"

Shelly stared in bewilderment at her mother. "I don't know—weed, acid, the usual."

"If you say so." Anne shook her head.

Mosey detached herself from the mother-daughter chatter, so as to explore the relevance of Schulte's alleged criminal past to the puzzling statement he'd made regarding a stalker. "So he doesn't want someone who knew him *before* to see a picture and—"

"—blow his cover." Shelly rounded out her theory.

"A little unexpected, if you ask me," Anne opined, "but it explains his behavior, I suppose." Apparently, the sheer force of the notion that Arnold Schulte, a respected professor of American Studies, could at one time have peddled drugs sent a mild shudder down the length of her slender frame.

"Maybe he sold drugs, maybe he didn't," Mosey threw out, hoping to provide some relief, "but even if he didn't, the notion of a cover—that makes sense. He doesn't really have a stalker, but he doesn't want to be recognized."

"That's what I think," Shelly said, prepared to relinquish her story. "Or who knows?" she added. "It could be a dumb rumor."

"You kids shouldn't say such things about the faculty," Anne said.

"Mom, we aren't kids, for crying out loud."

"I know, I know, but sometimes you act like it."

The three women progressed along the sidewalk— Anne emitting the occasional sigh, Shelly plucking childishly at her lower lip—until they came to the place where, a couple of hours before, they'd stopped to listen to Dr. Schulte's account of Palmer Shoemaker's tumble into the gorge. Down below, several men in black coveralls and yellow boots were scouring the rocky slope where a person less fortunate than Shoemaker had fallen to her death. One of the officers picked up an object in his gloved hand and held it up for his fellow officers to see.

"What you got?" called out one of the men.

"A switchblade."

"Bag it. Bring it up."

He slipped the knife into a plastic bag and, taking hold of a rope, climbed up the side. When he reached the top, another policeman took the evidence and passed it to a man who wasn't in uniform. He was tall and wore a wide-brimmed hat and Western shirt and boots. "Good work, Jernigan. Tell the others to come on up."

"Who's that?" Mosey said to Anne.

"Chief of Detectives Dunavent Judd."

"Westford has a Chief of Detectives?"

"Yes, indeed."

"Didn't know there was much crime around here."

"The border is, what, fifty miles from here, seventy-five?"

"Oh, I see," she responded, though she didn't *really* see, not entirely, since Easterners, in general, were slow to grasp the paradigm of the Southwest. Diverse cultures—Anglo, Mexican, Mexican American, Native American—and a jumble of border issues that, easy enough for locals to spot, were hard for a stranger to work out. Mosey might as well have been in a foreign country. "Stranger in a strange land..." she muttered.

"What was that?" Anne said.

"Nothing. I must be a little homesick for Hembree." Mosey leaned against the railing, shading her eyes from the rays of the afternoon sun. "God, it's hot."

"Where's your water bottle?" Anne said.

"Must have left it at the Silver Star."

"Better get some water. You can dry up in a second out here."

"That's what Robert says."

"Better get out of the sun and have something to drink."

"I think I'll do that." She fanned herself with her hat. "I'll see you ladies later, at the banquet, maybe."

"We'll be there."

Mosey walked away from the gorge, looking for a place to cool off. She passed the house with the corner door and noticed the door was open, just a crack. She approached the front stoop, then looked around to see if anyone was watching. The house was a good forty feet from the yellow tape that stretched along the sidewalk, and the only spectators who were standing near the house appeared to be fully focused on the investigation. The police officers, directed by Judd, were starting to pack up their gear.

"They must be getting ready to head to the crime lab with that lackluster piece of evidence," Mosey uttered to no one but herself. "A switchblade! Who kills with a knife?" In the short time that had transpired since the recovery of the implicit weapon, she had concluded that the knife was not the direct cause of the hapless woman's demise—assuming she had, in fact, been murdered. That's what the investigation suggested, especially the large number of officers at the scene.

Apparently, to Judd and company, the preliminary findings pointed to homicide.

Before going into the house, she glanced back at Judd. Though superficially faithful to the standard image of a Western lawman, he seemed a cut above the expected. Despite his typecasting down to the brass buckle and lasso tie, she had a feeling Westford's high-ranking officer knew more about crime than a New York City policeman. But what sort of crime? Likely border stuff—drugs, illegal entry. "Humm, what else?"

Before the police departed—and she'd squandered her chance to make Judd's acquaintance (she had the perfect pretext, after all)—she made up her mind to inquire point blank about the victim's identity. "Lieutenant Judd," she shouted, just as he was about to get into his vehicle. She came around the back of the squad car and reached the passenger side an instant before the door closed. "Lieutenant Judd."

He removed his hat and cracked a quick smile. "Yes, ma'am."

"Sorry to bother you. I know you're busy, but I was the one who made the 911 call. I'm Mosey Frye." She timidly extended a hand.

Half in, half out of the car, he put both boots on the ground and stood up before taking Mosey's hand. "Why, yes, I was meaning to call you…to thank you for reporting the accident before anyone had a chance to do anything dumb, like shimmy down the side of that gorge. You'd be surprised at the things people do."

"Oh, of course, that was my first thought…call the police."

The sun beamed directly behind the lieutenant's broad shoulders.

"I have this terrible feeling I might know the woman." She shaded her eyes. "It isn't Selena Billings from the Lost Dog, is it?" Even if the question was more direct than she would have liked, she needed to reach her objective quickly, before the detective decided to get on with his business.

"Do you know Selena Billings?" he said, looking her squarely in the eye.

"Well, she's a friend of a friend."

"What friend?"

Should she say? How could she *not* say? "Hugh Jessup…he's doing some research in the area. He's an anthropologist."

"Hugh Jessup, eh?" Judd unsnapped his shirt pocket and pulled out a small tablet and pencil, then wrote down the name. "And you are Ms. Frye, you said."

"That's right, Mosey Frye."

"How do you spell that?"

Mosey spelled her name for him, though she was a little uneasy at seeing it jotted down on his pad.

"And how can I get in touch with Mr. Jessup?"

"He's staying at the Velvet Arms. I'm there, too, with my husband."

"Ms. Frye." Judd put on his hat. "I've got to run, but I'll be in touch, maybe later today."

He was back in the car and closing the door, and her only option was to back away, giving Judd's driver space to turn the big vehicle around. He quickly backed up and turned, then switched on the siren and sped off toward First.

She took a deep breath and put on her hat. Her hunch regarding the lieutenant's competency in dealing with crime matters seemed spot-on. She'd learned nothing from him. He, on the other hand, now had her name, Hugh's name, and would be calling Hugh later for questioning.

Nice, Mosey—just perfect! came the words of her father.

"You don't have to be so dang sarcastic," Mosey grumbled.

Don't get your dander up, young'un. That was not *a smart thing to do, and you know it. Couldn't you stay out of it just this once, if not for your sake, for Robert's?*

He had a point. She was in Westford at the behest of her distinguished husband—at least in those climes—and she ought to behave herself. On the other hand, she had a ton of time on her hands. She had to do something.

She reached for her cell phone but paused before placing the call. Given that Hugh and Robert were in a session, unlikely their phones were on. No matter—she decided to leave a message. She scrolled to Hugh's number, pressed the call button, and continued walking toward the hotel.

Chapter Five

Scheduled to deliver the keynote speech at the banquet that evening, Hugh had convinced Judd to conduct his questioning at the hotel instead of the police station. The lieutenant arrived shortly before six. The cocktail hour preceding the banquet was set for six-thirty.

Judd trudged up the stairs of the Velvet Arms and, taking the hall to the left, stopped in front of Hugh's door, one down from Robert and Mosey's room. Mosey, as she was putting on her make-up, heard steps in the hall followed by a knock, a door opening, and then Hugh's voice.

"Come in. Lieutenant Judd, I presume? I'm Hugh Jessup." The door closed.

Judd sat in a straight-backed chair in the corner of the room near a window. The room was warm, despite a draft of air from the fan that whirred overhead. Hugh pulled up a chair close to the lieutenant's. Then, remembering he hadn't put on his tie, he stepped to the dresser. "Go ahead, Lieutenant, I'm listening." His blue silk tie was draped over the mirror. He flipped up his crisp, white collar, slipped the tie around his neck, and made a knot.

"Well, it seems we have a bewildering case on our hands," Judd said. "Dr. Jessup—"

"Call me Hugh."

"Okay...Hugh, as I was saying, the facts of the case don't seem to point in any one direction."

"How's that?" he said, struggling to correct his knot, which was slightly twisted.

"Let me start with this," Judd said, leaning forward. "Ms. Frye mentioned to me that you were friendly with Selena Billings."

"I wouldn't say friendly, exactly. I've talked to her several times at the Lost Dog. I've been doing some research out at the cliff dwellings, and after work, I usually stop off at the bar for a beer."

"Were you there yesterday afternoon?"

"Yes."

"What time?" Judd reached for his tablet and pencil.

"Four till around five, give or take ten minutes."

"And Ms. Billings—she was there the entire time?"

"I think so. She served me a beer, and we conversed off and on while she was cleaning around the bar."

"Who else was in the bar—did you notice?"

His tie satisfactorily knotted, Hugh picked up his sports coat, hung it over the back of the dresser chair, and took a seat. "Three guys were playing pool...maybe one or two people were at the bar. There was a biker standing outside—he came inside once, I believe."

"Did Selena seem her normal self, or did she say or do anything unusual?" Judd lifted his chin and narrowed his eyes.

Hugh paused for a second, not sure if he wanted to tell Judd everything he knew. "Mind if I ask you a question, Lieutenant?"

Judd's response was reticent. "What question is that?" he said, chin still raised.

"Selena…she wasn't the one they found in the gorge, was she?"

"No, it wasn't Ms. Billings."

"I'm glad to know that. Why all the questions about Selena, then?"

"No one has seen her since yesterday around five. You may have been the last person to talk to her. That's why it's important for you to tell me whatever it is you know."

"I don't think I know anything really."

"The smallest thing could be crucial."

"Selena repeated a conversation to me she'd had with someone else at the bar. I don't know exactly when the conversation took place."

"Do you know that person's name?"

"Yes, actually it's someone I know, not well, but I've met her. Her name is Eleanor French. She's here for the conference—though I'm not sure why. She's a retired publicist."

"What was the conversation about?"

"French had a nervous collapse some years ago— had to do with her work—and she went through some hard times. Lost her job, was hospitalized. It was during that time that she developed a complex of some sort, thought she might be responsible for someone else's death—several people it was."

"Was she brought up on charges?"

"No, no, nothing like that. It was all fantasy, a delusion. She never hurt anyone, as far as I know."

Judd cocked his head. "And what did Ms. Billings have to do with any of that?"

"Nothing. French told Selena her story, that's all. She thought it was strange, and she repeated it to me."

"Was she afraid of Ms. French in any way?"

"I don't think so. French is harmless. She's fully recovered. If it weren't for that story, you'd never suspect she'd been ill."

"I see. Anything else you can think of? The biker you mentioned before...do you know his name?"

"No."

"Could you describe him?"

"Six feet tall, dark-complexioned, had a tattoo on his arm, maybe both arms."

"Did you see him speak to Ms. Billings?"

"Yes, they seemed to know each other...maybe. Not sure about that."

"Did they seem friendly?"

"I guess you could say that. He put something in her pocket. Could have been money, a note. Not sure what it was."

Judd brought out a photograph from between the back pages of his tablet and handed it to Hugh. "Do you recognize this man?"

"That's the biker."

"You're sure?"

Hugh hesitated. "Yes, this is the guy, but he wasn't dressed like that." The man in the picture looked clean-cut, professional, with ordinary clothing.

"Okay, anything else you can think of...anything at all?"

Hugh shook his head. "No, nothing, not really. I suppose I should mention that I had some misgivings about the biker. Not sure why. He seemed pleasant."

"Well, I might as well tell you. You'll read about it

in the paper. This guy's an undercover agent. He's gone missing as well. His motorcycle was found wrecked out on 65 near the cliff dwellings."

"I see." Hugh was surprised to learn that the biker he'd suspected of mischief was, in reality, a spy. "And the woman in the gorge?"

"Well, that's another can of worms." Judd got up and moved toward the door. "Thanks for your help. And good luck with that speech. Sorry to have held you up."

"Glad to help." He opened the door for Judd.

Judd turned back and handed Hugh his card. "Where is your banquet, by the way?"

"The Alameda. Cocktail hour should be starting in less than half an hour."

"If you think of anything else, give me a call." Judd tipped his hat and left.

As soon as Judd had reached the top of the stairs and begun his descent, another knock came at the door.

"It's open," Hugh shouted.

"Damn." Robert poked his head in. "He was here long enough."

"Not so long. You ready?"

"Mosey's changing her purse."

"Let's go." Hugh checked his watch. "Good God, tell her to get a move on. It's after six."

"I'm ready." Mosey slipped in next to Robert, who'd remained in the doorway. "Who's driving?"

"Mind if we take your car? The jeep's covered in dirt."

"Not a problem," Robert said.

They scurried down the steps, then through the lobby, barely pausing as they passed small clusters of conference participants gathered in the reception area. If they'd stopped for a second, they might have seen that Judd had stayed behind. He'd stationed himself inconspicuously behind a king palm to await the arrival of Professor Addison Boatwright, bio-archeologist, specialist in wildflowers of a particular kind: species that, if touched or ingested, could lead to illness or death. Hugh and Robert knew Boatwright from several conferences. Mosey, too, was vaguely acquainted with the professor, for, yes, he was the octogenarian, indeed, the man in the slouch hat with whom she'd brushed elbows earlier in the day, the man who'd warned her of the danger of blue flowers.

Chapter Six

Mosey was no fan of conference banquets. Absurd, she thought, to eat a three-course meal, then remain seated for an hour, pretending to digest the academic trivia—common fare at such events—offered up by a ripened, if not over-ripe, scholar. Intolerable. This particular banquet, on the other hand, was different, as Hugh, provider of the evening's entertainment, had held everyone's attention—even hers—with a remarkable account of recent work on the Clovis people, believed to have established settlements in North America around 10,000 BC.

Robert was the first to congratulate his colleague. "Hugh, amazing talk, amazing...fine job." His face, if not his tone, suggested that his response had been just a little automatic. But why automatic, she mused. Was Robert jealous of his junior colleague's swift rise to prominence in the association? Or was the talk not of the same high quality he required of his own work?

"I didn't nap even for a second," she interjected enthusiastically.

"I thought I saw you nod a time or two," Robert said.

She lobbed back with an appropriate reproach. "Not once."

Hugh stepped away and, moving from one smiling colleague to the next, accepted their accolades and those of their spouses.

Mosey, who would have enjoyed basking in Hugh's limelight, settled instead for a scan of the room. She could pick out a few anthropologists whose acquaintance she had made at previous conferences. "Robert." She tugged at her husband's arm. "I think I know that man." She pointed discreetly at a tall, thin man who was accompanied by a short, squat woman. "That's what's his name—the man I met at the Aberdeen conference."

"John Metcalfe, you mean."

"His wife is pregnant. And that man they're talking to—isn't that the guy from Canada, the one I met in Telluride?"

"Andy, Andy Gibson."

"Andy, of course. I liked him. He's interesting."

While Robert continued on around the hall, Mosey went first to the ladies' room, then the bar, where she encountered the older gentleman she'd spoken with that morning at the reception desk. No longer wearing his slouch hat, he was looking rather dapper in his navy blue pinstripe and bow tie.

"We meet again." He offered her his bar stool.

"Oh, no, keep your seat," she responded.

"My mother taught me better than that. I wouldn't be able to sleep tonight."

"Oh, well, okay." She wiggled onto the stool.

"Waiter," he called, "this young lady would like to order something to drink, I believe."

"Champagne."

"I'll have a Glenlester neat," added the gentleman, whose identity still remained a mystery to Mosey.

"I haven't been out drinking with a stranger, not

lately anyway," she said.

Before introductions could be made, Anne and Lionel Howard approached. "Mosey, I didn't know you and Addison were friends," she said.

"Well, if you mean this gentleman, I'm not sure that I've had the pleasure."

"Pardon me. I'm Addison Boatwright."

"Mosey Frye."

"Mosey, I believe you know my husband," Anne said.

"Yes, of course, good to see you, Lionel."

"Your friend Hugh gave a first-rate keynote," Lionel said.

"He surely did," Boatwright agreed. "And," he said, smiling at Mosey, "I now know where I've seen you. You're Robert Ellison's wife."

"That's right," she said, "but refresh my memory—where exactly did we meet?"

"At the bio-archeological lab in Ruidoso. I think you and Robert were newlyweds."

"Oh, gosh, you're the wildflower man!"

Anne and Lionel laughed at Mosey's description.

"The world authority on poisonous flowers, to be precise," Lionel amended. Then, turning to Boatwright, he said, "I hear you've been in Australia."

"Got back last week. They've got quite a problem with *Cycas armstrongii*. Killing the cattle."

"Didn't know you were interested in that sort of thing."

"Well, it paid for the trip, and I got to poke around in the bogs while I was there. I had heard about some interesting specimens in the south, but they weren't particularly different from some of the examples of

Zigademus venenosus I've run across around here."

"That's why you said 'blue flowers can be dangerous.' " Mosey passed Boatwright his chunky glass of scotch.

"Not a bad line for an old man." He chuckled.

"So...blue flowers?" she prodded, lifting the slender flute of champagne to her lips.

"Oh, my goodness, don't get me started," he replied.

"*Zigademus venenosus* isn't blue, is it?" Lionel said.

"No, as a matter of fact, that's a yellow one, unlike its close cousin *Camassia esculenta*, which, by the way, is perfectly safe to consume and is a primary root food of the western North American groups. The Maidu are quite taken with it."

"Who are the Maidu?" Mosey said.

"A California group. Ask Robert about the Maidu."

"I didn't expect to see you here this year, Addison," Lionel put in, lifting a palm full of cashews to his mouth.

"I hadn't really expected to make it, but Arnold wanted badly for me to come." He pushed the bowl of nuts toward Mosey. "Care for some, my dear?"

Taking no notice of the polite gesture, Mosey locked glances with Anne.

"Arnold," Anne said, "gave us spouses a tour of the downtown area this morning."

"Yes...he tells me he's putting together an article on Shoemaker."

"So, then," Mosey dared, "you must be friends with Dr. Schulte?"

"He was my student at CSU...I won't say how

many years ago."

"His degree is in anthropology?"

"American Studies."

"He ought to write a book on Palmer Shoemaker," Mosey said. "Amazing man."

"I doubt he'll do that—but who knows?"

Before Mosey could make out the full connection between Boatwright and Schulte, Robert and Hugh joined the group.

"I see you've met Professor Boatwright." Robert smiled broadly.

Boatwright set down his scotch and gave Robert's hand a firm shake.

"You don't remember, either," Mosey looked at Robert, "but *he* remembers."

"Remembers what?" Robert said.

"That he and I met years ago, in Arizona at the lab."

Robert nodded. "Yes, I'd forgotten about that." Then, turning to Hugh, he said, "You know all these folks, Hugh?"

Hugh, who had been talking to Lionel, stopped to acknowledge Boatwright. "Of course, Addison and I were on a panel together—where was that, UT?"

"You are correct, sir, UT. I was a gatecrasher there. That one had nothing to do with wildflowers." He took a slow sip and glanced at the clock above the bar. "Wish I could continue this, but it so happens, I've got to meet someone back at the Velvet Arms."

"Late date, eh?" Lionel winked at Boatwright.

"No such luck." He chuckled. "Unfortunately I've got some business—I guess you could say business." He patted Hugh on the back and left the bar.

"That's the guy," Mosey whispered to Robert, glancing after Boatwright.

"What?"

"I told you."

"Told me what?"

"At the hotel."

"When I was in the shower?"

"Yes, didn't you hear a word I said?"

Robert ate a nut, then pushed the bowl away.

Mosey twisted around to face the bar and, placing a napkin in front of her, reached for a bowl of pretzel sticks. Picking out the longest sticks from the bowl, she formed several horizontal and vertical lines. A nudge from Hugh brought her diversion to a halt.

"Let me guess. You're into schemata."

"Schemata…la-ti-data," Mosey rejoined.

"So what *is* that?"

When Mosey had finished plotting her mysterious diagram, she reached for the bowl of nuts and began placing cashews strategically alongside the pretzels.

Hugh plucked the largest cashew from its spot and popped it in his mouth.

"What's that?" Robert insisted.

"This is downtown Westford, and the cashew Hugh just ate was Addison Boatwright. He's the first oddball I met today."

"Oddball?" Robert protested.

"And who is that?" Hugh pointed at another nut.

"Arnold Schulte, who has a stalker or, to the contrary, may *not* have a stalker."

"May *not* have a stalker?" Hugh furrowed his brow.

"Correct."

"Before, you said he *had* a stalker." Robert, as it happens, had apparently only heard a few bits and pieces of his wife's harangue.

"He sold drugs, maybe, maybe not. He doesn't have a stalker, he just says he does, or maybe he *really* has a stalker."

Robert set the nuts down. "That's ridiculous."

"Arnold Schulte is Boatwright's former student," Mosey clarified. "Boatwright is here because of him. Arnold wanted him to come *badly*, he said."

"I somehow doubt that," Hugh opined.

"He said he'd just come back from Australia and…"

"How many of those have you had, my sweet?" Robert signaled with his own glass toward hers.

"One, and I don't know what you're insinuating."

"Nothing. *Tranquila.* I just wanted to know if you wanted another."

"Yes, please. Sorry."

Hugh, who had little patience for circumlocution, was adamant. "Out with it, Frye."

Mosey set her glass on the counter in expectation of a refill. "Dunavent Judd," she said to Hugh, "what happened with Judd?"

"Oh, that." Now it was Hugh who was hedging. "I told you. Selena's alive. Her biker friend is a spy, by the way. They're missing."

"So…the woman in the gorge—who was it?"

"He didn't say."

Robert began a rollcall of the cashews that remained on his wife's napkin. "Boatwright, Schulte, who else?"

"Eleanor French."

"She's not a nut," countered Hugh.

"Obsessive compulsive, but you're right," Mosey conceded. "I think Eleanor's okay."

"What's that?" His reference was to the sunflower seeds she'd arranged in an even row close to the spot where the original Boatwright cashew had been.

"You can't guess?"

"The goths," Hugh answered.

She nodded with a smile. "Very good."

Hugh picked up the plump raisins he'd taken from a bowl of trail mix and lined them up in a snug little row along the pretzel "street," an inch, inch and a half from the sunflower seeds.

"Hey, this is my schema."

"Bikers." Hugh grinned slyly. "And this one," he said as he poked it with a toothpick, "is *the missing spy*."

Chapter Seven

Lieutenant Judd stood at the end of the Spanish colonial bureau, glancing between the desk clerk and the door.

The clerk looked up from his paperwork.

"I'd like to leave a message, please, for Addison Boatwright."

"The professor isn't—" He stopped mid-sentence, targeted by a piercing stare from Judd's blue-gray eyes.

"If you'd just make sure the professor gets this, soon as you see him…" He shifted his stare to the clerk's nameplate. "…Mr. Al-ca-lá."

Alcalá slipped the folded page into Boatwright's box, and Judd passed through the door onto Silver.

He trod wearily along the street and, coming to the corner, turned left onto First. He passed the Carcajou, with its assembly of goths, and, a few minutes later, the Lost Dog, where the usual row of bikers occupied some twenty feet of sidewalk. It struck him, as he walked on toward Shoemaker House, that, when you got right down to it, First Street was a dadgum stakeout, or close to it. He turned around and headed back to the Carcajou and, crossing the threshold, strode to the counter at the back. "Can you tell me," he said to the attendant, "what time you guys close?"

"Just like it says on the door, one a.m." The youth, who was wearing black pants and a black vest, lifted a pair of green goggles and pushed them back into a passel of synthetic dreadlocks.

"Every night?"

"Except Monday."

"Give me a large coffee…black."

Judd opened his worn leather billfold, slapped a five on the counter, and told the attendant to keep the change. He picked up his cup and saucer and headed to a table near the front, sloshing coffee as he went.

Through a wall of plate glass, Judd scrutinized the backs of a dozen Carcajou 'sentinels,' black-clad and zombie-like. He hadn't paid them much attention. He preferred as a rule to look *through* not *at* the freak show he often encountered at the Carcajou. He gently blew the coffee that had spilled into the saucer and watched the *tableau vivant* from the back. Yep, he said to himself, perfect little setup. Nobody looks at those guys anymore. Judd took a slurp of the dark brew. It'd be easy to slip in a spy, now wouldn't it? The biker was a spy, so why not a friggin' cyber punk? But he quickly changed his mind, realizing they were too young for Intelligence.

When he'd finished his coffee, he approached the counter again. "Mind if I ask you a couple of questions?" He showed the attendant his badge.

"About what?" The young man, setting up for the late-night crowd, was placing bagels alongside a row of raspberry scones.

"I was just wondering if you happened to be here last night?"

"I was."

"And did you close at one, like you said before?"

"I locked the door about then. I didn't get out of

here till two."

"Did you see anything unusual on the street?" He paused to wonder what "unusual" might mean to the attendant. "You know, strange…out of the ordinary."

The young man thought.

"Well, did you?" Judd urged.

"I'm thinking."

"Take your time." He leaned on the glass counter, examining the layout of pastries and cupcakes.

"I left here around two, like I said, and walked down to the theater where I park my car. Nobody was outside the café, but there were a couple of guys in suits outside the Star."

"The Silver Star, you mean."

"Yeah, so I got to the Lost Dog—must have been around two-fifteen, two-thirty—and the bikes were there…but the bikers weren't there."

"The bikers *weren't* there."

"I don't think so. The bikes were there for sure, backed up to the curb like they always are. But there wasn't anyone on the street outside the bar."

"You're certain about that?"

"Yeah, I'm certain. The bar was empty, I'm pretty sure. I mean I didn't go in or anything."

"Were the lights still on?"

"I don't believe so." He glanced at his watch and, opening the case, pulled out a single cruller and set some blueberry cupcakes next to the scones. "It was dark in the bar, but not pitch black, like when all the lights are off."

"You didn't see anyone at the bar?"

"The door was open, but I don't remember seeing anyone inside."

"Thanks for the information." Judd handed the man, whose name was Dave, his card. "Call me if you think of anything."

"Hey, Lieutenant," Dave called after Judd. "You don't know who that girl was, do you?"

"Why do you ask?"

"Just curious," he said with a shrug.

Judd left the Carcajou, taking a quick look at the sentinels, who hadn't budged from their lookout by the door. "You guys get bored?"

No one answered—or even blinked, as far as Judd could tell. "If I ever need extras for a stakeout..." He trailed off. He tipped his big hat and sauntered off toward Shoemaker House. Passing the Lost Dog again, he saw that the bar was open, but the bikers were nowhere in sight, neither they nor their motorcycles. He took out his cell and called Sergeant Jernigan. "Are the forensics people there yet?"

"Been here."

"I'm on First, at the Lost Dog. Tell them I'll be there in a minute."

"Yes, sir."

Judd got to Shoemaker House and, rounding a black SUV with Texas tags, went in through the corner door, avoiding the area marked off by yellow tape. Two men, hunched over a red stain on the pine floor, straightened up when he entered the room. "Thanks for driving over," he said. "What you got so far?"

"The blood stain is a match," said the taller of the two men. "But I guess you knew that." He dutifully flashed his ID and introduced himself. "Special Agent Warner, FBI," he said, "and this is Sergeant Barbour." Barbour crouched again, then stood, stepped back, and took a snapshot of the stain.

"I know Barbour," Judd said. "Find any prints?"

"Oh, yeah," Barbour said. "Five fresh ones just in here."

"Where?"

"Right here on the floor."

The white powder, dusted around the bloodstain, had been lifted in five distinct spots. Blood droplets, leading away from the larger stain, were marked off with tape.

"What do you make of it?" Judd stepped closer to the spot where the victim had lain.

"We need to the see the body first," Warner said, "before we can put all this together, but, for the time being, I'd say she was killed right here, then lifted—not dragged—and taken out that way." He pointed toward the door.

"See those?" Barbour aimed his camera at a set of footprints that led away from the largest of the blood stains. "We got two sets, one, about a size twelve man's boot, and the other, I'd say about a size nine woman's boot."

"So two people, you think, maybe a man and a woman, carried her out of here." Judd pulled out his tablet and jotted down the information. "Doesn't mean they're the killers—or does it?"

"No, but logic tells you that, if they *weren't* the killers, they had a damn good reason not to report the murder."

"So we're talking murder here…for sure," Judd said.

"We're not talking anything till we see the body," Warner replied with a hint of impatience. "Barbour, go ahead and photograph those tracks outside the door." Then, he turned to Judd. "We found another set of fresh footprints on the stoop. Looks like a woman's shoe but a little smaller than the woman's boot prints in here."

"That could be anybody's prints. A whole slew of people's been around here today."

"Right, but these are close to the building," Warner explained. "There's also a handprint on the outside doorframe."

Barbour, after he'd snapped pictures of the prints on the front stoop, came back into the room. "Ready to pack up, Agent Warner?'

"Yeah, go ahead. We'll have to come back after we've checked the body, but we're finished for now. Run those prints through the data bank."

"Jernigan," Judd called to his sergeant, who'd remained outside, "go on and stick around here for the time being. You need anything?"

"No, Lieutenant, I'm fine." He popped a sunflower seed into his mouth.

Warner and Barbour loaded their equipment into the back of the SUV and took off, spinning a dust cloud off the rear tires. Judd pulled in front of them at the corner and led the way down First onto the highway. In five minutes, they reached the police station, and, making their way through a higgledy-piggledy arrangement of desks and cabinets, entered the morgue, where the coroner, in the presence of two officers, was examining the victim's body.

Judd introduced the coroner first, then the agents. "This is Dr. Tremble…Special Agent Warner, and you know Sergeant Barbour."

The coroner, who was standing in the middle of a

room no bigger than a workroom, looked at Barbour. "Hey, didn't expect to see you around here today."

Barbour removed his hat and nodded to Tremble.

Judd stepped into the stream of light from the surgical lamp above the dissection table. "What you got there, Tremble?"

"Asphyxia looks like," the doctor said. "On the other hand, I wouldn't bet on it." He looked up. "When's that professor getting here?"

"I need to pick him up over at the Velvet Arms." Judd checked his watch. "But not quite yet. We're meeting around eight."

"Preliminaries don't add up." Tremble directed the onlookers' attention toward a cut on the victim's arm.

"I thought you said asphyxia," Warner said.

"That's right. It seems like asphyxia—*seems* being the operative word. The heart and lungs suggest that, but look at the throat."

Barbour, who'd been standing at the victim's feet, moved toward the upper part of the torso. "No bruising."

"Right," Tremble confirmed. He pointed his scalpel toward the victim's arm. "Under ordinary circumstances, a cut like this wouldn't be fatal, though it can spill a lot of blood. But look at this."

A broken circle of white powder stood out against the dark skin of the victim.

"Looks like some sort of residue," Warner said.

"And now this." Tremble grasped the victim's jaw and inserted a wooden tongue depressor into the mouth.

"What is it?" Warner said.

"Looks like some kind of plant bulb," Tremble suggested.

Barbour leaned over the victim and cocked his head. "More like a tuber."

"I'm hoping the professor can shed some light on this." Tremble removed his gloves. "Does this lady have a name?"

"We're waiting for confirmation, but the cell phone found on the body belongs to Mariah Weatherford of San Angelo."

"No handbag found at the scene?"

"Nope."

"Any prints on the switchblade?"

"Wiped clean."

"Could have been the instrument that made the cut," Tremble said.

"What's the time of death?" Warner said.

"She's been dead a good twelve hours, maybe a little more."

"Find anything under the fingernails?" Judd said.

"There aren't any defensive wounds on the body, but we'll know when we get the report from the lab."

"Okay, Doc." I'll be back with Boatwright soon as I can. He looked over at Warner. "And in the meantime, maybe you could check on those prints?"

It was Barbour who answered. "I'll get right on it, Lieutenant."

Judd left Warner and Barbour with the coroner and returned to the Velvet Arms.

Chapter Eight

"Here he comes now," Judd mumbled to himself, "in his suit and bow tie." Able to muster only a modicum of respect for occupants of the ivory tower, Judd grunted, rose lethargically from his wing chair, and took a step in the professor's direction. "Professor Boatwright," he called out as the senior gentleman pushed through the door.

"You beat me back, I see." Boatwright took off his hat and twirled it between his nimble fingers.

"They're waiting for us at the station."

"Let's get on with it, then, Lieutenant." He politely gestured with his hat toward the door. Judd went out first and, in a few long strides, got to his truck and opened the cab door for Boatwright.

"Not sure what my role is in all this." Boatwright stepped in.

"The coroner wants your opinion about something related to the case—what we spoke about before."

"I'm not a forensic anthropologist. There're a few of them here at the conference, if that's what you're looking for."

"I think you're just the man for the job, Professor," Judd replied, rolling down the window.

"And what makes you think so, if you don't mind my asking?" Even at eighty, Boatwright apparently had not yet recognized his own eminence.

"I've got my sources," answered Judd, with a slight grin.

Boatwright didn't press the matter and sat straight-faced till they'd reached their destination. "I myself am not a suspect, am I?" he said as they entered the station yard.

Judd shook his head.

Agent Warner and Dr. Tremble were waiting on the patio of the small adobe house that served Westford as a police station. Tremble smiled upon seeing the professor come through the gate.

"Professor Boatwright, I presume," the good-natured man began, approaching to shake the professor's hand. "Glad to finally meet you. I've heard quite a lot about you."

"Really—from whom?"

"Arnold, of course." He opened the screen door.

"Oh…I didn't know you and Arnold were friends."

"Arnold and I go way back, college, in fact. We both went to Elmore. Go on in. The morgue is through here. You've seen a dead body before, I'm guessing."

"Well, yes, but not—" Boatwright didn't seem to know exactly how to finish.

"Not dissected?" Tremble said.

"Yes, not dissected."

"Here, let me take your coat," Tremble said.

Boatwright took off his suit coat and handed it to Tremble, who hung it behind the door and handed him a pair of latex gloves. "You're okay with this?"

He nodded. But when Tremble closed the door and pulled back the sheet, he momentarily turned away from the open chest cavity from which the heart and lungs had been removed. He drew a handkerchief from his pants pocket and placed it over his mouth and nose.

"I'd like your opinion of this." Tremble cleared his throat, then pointed to the victim's right arm. "The obvious cause of death is asphyxiation, but there's no sign of strangling or choking. Some blood gushed out here, enough to leave a good size stain on the floor, but not enough to end a life. Something has been introduced into the lesion, as this residue would seem to corroborate. Do you agree?"

"Let's take a look." He took the magnifying glass Tremble handed him and aimed it at the sprinkling of powder.

While Boatwright examined the wound, Tremble inserted a tongue depressor into the victim's mouth. "And we also have this."

Boatwright lay the magnifying glass on the metal side table and turned his attention to the object inside the dead woman's narrowly parted lips. "I suppose you're thinking there's a connection between the residue and *that*, whatever it is."

"Hopefully, your guess is better than mine."

"Can you remove it?"

Tremble picked up a pair of tweezers from the table, pulled out the object, and held it up. "There."

"Okay," Boatwright said, "now that's obvious. It's a tuber, and, if you're thinking poison, sometimes the tuber or root is the most virulent part of the plant."

"A tuber," Tremble said. "I thought it was some sort of bulb. Ever heard of administering poison that way?"

"I know of a flower, a member of the buttercup family—the genus is *aconitum*. Many species exist, several dozen." Boatwright stepped back from the body and daubed his forehead with his handkerchief.

"Aconitum," Tremble said. "Yes, I'm familiar with it."

"*Eranthis hyemalis*...you may know it as wolf bane or monkshood—it's even been called women's bane. It's among the most toxic plants in cultivation. According to legend, women have been killed by having tubers forced into their mouths." He reached for the tuber Tremble had placed on the table. "In crude form, it's very dangerous. Death could be almost immediate."

"Then, wouldn't it be overkill to slice open an arm and sprinkle a bit of poisonous powder on the wound?"

"Maybe, but applying the poison in powdered form to abraded skin is rather common...and effective. Maybe the perpetrator wasn't entirely aware of the potency."

"I guess we need to send the tuber and some of the residue along with a blood sample to the lab."

"That's what I would do." Boatwright passed the tuber to Tremble.

Tremble dropped it into a plastic bag and labeled it with the Latin name. "*Eranthis hyemalis*, you said."

"Yes, and, mind you, I would need to run some tests to confirm that."

"Won't be necessary. I'll send this to the lab along with the other evidence. We'll just point them in the right direction, save them a little time."

Tremble and Boatwright removed their gloves and left the morgue to join Judd and Warner on the patio. Passing through the front room, they nodded to Barbour, who'd set up his laptop on a metal desk in the corner.

"The professor's been very helpful," Tremble said. He reached into the cooler for a soft drink. "Cool drink, Professor?"

"I'll pass, thanks."

"I'll take one of those," Warner said to Tremble.

"Looks like we have a theory for the cause of death," Tremble said.

"What's the theory?" Judd said.

"Poisoning," he responded. "Wolf bane."

Warner took a sip of his drink, then a languid puff off his cigarette. "You're certain it's wolf bane?" He appeared more curious than astonished.

"We'll need confirmation from the lab," Tremble said.

Warner puffed again and stared out at the night sky. "We've seen two cases of aconite poisoning in the last eight or nine months."

"What?" Judd took off his hat as if better to hear Warner's words. "Two cases? Where?" He tossed the toothpick from his mouth toward the scant grass that bordered the patio.

"Both were around here, more or less," Warner said. In anticipation of Judd's next question, he continued: "We didn't report the exact cause of death." He sipped his drink again and took a final puff off his cigarette before squashing the butt on the tile floor. "Not publicly, anyway." He squared his jaw, prepared for rebuff.

"Why's that?" Tremble said.

"Asphyxiation was the more obvious cause, and, for internal reasons, the deaths were reported as such. The press was told the women had been strangled."

"*Internal reasons*, huh?" Might as well have been

swear words, the way they rolled off Judd's tongue.

"Yes, internal reasons," Warner repeated.

"Meaning?" Judd poked.

"Serial killer. A serial killer with a bizarre *modus operandi* probably committed those murders and now this one."

Judd's expression darkened.

"This piece of information was withheld?" Tremble took a pipe from his pocket, clinched it between his teeth, and struck a match on the adobe wall.

"Damn right." Warner was apparently peeved at Tremble's insinuation.

"And for the usual reason, I suppose," Tremble said.

"If you mean false confessions, yes."

"You'd better fill us in, Warner." Judd backed up to a wooden post and, leaning back, crossed one dusty boot over the other.

"Other than the physical evidence, which is much like what we have here, we don't have a lot to work with. Both women were real estate agents, young— neither over thirty-two. The first was found in a parking garage in Dallas. Not long after that, a similar case turned up in Beaumont."

Judd, who'd pulled out his tablet, was quickly jotting down the information. "Was Mariah Weatherford a realtor?"

"Maybe," Warner said. "We're waiting for prints to confirm the identification. More reliable than a phone."

"Can you put a rush on that?" Judd said. "If I've got a serial killer in Westford, I'd damn well like to know it."

"As would we," Warner said, "as would we. There's more evidence here than what was found in Dallas or Beaumont. Looks like the killer's getting sloppy, which is often the case." Warner pulled a pack of cigarettes out of his pocket and offered it around.

"Those other women—were they Anglos?"

"Dark-skinned, like this one."

"Lieutenant Judd, sir," Boatwright said, declining Warner's offer, "if I'm finished here, would you mind dropping me back in town?"

"Certainly. You'll be around tomorrow, I assume."

"Yes, I expect to be here through the weekend."

Judd put his hat on. "Warner, give me a call, or, better, I'll call *you*."

Judd and Boatwright departed. Tremble and Warner remained on the patio, sipping soft drinks, smoking, and waiting for information.

Chapter Nine

A sudden eruption of merriment followed the banquet and, in next to no time, anthropologists and their guests abandoned the Alameda for a different sort of venue. Fernando Law and Eleanor French said they'd be at the Lost Dog should anyone want to join them. Hugh, Robert, and Mosey left for the Silver Star, with an interim stop at the Velvet Arms.

Back at the hotel, Addison Boatwright stepped down from Judd's truck and, waving good-bye, entered the lobby. "Any messages for me?" he said to the clerk, who checked the appropriate cubbyhole and handed him a folded slip of paper.

"Thanks." He opened the note and read the signature at the bottom. "Arnold," he murmured. Then, hearing someone call his name, he looked up to see Mosey scampering down the stairs. "Ms. Frye, I thought you'd be in bed by now."

"Indeed, not. The fun's only beginning. Won't you join us at the Silver Star?"

"Actually, I already have a *date*."

"A date, eh?"

He chuckled. "Just meeting an old friend, a former student, over at the Lost Dog. He's challenged me to a game of pool."

"You're kidding."

"Yes, I'm kidding."

"You've got something more interesting to do, I suppose?"

"You're not entirely wrong there." He opened the door for Mosey, whose companions were waiting outside.

"Come with us, just for a drink," she insisted.

"Yes, do," Hugh seconded, sticking his head in. "You can tell us about your trip to Australia."

"I need to go upstairs and get out of these clothes, but I'll be down directly. If you bump into Arnold Schulte at the Silver Star, please let him know I'm running a little late."

"Certainly," Hugh said. "So we'll see you later, I hope."

"Maybe so."

Mosey looked back to see Boatwright cross the lobby and plod up the stairs. "Well, that was evasive. First, he said he was meeting him at the Lost Dog, and now he says we may bump into him at the Silver Star."

"Arnold, eh?" Hugh said.

"The very same," Mosey said, now staring ahead.

"This could get interesting," Robert said.

"Especially," Mosey said, "if Eleanor French shows up."

"You're still on that one?" Hugh said.

"Not so much."

The threesome reached the Silver Star, and Robert opened the door for his wife and friend. "Robert, mind ordering me a martini? I think I'll deliver Professor Boatwright's message." She left Robert and Hugh at the bar and headed to the large, round, corner table where Arnold Schulte sat alone, writing in a notebook. "Dr. Schulte." She pulled out a chair. "Mind if I join you for a second?"

He stopped writing and removed his reading glasses. A faint smile suggested he didn't mind the interruption.

"Professor Boatwright will be along shortly. He said that if I ran into you, I should let you know."

"Thank you." Schulte smiled again. "You wouldn't know what he's up to, would you?"

"He left the banquet to meet someone at the Velvet Arms. Said it was business. Now he's back at the hotel."

Schulte checked his watch. "So…are you enjoying the conference?"

"More than usual. I didn't see you at the banquet."

"No, I'm not a fan of banquets." Schulte stared past Mosey at Boatwright, who'd just come through the door. He rose from his chair and waved. Mosey also stood, offering Boatwright her seat next to Schulte.

"What took you so long?"

"I had a *date*," Boatwright said.

"Not that again!" Mosey rolled her eyes.

"Keep your seat," Boatwright said with a flirtatious grin. He borrowed a chair from a nearby table and placed it next to Mosey. "With a young woman, maybe younger than you," he said, "who was quite dead." He opened his eyes wide, waiting for a reaction.

"Jaw-droppers are Addison's specialty," Schulte said. "Don't pay him any mind."

"You are mistaken, my friend." Boatwright sat. "In fact, I've just come from the morgue and, considerate fellow that I am, I stopped at the hotel to wash up."

"Why the morgue, for God's sake?" Schulte looked from Boatwright to Mosey. "Hear that? The morgue, he says."

"Don't act so surprised, Arnold," Boatwright said.

"Why?"

"The woman they found in the gorge—you two know all about that, I assume. Seems that she had an interesting mouthful before departing life."

"Good God, Addison, what are you talking about?"

"Wasn't a flower, which wouldn't have been entirely unexpected—the best restaurants serve them these days. It was a common tuber…well, not a *common* one exactly, though they are found in the American West, especially on breezy hillsides."

"Addison, you're rambling." Schulte took another sip of his drink.

"Women's bane."

Mosey stared into his face with amusement more than consternation, not sure if he was dead serious or pulling their legs. "Poison flowers seem to pop up everywhere when you're around, Professor."

"As when *you're* around, Ms. Frye," he rejoined.

"I wasn't aware you and Ms. Frye were well acquainted," Schulte remarked. He looked at one, then the other. "She's too young to have been your student," he said, staring at Boatwright. "You've been retired from teaching for a good fifteen years, haven't you?"

"We've known each other for years."

"He never passes up an opportunity to get my goat," Schulte said to Mosey. "Spill it, Addison." Schulte's patience seemed to be wearing down.

"*Cálmate, amigo.*" Boatwright patted Schulte's hand.

"*Cálmate tú, tonto,*" Schulte replied crossly.

The little spat between the two ended when Robert

approached. "Addison." Robert set two whiskies on the table. "I assumed this would be your drink of choice."

Boatwright stood and scooted his chair to make room for Robert and Hugh. Then he took the drink in his hand, checked the color, nosed it, and took a sip. "Yes," he nodded. "Thank you, Robert."

"The professor was just telling us—"

"About my *date*," Boatwright interrupted.

"With a corpse!" Mosey added.

Schulte looked across the table at Robert. "I think Addison has met his match, don't you?"

"Who, Mosey or the corpse?" Robert said, deadpan.

The entire table laughed out loud.

"Very funny, Ellison." Schulte's ill humor had apparently lifted. "No, not the corpse. Your wife."

"We make a handsome couple, don't we?" She gave Boatwright a pat on the arm. "Tell us, Professor, what *were* you doing at the morgue?"

"Simple. The victim had a tuber in her mouth and, besides that, a nasty cut on her right arm. Tremble, the coroner—" Boatwright stopped, setting his eyes on Schulte. "I believe I have *you*, Arnold, to thank for that."

"So...he told you," Schulte said.

"Yes, he told me—did you think he wouldn't? As I was saying, the coroner wanted my opinion."

"I gather we're talking about the woman in the gorge?" Hugh clarified.

"Yes, the woman in the gorge, who didn't die in the gorge—well, I don't *think* she died in the gorge. The poison was administered at Shoemaker House."

"Oh, my." Mosey crossed glances with Schulte.

"How do you know that?" Schulte said.

"They told me. Tremble and Judd. The FBI was there, too. Agent Warner and—I forget the other man's name."

"How do they know that?" Schulte persevered.

"That I'm not sure, but blood—the victim's blood—was discovered on the parlor floor. Someone must have seen it."

"But you said she was poisoned," Hugh said.

"I'm fairly certain she was. I was telling Arnold and Mosey—you don't mind if I call you Mosey, do you?—about the tuber found in the victim's mouth. Women's bane or wolf bane. Technically, *Eranthis hyemalis*, also known as monkshood."

"Women's bane," Robert said, a hint of levity in his voice.

Mosey stared blankly at her husband.

"Maybe they should call it realtor's bane," the professor added pensively. "Two—could be three now—real estate agents, all women, all dead from aconite poisoning in less than a year." He sipped his whisky. "And all three close by, relatively speaking."

As if members of a synchronized drinking team, Mosey, Robert, and Hugh lifted their glasses, paused, then exchanged glances.

"Did I say something?" Boatwright questioned.

Hugh, the first to recover his composure, explained. "As it happens, Mosey is a real estate agent, and she, well, all of us, heard about two such cases within the last year. Both were women…strangled in Texas."

"I see." Boatwright shook his head. "Well, they weren't strangled. The paper reported it that way, but they were poisoned. Tubers in their mouths, just like this victim."

"Have they identified the body?" Schulte said.

"Maybe. They found a cell phone registered to—what was her name? Mariah something or other."

"And she's a real estate agent?" Mosey said.

"They aren't sure. They're waiting for confirmation of her identity—from fingerprints."

"Why was she at Shoemaker House?" This piece of the puzzle ostensibly aroused Schulte's interest.

"No clue," he replied. He took a last sip of whisky.

"Can I get you another one of those?" Hugh said.

"One more wouldn't hurt, I suppose, but let me get this round."

"No, no, stay put." Hugh picked up his, Robert's, and Boatwright's glasses. He turned to Schulte, seated on his right, and asked if he'd care for another drink.

"No thanks, Hugh, I'm good."

"Is Shoemaker House occupied?" Mosey turned to Schulte.

"Hasn't been for some time," Schulte said. "The heirs moved away from Westford in the 1980s. There's been talk of turning it into a museum, but, for lack of funding and interest, it's stood vacant. The heirs prefer not to sell it to an individual or to rent it, and the town can't afford to buy it."

"It's usually locked up, then," she said.

"I would say so."

"I was by there around one o'clock, and the door was open," Mosey said.

"I suppose the police might have opened it," Schulte said.

"Or the killer," Mosey said.

"Possibly. But why there?" he mused.

His words prompted silence. No one had an answer.

Chapter Ten

The murder of the woman provisionally identified as Mariah Weatherford had eclipsed the disappearance of Selena Billings in everyone's mind except Hugh's. It occurred to him on his way from the bar to the table that perhaps Professor Boatwright had heard something. No, impossible—Judd was tight as a drum. He wasn't going to reveal anything to anyone, unless he expected to gain something in return. Hmm. Had Judd, in point of fact, already discovered her whereabouts?

He set the whiskies on the table and passed one to Boatwright, the other to Robert.

"Thanks, Hugh," Boatwright said.

"By the way," Hugh said, "while you were at the station, did you hear anything about the missing woman, Selena Billings?"

"Oh, yes, I heard something about that but not at the station."

"What'd you hear?—if you don't mind my asking."

"That she was missing," Boatwright said, "nothing more. When I was waiting for Judd, I heard two people in the lobby. They said the girl who works at the Lost Dog had gone missing, and they were afraid she might be the woman in the gorge."

"Who were they—do you know?" Robert asked.

"You know them," he said. "I saw you speak to

them at the banquet. Law, I think, yes, Law, and that sidekick of his—a woman."

"Eleanor French," Hugh said.

"Could be. I don't really know them. But later on I ran into them again, in the hall when I was going to my room to wash up. I told them the dead woman wasn't Selena Billings."

"Really?" Robert said.

"Yes, and they thanked me for letting them know."

"She's been missing for a full day now, a little more," Hugh said.

"Well, that's not so long. She'll show up. Law's friend, she mentioned something about stopping by her place."

"Her place?" Hugh said.

"Right, said she knew where the woman was staying and had passed it on the way to the cliffs."

Hugh paused. "Come to think of it, I think I may know the place she's referring to."

"Where's that?" Robert said.

"There's an old cabin off the road...off 65...going up to the cliffs. I pass there every day. I've seen some of the bikers up there."

"Bikers. What's that got to do with Selena?" Robert said.

"Judd told me Selena's friend—the biker I saw her talking to at the Lost Dog—was missing as well. Judd said it would be in the paper tomorrow. One of the bikers is an agent from DC—an intelligence agent."

"FBI?" Robert said.

"Could be FBI, or I'm wondering DEA, maybe."

"Drugs," Boatwright interjected. "Not surprising, not around here."

Robert concurred.

"Westford's on the drug route between Mexico and several large American cities," Boatwright said. "Think about it. Albuquerque, Amarillo, Oklahoma City…" He leaned forward and addressed Schulte and Mosey, who were seated on his left. "You folks okay?" Both glanced back at him, smiled, and continued their conversation. "Wouldn't you like something else to drink?"

"I think we're fine." Schulte glanced at the martini Mosey had hardly touched.

"Yes, I see what you mean," Robert said, addressing Boatwright. "There're cops by the dozen around here. I wondered what that was about."

"I've thought about that myself," Hugh said. "But drugs. I didn't think of the drug angle. I assumed they were after undocumented immigrants."

"That, too," Boatwright put in. "We're practically on the border here. Drugs, immigrants, smuggling… and other things."

"Other things, you say?" Robert said.

"Hate crimes against Indians, for one."

"And?"

"Land rights, mineral rights corruption."

"I haven't heard anything about that lately," Hugh said.

"It isn't likely to make national news," Boatwright said.

"So, what's up with that?" Robert said.

"For years now, there's been an ongoing struggle between the oil companies and the local Indians. As you well know, Robert, the indigenous population found oil in seeps around here, well, not just here, all over the country, before the Europeans ever arrived."

"That's true," Robert said. "But what's that got to do—"

"With this business around here?" Boatwright cut in. "Nothing, maybe"—he shrugged—"but it's just one more ticklish area. A lot of bad deals went down between the prospectors, the oil companies, and the natives. The last century is riddled with it, ever since that big gusher in Beaumont...1901."

"So, you think that has something to do with the murders?" Hugh said.

"Probably not," Boatwright replied, "but there is something about these murders. I mean the killer's method, real estate, the places where the murders occurred...Dallas, Beaumont." He took a sip of his drink. "Sounds to me like revenge could be a motive, but, on the other hand, it's too obvious."

"Revenge," Hugh repeated. "You mean a Native American murdered these women as a vendetta for past wrongdoing?"

"This last victim—I'm pretty sure she *is* Native American. But, of course, Native Americans haven't always seen eye to eye on these issues—tribal lands, mineral rights." Boatwright paused. "There's a certain logic to it. After all, the method sort of points at the native population. Which is suspect, if you ask me."

"That's a clever theory," Hugh said. "Could be the murderer used this bizarre method in order to point law enforcement in the wrong direction."

"That's what I'm thinking, but I don't know if it's working."

"Why not?" Robert probed.

"Well, it's too soon to say, but Warner had all the facts about the Texas murders and never once suggested the murderer might be Native American. Judd, he's from around here. Once he's had time to think about it…"

"I guess Warner didn't mention oil, either," Hugh said.

"Not while I was there, but I didn't talk to him much. My contact was with Judd and then Tremble. But Warner seemed to be holding back." Boatwright took another sip of whisky. "Yes, I think so. And Judd wasn't pleased."

"No, I wouldn't think Judd—"

"*Hablando del rey de Roma*," Boatwright cut in.

"Beg your pardon?" Robert said.

"Judd." Boatwright signaled with his head toward the door.

Robert and Hugh twisted around just when Judd, Warner, and Barbour passed the threshold.

"What is it?" Mosey said, seeing Robert craning his neck and twisting in his chair.

"Judd and the FBI, over there, just inside the door."

"Oh." Mosey's eyebrows raised.

"*El mundo es un pañuelo*," Boatwright observed.

Schulte shook his head and tittered. "That's not what that means."

"Sure it does," Boatwright retorted.

"No, it means, 'It's a small world.' "

"Exactly."

"Not in a mundane sense, as you're using it."

Mosey rose in her seat. "If you guys will excuse me, I think I'll run over to the Carcajou before it closes. I need to check my e-mail."

"They're open till one, I think," Schulte said.

"Well, guess I could finish this martini first." She

sat back down.

"Looks like Judd's heading our way," Hugh said.

"Surely he's not going to drag me back out to the morgue at this time of night," Boatwright complained.

Judd stopped at a respectful distance from the table and took off his hat.

"Lieutenant Judd." Hugh stood. "Would you care to join us?"

"Actually, I need to speak to Ms. Frye." He nodded at Mosey.

"Me?" Mosey exclaimed.

Robert, who was getting up, dropped back in his chair and leaned toward Mosey, as if to defend against Judd's next move.

"Yes," Judd said, "if you wouldn't mind walking with me over to the Velvet Arms. We could speak a little more privately there."

"What's this all about, Lieutenant?" Robert stood.

"I'm sure it can be cleared up quickly."

"Well, certainly, if I can be of help." Mosey slipped her arms into her jean jacket, lifted her handbag off the back of the chair, and, squeezing past Boatwright, gave Robert a pat on the shoulder. "It's fine. I'll see you back at the hotel. Do you have your cell phone?"

Robert checked his pocket. "Yes, call me when you're finished."

Chapter Eleven

Like a fighting bull in the ring, the Chief of Detectives had returned to his *querencia*—which, in this case, was the comfortable if slightly saggy and worn wing chair that stood in the corner of the Velvet Arms lobby. Mosey had gone to the ladies' room, and Judd sat alone.

A guest who was checking out thanked Mr. Alcalá for his service, and he came from behind the bureau to help the woman out with her luggage. "Your ride is here, *señorita*."

"You say it's half an hour to the airport?"

"About that. You've got plenty of time to make your flight."

"*Muchas gracias*." She pushed her briefcase into the back and climbed in.

"*De nada*. Hope to see you next trip." He closed the door and backed away. Spying Judd, he looked straight ahead and mumbled. "Damned flatfoot. What does he think this is—his interrogation room?"

"Okay, Lieutenant." Mosey rounded the big palm. "I'm all ears. How can I help you?"

Judd stood and offered her his chair. "Would you prefer to sit here?"

"Thanks, this chair's fine." She pulled up a petite rosewood, sat, and crossed her legs.

"Ms. Frye, I need to follow up on something," Judd

305

began. "We've just received information identifying the prints we discovered at the crime scene. I'm talking about the murder of Mariah Weatherford."

"So you've identified the body."

"It turns out a set of prints at the crime scene was identified as yours, Ms. Frye."

"Oh, my." Mosey's eyebrows arched sharply. "I'm not a suspect, surely."

Distracted momentarily by the leopard ballet flat that dangled from Mosey's left foot, Judd coughed and continued. "Like I say, your prints were found at the crime scene."

"Where exactly?"

"I'll ask the questions, if you don't mind."

"Of course, sorry." Mosey put both feet on the floor and smoothed her skirt.

"Now, then." He took out his tablet and turned to a fresh page. "Can I get your whereabouts last night, say around eight o'clock?"

"I was with Robert...Robert Ellison, my husband. We got in about five, checked in. We were going to meet Hugh Jessup at the Lost Dog, but we were exhausted—long trip, a good eight hundred miles—and decided not to go."

"So you didn't go to the Lost Dog at all last night—is that correct?"

"No, we didn't. We went for a walk later, along First. We passed it but didn't go in."

"What time was that, you think?"

"I'm not exactly sure. We had dinner at the Rancho Grande. I guess we left around nine. Then we walked back to this end of First. We must have passed by there a little after nine. I'm pretty sure it was...let me think, yes…nine or nine-fifteen."

"So, you would have passed near Shoemaker House right before then, say between nine and nine-fifteen?"

"That's about right. We could check with Robert or Hugh—he was with us—and then the three of us came back here."

"You didn't leave First, then."

"No, not till we got back to Silver."

"You didn't step over to Shoemaker House, even for a minute?"

"No," Mosey emphasized. "I was never there till today, on the tour with Dr. Schulte. Why do you ask?"

"Did you go into the house?"

"No, we stood near the entrance. Dr. Schulte explained about the corner door, about how only the well-heeled—"

"I see," Judd interrupted. "At no time did you approach the house?"

"No, I didn't say that. I did go up to the door later on."

"When was that?"

"After the body was discovered. Well, not right after. It was later, after the police arrived. That was when I saw you—remember, Lieutenant?"

"Okay. So, you didn't enter the house at any time until after the police arrived."

"I didn't go into the house at all. I've never been inside. The door was open, and I walked over to the steps and stood on the stoop…just a second. But then I saw you getting into your car."

"Did you see anything inside the house?"

"Nothing. The door was barely cracked, and I was

only there for a minute, less than a minute."

"You didn't go inside, didn't disturb anything, didn't see anything inside the house."

"Nothing, Lieutenant, nothing at all."

"Okay," Judd said. "I guess your story corroborates the evidence."

"What evidence exactly do you mean?"

"Your fingerprints were found on the doorframe, and an unidentified footprint was found on the stoop. What size shoe do you wear?"

Mosey glanced down at her ballet flats. "Seven and a half, eight." She pulled one off and extended it toward Judd. "These are thirty-eights...European sizing."

"No need." Judd threw up a hand. "According to the data bank, the tread is from a Camper. Do you happen to own a pair of Campers?"

"Yes, I was wearing them earlier today."

"Well, I guess that takes care of that."

"I'm not a suspect, am I?"

"No, I wouldn't say so."

Mosey was relieved. *Nosey Mosey*, she admonished. She might as well say it herself, since Nadia wasn't around to say it. "Lieutenant," she began, disregarding her own caution, "I happened to hear that Mariah Weatherford was a real estate agent, as am I. I was just wondering—does this case link up with those other cases earlier this year? I read about it in the paper. Two women—"

Judd abruptly stood. "Ms. Frye, your line of work is selling houses. Now isn't that so?"

Mosey stood, too. "Yes, that's what I do now—sell houses."

"Ma'am, I strongly suggest—"

"I stick to selling houses," she said, crestfallen. "I know, you're right. I'm sorry. You're a very busy detective with a murder case to solve. I oughtn't to be asking questions, holding you up like this." She reached around Judd and picked up his white ten-gallon, which he had propped on the floor beside the palm. Flicking a piece of fuzz off the brim, she offered him the hat and smiled. "Here's your hat."

The sudden salvo of sweetness had apparently disarmed him, but rather than succumb to the charms of a woman twenty years his junior, he pocketed his tablet and pencil, put his hat on, and said nothing at all. He left the hotel and headed down Silver back to the Silver Star.

Chapter Twelve

Mosey took another seat but this time on the colorful, striped velvet window seat that stretched across the front of the lobby. She watched out the window until her interrogator had reached Silver. Then, she left the hotel, cell phone in hand. "Robert…"

"What happened?"

"Not much. They traced some prints left at the crime scene to me."

"What the heck?"

"Nothing important. Judd had a few questions."

"You're not a suspect, are you?"

"Good grief, no…well, not now."

"Stay put," Robert insisted. "Hugh and I will be over in a minute."

"I'm headed to the Carcajou. I'll meet you later at the Silver Star."

Mosey brushed past the goths at the entrance to the café, went inside, and ordered a caramel latte with whipped cream. "Okay if I use a computer?" she said to the attendant.

"Sure, go ahead. It's three dollars for the first thirty minutes."

"Charge me for half an hour. I'm in a bit of a hurry."

"Fine. That'll be four dollars for the latte and three for the computer, and with tax…"

"Never mind." Mosey handed him a ten-dollar bill. "Keep the change."

"I'll bring the latte to your table. The password is Frankenstein."

Mosey sat down at a laptop similar to her own, keyed in the password, and called up the web site for the *Beaumont Enterprise*, then for the *Dallas Morning News*. Within minutes, she had ascertained the names of the murdered real estate agents: Angela Spivey and Magda Kelly—the women she'd read about months earlier in the *Gazette*. "Interesting," she mumbled. "Hispanic given names...Anglo surnames."

Once she'd retrieved the victims' names, she turned to a source that she'd often used to access information on properties. This could be tricky, she thought, since the agents are dead...but with a little luck... Yes! Spivey's name was still listed by the National Association of Realtors. "Profile...yes!" She clicked on the photograph of Spivey. Angela Spivey, she read. Average listing price, 459,000 dollars. Specializations: land, waterfront, residential. Languages spoken: Spanish, Tsalagi. How common is that? She moved on to the profile of Magda Kelly and soon determined that both women had been associated with prominent firms, had specialized in land and residential properties, and had begun their careers in real estate in 2008. Under "languages spoken," each listed Tsalagi.

"Tsa-la-gi," Mosey mouthed. She'd heard of that. She keyed it in. Tsalagi...language of the Cherokee Indians. Hmm.

She was up from her chair and back at the counter. "I've really got to run. Could you give me that latte to go?"

The attendant poured the latte into a paper cup, topped it with whipped cream and a drizzle of caramel, and set it on the counter. With a quick "thanks," she was on her way.

She entered the Silver Star and, passing through the bar, came face to face with Judd. "Lieutenant...we just keep bumping into each other, don't we?" She smiled and nodded to Judd, Warner, and Barbour, and continued walking toward the corner table.

Robert pulled out a chair. "Well?"

"Well what?"

"What did you find out?"

"Interesting stuff." She slipped off her jacket before sitting.

"You've been surfing over at the Carcajou, I guess," Boatwright remarked.

Mosey smiled and took a sip of her latte.

"Well?" Hugh said.

"I don't know what the lieutenant and those spook friends of his know about those women—I mean the murdered real estate agents—but I don't mind telling you," she paused, casting a glance toward the bar, "they spoke the same language, Tsalagi."

"Bizarre," Hugh exclaimed.

"Un-huh." Boatwright shifted in his chair.

"Amazing," Robert said.

"Quite," Schulte said. "You learn anything else?"

"Well, from their pictures, they were youngish, attractive, dark-complexioned. Oh, and there was one other thing. They started selling houses in 2008—both of them."

Boatwright stared into his glass, shook his head, and then downed the last drops. "If you ask me, there's something highly intentional about these murders."

"Intentional?" Schulte said.

"Yes, intentional."

"How could they *not* be intentional?" Robert said.

Hugh interceded, looking at Boatwright. "I think I see what you mean. It isn't what you'd expect of serial killings."

"I agree," Schulte said.

"You're right," Mosey said. "There is a sort of randomness to serial killings, isn't there?"

"Randomness, yes," Hugh concurred, "even though the victims often have something in common. Either they're all children—all boys, all girls—"

"—or prostitutes," Schulte interjected. "Or women with similar traits—blondes, brunettes."

"More often than not that's the case." Boatwright shook his head. "But in this particular instance, there's *too much* of an overlap. Either that, or those women didn't speak Tsalagi. It's too much of a coincidence, if you ask me. Cherokee women or real estate agents, but not Cherokee real estate agents. Couldn't be."

"Maybe these profiles can't be trusted," Robert said.

"Of course, they can be trusted," Mosey rejoined. "I've never once run across one that was in error—not regarding a realtor's profile."

"Nothing on the Internet is fool-proof," Schulte opined. "Robert might be onto something."

"That's true," Mosey said.

"Maybe the profiles were tampered with," Hugh said.

"I think you're all on the wrong track." Boatwright paused to catch the waiter's attention.

"Can I get you something?" He gathered the empty glasses and placed them on his tray.

"Men, will you join me in another whisky?"

Robert and Hugh passed.

"Just one, then," he said to the waiter. "Make it a Glenlester neat. Arnold, Mosey—care for something?"

They passed, too.

"Let us assume, for the sake of argument," the professor continued, "that the information is correct." With his index finger, he tapped off the commonalities on the rough-hewn table. "Two Cherokee women, relatively new to the real estate business, victims of aconite poisoning." He wiped the table with the flat of his hand. "Not only could this not be a case of serial killing, whatever it is that *really* connects these murders has yet to surface." He tapped the table lightly with his finger.

Hugh frowned. "You're suggesting we know *who* they are, but we don't really know—"

"—what they did," Robert finished.

"Exactly," Boatwright said.

Mosey tilted her head and stared at the table, as if the solution might be scratched into the surface. "These weren't hate crimes, then...though I've heard about hate crimes committed against Native Americans. Those particular women must have done something."

"Substantial enough to cause someone to come after them," Schulte said, "and stuff a poisonous tuber in their mouths."

"Whatever it was," Robert said, "the two women must have been involved."

"Maybe three," Hugh said.

"In Mariah Weatherford's case, the killer's method

is certainly the same," Boatwright said.

"What do we know about Mariah Weatherford?"

"Is that the dead woman's name?" Robert said.

"Judd said they'd confirmed the victim's identity," Hugh said.

"You didn't look for her profile?" Robert said to Mosey.

"I guess I got distracted when I saw that the others spoke Tsalagi."

Schulte reached into his jacket pocket. "Never mind, I have my iPad."

"Excellent. Go to REALTOR.com."

"Okay, now what?"

"Since we aren't sure where she lived, put in her name," Mosey directed.

"Oh, gosh, looks like there's a bunch of Mariah Weatherfords."

"Where do they live?" Mosey said.

"Here's one in Texas."

"Check that one."

He clicked on Weatherford's picture. "San Angelo, Texas. San Fernando Realty. Specialization: land and residential. Languages spoken: Spanish, Tsalagi."

"Jackpot!" Boatwright said.

Chapter Thirteen

Hugh got up to check on Boatwright's order, leaving his companions to ponder the mystifying facts of the murders. He stood at the bar, waiting to catch the bartender's attention. "The Glenlester we ordered?" He aimed a thumb in the direction of the corner table.

Agent Warner put out a cigarette with his foot and looked across at Hugh. "Professor Jessup."

"Yes, and you are…?"

"Special Agent Warner."

"Hugh Jessup." He extended his hand. "I think I saw you earlier with Lieutenant Judd." He glanced around. "Where *is* Judd, by the way?"

"He'll be back." It was Sergeant Barbour who responded.

"Nothing yet on Selena Billings?"

"Billings, right," Warner said.

Evasive lot—thought Hugh, his question having been left unanswered. "Lieutenant Judd gave me his card." He reached into his lapel pocket. "Said I should give him a call if I thought of anything."

"He'll be back," Warner said.

The agent's reticence was a prod. "The FBI agent I saw with Selena in the bar, you wouldn't know—"

"Isn't FBI," Barbour corrected.

"Oh." Hugh paused. "I didn't think so."

"Why's that?"

"Doesn't compute, exactly."

The bartender returned with the whisky. "He didn't want water," Hugh said. Before the barman could whisk away the drink, Hugh picked it up and nosed it. "Add it to my tab."

Turning again to Warner and Barbour, Hugh rattled on. "Selena Billings wasn't much of a bartender."

"Really?" Warner said.

"She wasn't a criminal, either," Hugh said.

Before the agents could remark, Judd set a beefy hand on Hugh's shoulder. "Jessup."

"Lieutenant," Hugh said cordially. "I was chatting with your friends here."

"About what?"

"Witness protection."

Warner's eyebrows shot up.

"Witness protection," Judd repeated.

"That's what I said, witness protection."

"What about it?" Judd said.

"I've been scratching my head, trying to figure this thing out. It's the only way I can imagine that Selena and the agent—"

Judd reached for his tablet. "Go on."

"What you said," Hugh continued, "about the biker, or agent, rather."

"They're not *agents*, they're *marshals*," Barbour interjected.

"The marshal, then. Her exchange with the marshal who was pretending to be a biker—I thought it, well, strange. And besides that, Selena isn't a Lost Dog kind of girl."

"You mentioned that before, I believe." Judd flipped backward in his tablet.

"What if she was aware the biker was a marshal? And, by analogy, the biker knew Selena was—?"

"What?" Judd cut in.

"A witness."

"A witness to what?" Judd said.

Hugh remained silent, watching as Judd crossed glances with Warner.

"How do you know that, Jessup?" Judd said.

"I don't *know* it. But it makes sense—don't you think?"

The lieutenant looked quizzical.

Hugh wasn't sure at what point he should lay his cards on the table. Judd knew as much as he did—likely, a good deal more. Go ahead, raise 'em—he said to himself. Then to them, "If you would care to hear my theory…?"

Judd licked his finger and turned the page. "Go ahead."

"Angela Spivey, Beaumont, TX. Magda Kelly, Dallas. Now Mariah Weatherford, San Angelo. Three real estate agents, all dead from aconite poisoning. The same day Weatherford is murdered, Selena Billings and her biker friend go missing." He paused, sipped his drink.

"Maybe," Judd said, "we ought to continue this conversation down at the station."

"Why's that, Lieutenant?" Hugh put on his best poker face.

"You seem to know as much about this as we do—isn't that so, Agent Warner?"

Warner shrugged.

"Fine," Hugh said. "Mind if I…?"

"Go ahead."

Boatwright's whisky arrived and Hugh carried it to the corner table. "One Glenlester neat, as requested."

"Well?" Mosey said.

"Don't ask." Hugh stopped her in her tracks.

"Ask what?"

"Never mind. I've got to go to the police station."

"Why?" Robert said.

"I anteed up, he matched."

"Who?"

"Judd."

"Why you?" Mosey said.

"I've got a theory. Witness protection."

"Witness protection?" Schulte puckered his brow.

"Maybe, just maybe," Hugh said, "the victims were protected witnesses."

"Humph!" Boatwright shook his head and sipped his drink. "They did a damn good job of it."

Chapter Fourteen

While Judd pulled away in his big truck, Warner, Barbour, and Hugh got into the special agent's black sedan. From the back seat, Hugh offered up another part of his theory. "I've been considering…"

Warner waited for Hugh to tell them what he'd been considering.

"They could be at the cabin on 65," Hugh began, "or, if they aren't there, they might have left clues."

"Cabin on 65?" Warner said.

"Wednesday morning early, I was on my way to the cliffs. I passed the biker. I'm pretty sure it was him. That's where the wrecked bike was found—right?"

"The wrecked bike…"

"Has anyone checked?"

"Why don't you hold tight," Warner said, "till we get to the station, okay?"

"Sure," Hugh said.

Warner switched on the radio.

Hugh leaned back, staring out the side window into darkness. It was the season for falling stars. He searched the night sky but didn't see a single one. If Selena was a protected witness, he reflected, and the biker was a marshal, what was the purpose of the disguise? And why had this individual come to Westford? To protect her, maybe, or warn her of something? What if the lieutenant was wrong and the biker *wasn't* a marshal? He leaned forward again, placing a hand on the back of Warner's seat. "There isn't any doubt, I suppose, about the marshal's identity."

Warner twisted the volume knob. "Doubt? What are you getting at?"

"Lieutenant Judd's information."

"I suppose Judd knows what he's talking about." He reached for the volume knob, and Hugh leaned back.

In five minutes, they arrived at the police station. Tremble was standing at the open door, and Judd, who'd gotten there before them, had taken a seat next to the drink cooler. Barbour went inside, and Warner stayed on the patio.

"Tremble," Judd said as he stood. "This is Professor Hugh Jessup. Jessup, Dr. Tremble, coroner on the case."

"I've heard about you." Tremble shook Hugh's hand. "You're working at the cliffs, aren't you? I've got a friend who's interested in the cliffs, as a hobby more or less."

"Who's that?"

"Arnold Schulte. You know Arnold?"

"I've just come from seeing him. Some of us were at the Silver Star."

"*El mundo es un pañuelo*, as Arnold likes to say."

"Actually, that's the second time I've heard that tonight, except it was Addison Boatwright who said it before."

"Boatwright was there, too? Distinguished company you keep, Professor Jessup."

"Call me Hugh."

"Is Hugh here to see the body?" Tremble said to Judd.

"Nope. Just to answer some questions."

"He's not involved?" Tremble inquired.

Judd hedged. "He knows quite a bit, if you ask me, for someone *not* involved." Judd pointed toward an old cane-bottom chair. "Have a seat. Want something to drink?" Hugh shook his head, and Judd raised the top of the cooler. "Think I'll try one of these new sodas." He unscrewed the top and propped himself against the railing. "Now, then." He set his drink on the cooler and reached for his tablet and pencil. "Let's back up. What makes you think those other murders are related to this one?"

"I'd have to go back to last winter," Hugh began. "I read in the paper about two real estate agents, both women, strangled. Tonight Professor Boatwright told us that you said, or I guess it was Agent Warner who said, that the women *weren't* strangled. They died of aconite poisoning, like the woman in the gorge. Tubers stuffed in their mouths. *Eranthis hyemalis*, according to Boatwright. Robert Ellison's wife, Mosey Frye, who's in real estate, looked on line and found profiles of the first two victims. Both of them went into real estate in 2008, and both spoke Tsalagi."

"Tsalagi," Tremble said, "meaning Cherokee."

Hugh confirmed with a nod. "Of course, we thought 'serial killer,' but as the professor pointed out, that just couldn't be. That'd be too much of an overlap. Turns out Mariah Weatherford was a realtor as well and she, too, spoke Tsalagi."

"What did Boatwright suggest?" Warner took a step toward Hugh.

"Nothing. I left the table to check on the drink he'd ordered, and that's when—"

"Then this witness protection angle was *your* idea," Warner cut in.

"Yes, I guess it was. You see, I'm the only one who knew Selena, and what I saw at the Lost Dog yesterday didn't seem to fit. That's what got me thinking."

"What do mean it didn't fit?" Warner said.

"It didn't fit," Hugh repeated. "Not if you knew her. Unlikely the marshal was there to check up on Selena—I mean, I don't think she could be involved in anything criminal."

Warner moved closer to Hugh. "You think, then, Selena Billings *witnessed* a crime."

"Yes…as did the other women…maybe."

"And who do you suppose murdered these women and then made off with Selena Billings?"

Time to call?—pondered Hugh. No, not yet. Then he said, "How could I know that?"

"I expect you have some idea," Warner said.

Hugh rubbed his chin and walked to the edge of the patio, wondering if the plot he was spinning was utter nonsense. "My theory is…that these murders…well, had something to do with the Cherokee people…land rights, maybe. Whatever it was, and the motive could be any number of things, my best guess is someone committed a crime and went to prison for it."

Barbour appeared at the door, sparing Hugh additional elaboration. "Agent Warner, something's just come in. I think you should take a look."

Warner entered the station. The others remained on the patio, listening to the chirping of cicadas, then to a string of mild oaths coming from inside. The sound of a printer rose in the crisp summer air, followed by brisk footsteps.

Warner came through the door and handed a photograph to Hugh. "You recognize this man?"

"Sure do."

"Do you know his name?"

"*You* must know."

"I know his name but not necessarily his alias."

"I couldn't tell you his name or his alias," Hugh insisted. "But that's the biker, the one Lieutenant Judd said was an agent."

"We need to get going." Warner turned to Barbour and then Judd.

"Let me see that," Judd said.

Hugh passed him the photograph.

"What kind of firearms have we got in the car?" Warner said to Barbour.

"The usual. Couple of Glocks and a Springfield 1911."

"I expect that should do." Warner felt for his gun. "Lieutenant, you follow us."

Warner and Barbour climbed into the sedan and, gunning it, headed toward the main road. Judd followed in his truck, which, in the blink of an eye, disappeared into the cloud of dust raised by the sedan.

Chapter Fifteen

"Where would he take her?" Warner thought aloud.

"Might as well follow up on Jessup's theory." Barbour stepped on the brake at the crossroads of 240 and 65 and turned sharply to the right.

"The cabin on 65."

"Right."

"Call Judd," Warner said. "Tell him where we're going. Tell him to call the station for backup, then get Eleanor French on the phone and tell her not to leave town."

In ten minutes or less, they arrived at their destination. Fifty yards from the cabin, Barbour turned off the headlights and brought the sedan to a silent halt. Judd pulled up behind them and waited. Warner and Barbour stepped out, pistols drawn. Moving at a steady pace, they edged their way along the blacktop, then the shoulder of the road. Judd, rifle in hand, followed at a short distance.

A dog barked. A dim light streamed from the back of the cabin, which was surrounded by scruff and a low wall.

Warner and Barbour continued their approach, stopping and crouching behind the wall not far from the front door. Warner shouted, "FBI. We know you're in there, Hutton. Let the woman go. Come out with your hands up."

"He's got a gun!" shouted a woman from within the cabin.

"Selena's in there. Cover me. I'm going to see if I can get to the window."

Barbour nodded and took aim.

"Watch out for the girl."

Barbour nodded again.

Warner got to the window and peered in just as Selena's kidnapper leapt toward a rifle propped against a stucco chimney. Warner fired, and Hutton hit the wall with a thud, then slumped to the floor. He kicked open the door, Barbour now at his heels. They approached the wounded man. He was still alive. "Face to the floor!" Warner shouted. "Barbour, untie her."

While Warner patted down Hutton, who was bleeding from the left shoulder, the sergeant untied Selena and pushed the bandana down from her eyes.

Judd stood inside the cabin door.

"He killed her," Selena said to Judd. She was shaking hard, and perspiration rolled down her face. "He brought me here." She looked from Judd to Barbour. "Others are coming." Her voice broke, and she slumped to one side, as if she were about to pass out.

"Take it easy," Warner said. He grabbed her by the shoulders and pulled her upright. "What others?"

"I don't know. A drug deal. He's waiting for some men."

"You just sit there a minute. And here," Barbour said, taking the bandana from around her neck. "Wipe yourself off. I'll get you some water."

Judd flipped open his mobile. "Jernigan, where are you?"

"Close to the cabin."

"Hutton's in custody, and he's wounded. Better call Tremble and tell him to wait for us. The girl's here, too. She isn't hurt, but she's pretty shaken up."

"Good work, Lieutenant."

"We're not finished. Hutton's buddies could be here any minute. Drug deal. Set up a roadblock on 65, half mile east and half mile west of the cabin. Got that?"

"I'm on it, Lieutenant."

Chapter Sixteen

It was their last morning at the Velvet Arms, and Alcalá was beside himself. Dozens of anthropologists had formed a line that meandered through the lobby and doubled back into the breakfast room. "Where *diablos* is the limousine!" shouted the distraught desk clerk to the cleaning women he'd recruited to assist with the mass departure.

"On the way to the airport."

"Call them again. Tell them we need another *two* limousines…at least."

Mosey, Robert, and Hugh, suitcases in hand, descended the staircase to the landing, and seeing the line, stopped to consider their options.

"We can stand in the damn line," Robert said, "or we can grab some breakfast and come back later. Nobody's got a plane to catch, right?"

"I'd go for that," Hugh said. "Shall we drop the luggage off first?"

The threesome was headed back to Arkansas. Hugh, who'd flown out, was catching a ride back with Robert and Mosey.

After they'd packed the car, Mosey suggested they walk to the Square, where they were sure to find an assortment of pastries to delight their palates.

"That's several blocks from here," Robert said.

"So where do you want to go—the Carcajou?"

"No way." Hugh shook his head.

"Good grief," Mosey sighed. "Nowhere else on First serves breakfast."

"Let's go back to the Velvet Arms. The bagels aren't bad," Hugh suggested.

"Fine," Mosey said, resigned, for the next two days, to having her companions' bland choices trump her more sophisticated preferences.

They returned to the Velvet Arms, and, by keeping farewells to a minimum, soon managed to reach the breakfast room, where Special Agent Warner sat reading the morning news.

"Let's see if Agent Warner doesn't mind if we join him," Mosey said. "Looks like his booth is the only one with room for three more."

"Go ahead." Robert selected a ripe pear from the sideboard and stuffed it in his pocket. "Mosey, you want coffee?"

"Yes, please, and a bagel with cream cheese," she called back, already on her way to the agent's booth.

"Agent Warner, I'm Mosey Frye, Hugh Jessup's friend. Mind if we join you? The tables are full, and we're in a bit of hurry to start our trip back to Arkansas."

Warner folded his paper. "Sure, have a seat."

Mosey had already plunked down her handbag and was clearing a space for Robert and Hugh. "I'll just put these dishes over there. You've finished, right?"

"Yes, but you don't need—"

"I don't mind a bit. I don't see a busboy, do you?" She glanced around, then headed for the dirty dish bin.

Warner grimaced. It was his hallowed hour, his time to forget what he'd seen for the last twenty-four.

329

No rest for the weary, he sighed—or is it the wicked? With a covert shake of his head, he grudgingly scooted toward the wall to make room for his new acquaintances.

"Sorry to…" Hugh took the seat next to Warner.

"Dr. Jessup. Not a problem. Not a problem at all. In fact, I was hoping to see you before I left for Lubbock."

"Why's that?"

"To thank you for your help."

"I didn't do anything." In actual fact, Hugh had *done something*, though he was too polite to say it to the agent's face.

"If you hadn't told us where to look," Warner said, "we could have been scouring the desert till doom's day."

"Well…it worked out, and that's what matters."

Robert set down a tray of cups and bagels and reached in front of Hugh to shake Warner's hand. "We haven't met. Robert Ellison."

"Jack Warner."

"I suppose you're leaving, too, now the case—"

"The case," Warner interrupted. "Right. I was just telling your friend here that if it weren't for the information he passed along…"

"So, it's all wrapped up?" Mosey slid in before Robert could take a seat.

"You can read all about it in the morning paper." Warner pushed his copy of the *Westford Ledger* toward Mosey.

"I've already read the paper." She tossed away his suggestion with a flip of her hand.

He swirled the contents of his juice glass and took

a drink.

"But newspapers never tell the whole story," she continued, "and I'd rather hear it from you...especially the part about Selena's father. What was his name?"

"Rodger Billings."

"And what was that you called him?" she said. "They quoted you in the paper."

"An economic hit man."

"Economic hit man. Never heard of that before. I don't know how a man working for our government—intelligence no less—could turn into such a fiend." Mosey smeared half a bagel with cream cheese and held it out to Warner. "Care for some, Agent Warner?"

"No thanks, I've eaten."

You certainly have...razor soup, thought Mosey, whose abilities in mood detection were extraordinary.

"How does a thing like that happen?" She withdrew the bagel and placed it on Robert's plate.

"I suppose Billings picked up some bad habits along the way, like, well...killing people." He seemed to be eyeing Mosey, maybe waiting to see the effect of his words.

Mosey, undaunted, sipped her coffee and stared back. "But his own daughter?" She shook her head.

"Oh, I don't think he wanted her dead," Warner said.

"But kidnapped? What'd she ever do to him? I can't fathom such a thing."

"Selena left home when she was sixteen."

"Why?"

Warner picked up the *Ledger*. "Looks like they omitted that part of the story." He closed the paper and sighed, apparently resigned to a tedious regurgitation.

331

"Well…according to her brother, who drove over from San Marcos this morning, Selena found a letter that pretty much spelled out her father's contravention in Uruguay a good many years ago."

"Uruguay. What was Billings doing in Uruguay?" Hugh said.

"Nothing special." Warner stretched back. "Spying on a bunch of dissidents, torturing, killing."

Hugh wrinkled his forehead.

"I believe that's when he got his position in DC at NSA headquarters." He pulled a mechanical pencil out of his pocket and idly doodled along the edge of a column.

"Unbelievable," exclaimed Robert.

"In any event, it got him out of Uruguay." The doodle, which had started out as a triangle, was turning into a kite. "Later on, back in the States, he left the agency when Ingot made him an offer. He'd been a mining engineer before the government hired him."

"Ingot, right?" Hugh interjected.

Warner put down his pencil and gulped the last drop of juice. "Ingot was involved in open-pit mining in Utah and left a hole in the earth the size of a small town. They had huge volumes of material they needed to get rid of, and Billings came up with a scheme."

"Housing developments, I suppose," Hugh said.

"Yes, as a matter of fact. In the late 90s, the government allotted substantial funding for Native American housing and community development. The Cherokees in Oklahoma applied and received a grant to build homes, schools, parks…"

"How did Ingot get the contracts?" Robert said.

"That was Billings's doing. During his NSA years,

he'd made some connections in DC. He weaseled around and got contracts for a dozen projects, of which he completed five. Then one of the land developers, a Cherokee, had the soil tested at one of the new parks."

"And discovered it was loaded with what—lead?" Hugh said.

"That's right." Warner nodded. "Billings killed the man. Shot him in the chest."

"Good God," Robert said.

"How did they connect Billings to the murder?" Hugh said.

"The man's family knew he was the culprit, which is what got him arrested and ultimately convicted."

"What was the man's name?" Mosey said.

"Fred Day."

"His daughters must have been taken into protective custody," Hugh said.

"Yep, his wife was dead, and his daughters went into protective custody. That was in 2001. The oldest testified at the trial, and Billings was found guilty—first-degree murder. He got a life sentence."

"Too bad that couldn't have been the end of it," Robert said glumly.

"So what happened?" Mosey said.

"The girls' support was eventually cut off some four or five years after Billings went to prison. Funding was scarce, and the government dropped support to witnesses who were no longer considered vulnerable. Magda and Mariah moved away. Angela stayed on in Beaumont. Unfortunately, Billings had friends on the outside who were ready to do his bidding."

"Oh, gosh," Mosey said. "Who was it?"

"The biker," Hugh said before Warner could get

the words out.

Warner nodded. "That's exactly right, an old NSA associate of Billings's, guy by the name of A. J. Hutton."

"There's something I don't get," Hugh said. "Why did Hutton lure Mariah to Westford? Why not kill her in San Angelo?"

"He could have done that, but Billings told him to get Mariah to come to Westford, meet him at Shoemaker House, under the pretense of having her list the house."

"She met him there, and he killed her," Robert said.

"I don't understand Selena's involvement," Mosey said.

"Billings is a malicious son of a gun. He wanted her to pay for ditching him during and after the trial. He wanted her involved somehow, even if marginally. That was his revenge, the revenge of an abusive, narcissistic father."

"Seems like she could have gotten away," Mosey said.

"According to Selena, Hutton threatened to kill her and her brother if she refused to cooperate. So, she did what he told her to do. Helped him dump the body in the gorge. Then he tied her up and took her out to the cabin…which is where we found them."

Just as Warner finished his account, the clock in the breakfast room chimed.

"Nine-thirty," Robert said. "We need to get on the road."

"Selena," Hugh said, "she wasn't hurt, was she?"

"Traumatized but glad to be alive. She didn't have

any physical injuries."

Mosey glanced down at the *Ledger* splayed in front of her. "Eleanor French," she said, "how'd she figure in all this?" She picked up the paper and scanned the story.

"French worked for Ingot. Knew Billings and his family. When she saw Selena at the Lost Dog, she recognized her. Then she saw Hutton and recognized him, too."

"Eleanor French knew Hutton?" Hugh said.

"She didn't know him, but she'd seen him at the trial and, before that, at Billings's office. Didn't make any sense to her—Selena and Hutton being on friendly terms. And, besides that, she'd heard Selena call him by another name. So when she heard Selena had disappeared, she called up Judd, told him what she knew. Soon as we got an ID on the prints, we knew Hutton was involved."

"What do you think Hutton was planning?" Hugh said.

"He wouldn't have killed Selena, if that's what you mean. More likely he'd have left her at the cabin. But he got greedy. He was waiting for a shipment of cocaine. That's why he was still there."

"Drugs, eh? Doesn't surprise me." She closed the newspaper.

"Some of his biker chums were supposed to deliver a shipment to the cabin."

"If French hadn't gotten in touch with Lieutenant Judd," Mosey said, "nobody would have suspected Hutton."

"Correct. Rodger Billings, of course, was a suspect from the beginning, as soon as they identified Angela

Spivey as Amadahy, Fred Day's oldest daughter."

"Amadahy," Mosey said. "And the others?"

"Galilahi and Usdi."

"Usdi...Usdi," Robert repeated. "Baby."

"Right," Warner said, "the baby of the family. She was twenty-five."

"Wasn't there any way to warn them," Mosey said, "after their sister was murdered?"

"They *were* warned. Of course, they were. But there was nothing to link Billings to the crime...not directly. The Beaumont police couldn't make any headway. No physical evidence, to speak of. Billings was the only suspect, and he was in prison."

"Surely after the second sister was killed," Mosey said, "something could have been done to protect Usdi."

"She could have gone back into witness protection, but she refused to give up her friends."

"So sad, so terribly sad," Mosey said.

"Well, I'm sure Hutton and Billings will pay for this. With Selena's testimony..."

"Will they get the death sentence?" Hugh said.

"I'd say so."

Sergeant Barbour, who'd left Warner a quarter of an hour earlier, was back and picking over the buffet table.

"Sorry, there's Barbour. I've got to run." Warner raised a hand and motioned to Barbour.

Hugh got up. "Thanks for filling us in."

"Sure, and thank *you* for your help." He slid out of the booth.

"Have a good trip back to Lubbock," Hugh said.

"And you're going—where did you say?"

"Hembree, Arkansas."

"Right. Okay, well...have a safe trip."

When Mosey, Robert, and Hugh had finished breakfast, they returned to the lobby to face the line, which had dwindled to a handful of departing guests.

"Mind if I wait over there?" Mosey pointed to the window seat.

Robert answered with a nod.

Just as Mosey had settled into a cozy spot, a blotchy gray cat popped from behind the curtain, leapt to the wing back and then onto the floor. Exactly like Qittah, she thought. Qittah's twin flopped over on the rug and began cleaning himself. "Have a little modesty," she scolded, which under similar circumstances she'd have said to Nadia's cat. Nadia, she thought—we haven't spoken in days. Wait till she hears about all this.

"Mosey, my dear." It was Addison Boatwright who had broken her reverie.

"Professor."

"You're leaving, I see." Spotting Hugh and Robert at check-out, he waved his slouch hat in their direction.

"Off to Hembree," she said.

"I'm sticking around for a day or two. Arnold won't let me get away till we've taken care of a couple of things."

"That's what I hear."

"He took you into his confidence, I understand."

"Yes, he cleared up...well, you know...the business about the stalker. He'll be okay?"

"Of course, he will. No chance of his father doing any harm, not from where he is."

"I don't know if I'd say that."

"His father has no money, no power. A far shot from Rodger Billings," Boatwright said.

"Yes, poverty, strangely enough, can be a blessing."

"Selena Billings," he lamented, "another case of 'poor little rich girl.' "

"What will become of her, I wonder."

He shrugged.

"I bet she goes back to work," Mosey said, "goes right on as if nothing had happened."

"On the surface at least," he added.

"Yes, on the surface, that's the way it usually is—isn't it?"

He gave Mosey a hug and walked away.

She'd passed up her last chance to verify or dispel the rumors about Schulte. She couldn't see herself bringing up such tittle-tattle with a distinguished scholar like Boatwright. She'd concluded, though, after talking to Schulte himself the night before, that, regardless of past transgressions—and she seriously doubted there were any—she liked him a dang sight better than that blowhard Shoemaker, who'd managed to save his precious *house with the corner door*. "A badge of prosperity and privilege, indeed," she sassed, "affordable to a well-heeled minority." She curled up on the comfortable seat and, coaxing Qittah into her lap, spent the final moments of her stay soaking up the atmosphere of the unforgettable Velvet Arms.

You enjoy your vacation, kiddo?

"Daddy! As a matter of fact, I did."

And you didn't cause Robert any trouble?

"Not a bit." She fudged the truth a little.

She might have offered more, told him what a good

father he'd been, not at all like some she'd heard about. But their exchanges rarely waxed sentimental, so she let it go.

A word about the author...

Kay Pritchett was born and bred in Greenville, Mississippi, and attended Millsaps College in Jackson. She completed her education at the University of North Carolina, Chapel Hill, where she received her doctorate in Spanish Literature. After a long stint in Spain, she accepted an offer at the University of Arkansas and, at retirement in 2016, delved fully into fiction writing. *Murder in High Cotton,* inspired by childhood memories of the Delta, anthologizes her first short mystery novels. She lives in Fayetteville, Arkansas, with her husband Christopher J. Huggard.